I0681291

SINS OF EDEN

A SAM JENKINS MYSTERY

WAYNE ZURL

Copyright © 2018 by Wayne Zurl

All rights reserved. This book or any portion thereof may not be reproduced or used in any manner whatsoever without the express written permission of the publisher except for the use of brief quotations in a book review or scholarly journal.

ISBN: 978-1-68046-734-5

Melange Books, LLC
White Bear Lake, MN 55110

www.melange-books.com

Names, characters, and incidents depicted in this book are products of the author's imagination or are used fictitiously. Any resemblance to actual events, locales, organizations, or persons, living or dead, is entirely coincidental and beyond the intent of the author or the publisher. No part of this book may be reproduced or transmitted in any form or by any means, electronic or mechanical, including photocopying, recording, or by any information storage and retrieval system, without permission in writing from the publisher.

Published in the United States of America.

Cover Design by Lynsee Lauritsen

To Bazzie. Another one on the shelf. Thanks for a couple of those clever lines.

ACKNOWLEDGMENTS

Special thanks to the people who helped me create characters used in this book and develop the story line. They are:

Janetta Baker, for a character savvy in accounting, office management and the handling of two middle-aged detectives.

Holly Meissner, for teaching me what really happens on an all girls' vacation and providing a readymade cast.

Sylvia Whitehead Bedford, for extensive information about the place I chose to call Orr's Valley.

And to Jane Carver, my editor at Melange Books, for helping me take all these scribbled Sam Jenkins stories and create from them publishable pieces.

CHAPTER ONE

September 2011

THE PAINT WASN'T DRY ON THE WALLS BEFORE WE STARTED moving in.

"Ya know, Boss," John said, "we should have bought new office furniture. That would give the place a touch o' class. This old stuff, I don't know. Clients judge you by the appearance of your office."

No one will ever accuse former Detective John Gallagher of being financially savvy. And his wife is no better. They had living beyond their means down to a science—spending money like Crockett and Bowie the night before the Alamo fell.

I finished rubbing dark scratch remover into a scar on top of the old solid oak desk. "First thing, John, stop calling me *boss*. We're partners in this cockamamie private detective business. I have a first name. Please use it."

"Okay, B...uh, Sam. But you know how it is, old habits are hard to break."

"Let's put those words to music and get Bobby Vinton to sing it. The song should be more successful than we'll ever be." I shook my head. "I don't know why I let you talk me into this private cop venture."

John looked shocked that I'd question the sanity of his goofy scheme.

"It was a good idea," he said. "According to Lonnie Ray, we'll make lots of money."

"And we agreed to give Lonnie Ray Wilson seventy-five bucks for every hour he spends with us working on his computer, hacking into places where we shouldn't be. You think he's got a vested interest in suggesting we start this business?"

"Boss, you're the voice of doom."

I grunted and finished buffing the top of the old desk as I sneered at Gallagher. "There, see? These things have character. Between the Salvation Army and Goodwill, I bought four desks and eight chairs. After I tipped the kids who work there for helping me load this stuff into my truck, the whole shooting match cost us $320.00. You can't get a bottom-of-the-line new desk for that—and it would be made from some kind of poisonous Chinese flake board that would give us cancer. Who needs new furniture? These may not be genuine antiques, but they have a special kind of class. They give the place sort of a...hardboiled, Philip Marlowe look. Vintage. Like us."

John didn't have a chance to comment when Bettye Lambert walked into the outer office.

"Good mornin', gentlemen. How's the new business goin'?"

"Well," I said, "you're looking good. The new job suits you."

John jumped in with a compliment of his own. "Yeah, Sarge, uh, Sheriff, that outfit is way nicer than your old Prospect PD uniform."

For the five years I'd known Bettye, during our time together at Prospect PD, I often thought of her as the loveliest desk sergeant on the planet. Now she's the most beautiful sheriff. Her silky black blouse clung to her figure like one of the gowns worn by the Muses and Graces living above the clouds on Mount Olympus. Her straight beige skirt showed only an inch of knee and couldn't have been more appropriate for a newly appointed female sheriff.

John, on the other hand, looked like a slightly larger than usual leprechaun whose tie was always too short. Or were his pants always too low?

"Thank you both," she said. "I won't lie and say I wasn't overwhelmed when I started this new job, but so far, so good. I'm gettin' to like it."

John smiled.

I said, "Good."

"But listen," she said. "I came to see you guys and ask how you like bein' private eyes?"

I let Bogie answer, "Private *investigators*, doll-face. Save that private eye malarkey for guys like Boston Blackie. We're high class like Marlowe and Spade. We get twenty-five smackers a day plus expenses. And I love it when a dame like you visits the office."

"Well, thank you, Mr. Bogart. Have you been busy?"

"Honest answer?" John said. "I did one case—followed a cheating husband and his girlfriend to a sleazy motel. Not exactly the French Connection."

Bettye smiled before asking a question, the answer to which would change our lives for the next couple of weeks. "How would you like to work for me? I'm ready to put you two on the payroll and let you use those Special Investigator badges I gave you when I became the official interim sheriff of Blount County."

John jumped in promptly. "Yes, ma'am. I could use the money."

I played hard-to-get. "What's it all about, sweetheart? Come on. Spill the beans. I'm no sap. What am I gettin' involved in for my twenty-five bucks?"

"Will you stop with that 1940's act?"

"If I must."

"Good. This should be right up your alley. And you get a lot more than twenty-five dollars a day."

She took a moment to reactivate a smile I took in with my eyes but felt all the way down to my shoes. I have problems leaving my hard-boiled gumshoe character behind.

"Stanley got a missin' person case in Prospect that he passed off to us because he's goin' to be in Los Angeles for at least three weeks," she said. "His grandmother died. His family would like help handlin' her affairs, and Prospect PD is shorthanded now that we all left. I'm low on personnel, too, what with vacations still goin' strong and a couple of complicated cases that are keepin' CID busy."

"I like missing persons cases," John said. "The Boss does, too."

"John, I've asked you to stop calling me that. But you're right. I like MP cases. Always have."

"Ya know, Sheriff, the Boss, uh, Sam, worked missing persons cases when he first got to be a detective back in New York. He started out in Juvenile but didn't last long there." John lowered his voice and looked around as if he was afraid some nonexistent person might hear him. "He told me MP cases were easy because you didn't have to worry about Miranda or any of that stuff. He'd dangle someone out a window or hang them off a pier to get information about the missing kid."

Bettye looked at me as if she just learned I enjoyed pulling the wings off dragonflies. "Sam Jenkins, I will not allow you to dangle or hang or otherwise physically abuse some witness while you're investigatin' for me. Is that clear?"

"Yikes," I said. "Has she gotten tough or what? John, there's no doubt who's the new boss in town."

"Oh, stop," she said.

"Okay. When are you going to tell me about the case? I need to know a few things before we jump into this."

Bettye smiled. "I'll tell you all about it if you take me to lunch."

"I'll bet you've got an expense account, don't you?"

"Matter of fact, I do."

"Wow, a pretty woman with an expense account. I'd marry you if your father owned a liquor store. Let's go someplace pricey."

"Yeah, Sheriff, I mean, Boss," John said, "I can call you that, right?"

"Of course you can, John," Bettye said.

He finished with, "Where we going?"

"Not we, John," I said. "You have to write up your keyhole peeping case for the offended woman, and then you've got those four boxes of crap you want to hang on the walls to deal with. I'm gonna take my blonde lady friend here and buy her a glass of cheap white wine before she picks up the tab for our expensive lunch. I'll come back and tell you why she wants to hire us."

———

I COULDN'T HAVE ASKED FOR FINER SEPTEMBER WEATHER— seventy-two degrees, thirty-five percent humidity, cloudless Caribbean blue skies and a crop of colorful wildflowers—pale purple asters, black-eyed Susans, tall ironweed, golden rod and others—along all the roads in East Tennessee. A virtual Garden of Eden. What I needed was an easier job.

After working the missing person's case for several days, at 3:45 that afternoon, I parked my truck in the row set aside for police vehicles and walked from the blacktop lot toward the back door of Prospect PD. As I hit the concrete sidewalk, the chipmunk who lives at the Municipal Building stopped doing whatever chipmunks do and looked me in the eye, as if to say, 'Where have you been?' When I didn't provide a satisfactory answer, she scurried off and disappeared into her burrow next to the foundation. I climbed the concrete steps and entered the PD through the private rear entrance. My old four-digit code hadn't been programmed out of the electronic lock, and I still looked like I belonged there.

As I passed the doorway to the squad room and waved, PO Lenny Alcock called me.

"Hey, boss, got a minute?"

I stepped into the room and found Lenny sitting at one of the three computer terminals. An arrest report showed on the monitor screen. A familiar-looking, middle-aged geezer sat in the chair next to Officer Alcock. The man's right wrist was shackled to a three-inch metal ring attached to the desk by nuts and bolts. The man and his brown tweed sport jacket smelled sour and musty like you'd expect if someone just opened a tomb. Titus Haggerty carried a gold card in Prospect PD's frequent defendant's club.

"Stanley's the boss now, Lenny. I'm just another one of the sheriff's hired hands."

"Stanley's a great guy, but far as we're all concerned, you'll always be a boss around here."

It felt good hearing something like that. "Thanks, partner." I wanted to change the subject before my mascara started running. "What's this old cutthroat doing here?"

Haggerty smiled at me. "How're y'all t'day, Mr. Jinkins?"

I nodded at him. "What do you say, Titus?" And waited for Lenny to answer.

"Mr. Patel caught him shopliftin' two cans o' beer outta Git-N-Go."

I shook my head and looked at the old coot. "Have you thought about seeking help for kleptomania?"

He laughed, exposing a mouthful of nicotine stained, gray-green teeth. I was surprised he knew the meaning of *kleptomania*. "I's jest thirsty, but I ain't got no money."

"It's after arraignment time," Lenny said. "He's not drunk right now and eligible for twenny-five dollars bail. But like he says, he ain't got no money."

I put a hand to my forehead, shook my head and exaggerated exasperation. "Titus, Titus, Titus, why do you cause so much trouble?"

Lenny broke my spell before Haggerty could answer my rhetorical question. "Think I oughtta ROR his ass or put him in a cell for the night?"

I really didn't care what happened to the incorrigible old miscreant. "Do whatever you want. My advice—take him out back and shoot him."

Lenny laughed, and his dark Errol Flynn mustache stretched wide over his lip. Titus blinked, and his jaw ricocheted off his chest.

"Just kidding, Titus," I said. "We know where to find you if you don't show up in court. But you decide. You want a room at the Hotel Prospect and a couple of free meals, or would you rather get back on the street and fend for yourself?"

He showed me his offensive teeth again. "Shoot, Mr. Jinkins, I wouldn't mind some free food, if y'all don't care."

Considering my current opinion of Mayor Ronnie Shields and how paying one of the on-call cell guards always troubled his sense of fiscal wellbeing, I was happy to suggest keeping the old drunk overnight. "There you go, Lenny. Mr. Haggerty would love to accept your offer of accommodations. When I go up front, I'll tell Terri to call the next guy on the cell guard list."

Lenny Alcock thanked me, and I left the squad room.

Twenty-two paces later, I stood next to Police Officer Terri Donnellson who sat behind the reception desk in the PD lobby. I shucked off my lightweight navy blue blazer, tossed it at the coat tree behind the desk and to her left and missed. Terri heard the silver buttons hit the floor and looked at me.

"Any luck?" she asked.

"A lot of work. Not a lot of luck." I sat in the chair next to her desk.

"Are you waiting for me to pick up your jacket?"

I shrugged. "I thought you wanted to work the street. Did you volunteer to be the desk officer?"

"No, sir, I did not. I figured when Sergeant Lambert left, Joey Gillespie would take the job. But I guess it was okay for him to get *assigned* to work here, only *volunteering* for desk duty wasn't the manly thing to do. So, as last man in line, I was the one who got the inside job no one else wanted."

"Uh-huh. Seniority will get you every time."

Terri Donnellson looked like anything except a last *man*. She was an attractive twenty-eight-year-old, former military police sergeant whose dark hair and olive complexion favored her mother's Italian side of the family rather than her father's Scotch-Irish heritage. I had hired Terri only weeks before I got canned as chief at Prospect PD.

"Anything I can do to help you with this missing person?" she asked.

"Besides pick up my sport jacket?"

She frowned.

"I was in the neighborhood and figured I'd stop in to see if anyone left any messages for John or me. Or if there's been any progress closer to home. I assume the missing person hasn't come back yet?"

She shook her head. "Sorry. None of the above."

"This new job is not easy."

She smiled. "How about some help in your new business?"

I never expected that. "You want to go private now?"

"Just part time. I checked, and nothing in the city's rules forbids a cop from working security on their off time. I thought if you ever needed a female operative..."

"I guess you liked your undercover gig during the Leary case."

She smiled. "Yes, sir. That was almost Wild West stuff. I wouldn't mind working with you and John again."

"Hmmm. If John had an assistant, I wouldn't have to go to work as often. That sounds good. I'll tell him to give you my share of the case money."

"Really?" She sounded surprised.

"Yeah. That's a good idea. I'll tell John to call you. Don't let this get around, but I gave him fifty-one percent of the business so he'd call it Jenkins and Gallagher. But you don't have to call him boss—unless you want brownie points."

"I'll remember that. And thanks. Sure you don't need me to do anything to help find your missing person?"

"Not at the moment, but I might. I'm not sure where to go next. I'll see if Gallagher came up with anything useful. But since you've got no good news for me, I'd better schlep into the Justice Center and tell our new sheriff what's happening." I took a step toward my jacket and stopped. "Oh, I almost forgot. Lenny needs a guard for that old coot he arrested."

———

AFTER BEING ANNOUNCED BY BETTYE'S SECRETARY, CYNTHIA Wilkins, a thirty-five-year-old brunette not quite as lovely as her boss, but pretty good-looking in anyone's book, I walked into the sheriff's second floor office and grunted.

Bettye looked up at me. "What is wrong with you, Sammy?"

She dropped her granny glasses on the desktop and continued to stare at me. Her hair was the color of wildflower honey with a few carefully placed platinum blonde highlights. The highlights were new since she left Prospect PD.

I collapsed into the chair next to her desk like a wrecking ball dropped from twenty feet above the ground. "I hate these missing adult cases. Waste of time. Missing children or teens are easy—they're really missing."

Bettye took a deep breath and attempted to look conciliatory "You want coffee, darlin'?"

I shrugged.

"Is that a yes?"

"No. I want a drink."

"It's too early, even for you."

I looked at my watch. "It's 4:15. Besides, the drinks don't know what time it is."

She smiled, and I scowled as she sat in a classy, high back swivel chair behind a large desk John Gallagher would have loved to buy for his new office. If Bettye ever got bored with police work, we could turn her desk into a regulation ping-pong table.

"You told me you liked missing person cases."

"I lied?"

She smiled. "Gonna tell me why you didn't last in the juvenile section?"

I frowned. "I don't like to talk about my past."

"Yes, you do."

"Pfui. I only went there because they had an open spot, and I desperately wanted to get out of the *bag*. God knows I didn't want to rehabilitate the junior gangsters of the world. The family court judges said I didn't relate to the *clientele*. Not true. I could relate to those young scoundrels. I treated them like adults. It was the parents who couldn't stand me. All the rich people with big mouths and political clout never believed their little darlings would ever commit a crime." I raised my eyebrows. "I belonged in the general service squad to which they soon banished me."

Her smile widened. "Nothing ever changes, does it, Sammy?"

"What?"

She shook her head and changed the subject. "No luck so far?"

I shook my head, too. "Technically, he's a missing person. It's a lot more than forty-eight hours, and he's supposedly mentally challenged. I say hogwash. Half the people we deal with every day have IQs below eighty. This guy is smart by most standards."

"Didn't his parents say he's gone missin' before?"

"They did. So that gives me—and them—hope. And consider this. The weather is beautiful, Tommy Lee Helton is twenty-seven, and although he's not the sharpest tack in the carpet, he's a good-looking boy. Everyone I've talked to so far says he's highly functional. I think his mother claimed he's slow to get us motivated. Maybe he met a girl who liked him, and she whisked him away for a few of days of shoddy pleasure in a motel room with a heart-shaped hot tub in Gatlinburg. A long winter might be on the way. Why not sew a few wild oats before the freeze?"

Bettye gave me a sexy chuckle. "I'll bet your hormones outweighed your common sense when you were twenty-seven."

"I was a very mature guy in my twenties. When I hit thirty-five, I lapsed into my second childhood."

"Isn't that the truth?" She wrinkled her nose. "And you've never grown up."

I've always let many of the things she says go by the wayside to keep me out of trouble. "So far no one we've talked to says they've ever known Tommy Lee to abuse drugs or alcohol. His biggest vice is that god-awful sweet tea you people drink. It's got so much sugar he'll need dentures before he's forty."

She smiled and shook her head. "Not all of us, darlin'. If I drank sweet tea, my hips would be two nightsticks wide."

I felt obliged to mention how attractive her hips looked but didn't. I closed my eyes and tried to look frustrated.

"Is there anything I can do to help you find this boy?" Bettye asked. "I could probably free up a couple deputies for a day or two."

I shook my head. "You've done all you can, and I can muster up additional help if we need it. I'm not going to worry too much. The kid's got a good job at Prospect Hardware, and they owe him a paycheck and a couple weeks' vacation. Maybe he just forgot to tell Ervil he'd be taking off. John and I will look for him again tomorrow. There are a few more places for us to try."

———

JOHN AND I LOOKED FOR TOMMY LEE HELTON THE NEXT DAY, AND the one after that and still came up with bupkis. The surrounding police departments used a current photo Bettye's secretary faxed them and sent officers to visit every motel, resort, bed and breakfast, campground and flop house in the touristy towns surrounding the Great Smoky Mountains National Park. Negative results seemed to be the best anyone could turn up.

So, I looked to the women in my life for assistance. My wife appealed to her comrades at the Blount County Friends of the Library to volunteer a day of their time and walk the woodlands paralleling the Orr's Valley section of Prospect where Tommy Lee lived and frequently hiked.

A friend, Amelia Goodhardt, co-owner of Prospect Aviation, put me in touch with her associates at the local Civil Air Patrol to get a squadron of small planes into the air searching the foothills of the Smokies from above.

Another friend, but not a woman, John Leckmanski, a cameraman at WNXX TV in Knoxville, asked his station manager to put out a broad-cast requesting more assistance to comb the hills around Orr's Valley and made sure their competition did the same.

From all the publicity, I mustered a small army of volunteers that included a couple dozen Boy Scouts and a troop of my own cavalry. Twenty horse owners showed up in a caravan of trucks and trailers to provide mounted coverage. We saw good reason why Tennessee is called the Volunteer State.

Amelia and I jumped into a comfortable twin engine Cessna owned by her father, retired Air Force Lieutenant Colonel Charlie Goodhardt, and, like a proper battalion commander, I supervised the day long search from the air.

Remember what I said about bupkis? That just didn't go away. Twelve hours and many cumulative miles later, no one knew any more than I did before we started. No Tommy Lee Helton and no 1999 white Ford Focus owned and operated by our missing person.

Before we dispersed, almost half my ground force volunteered for a second day of combing the domes, hollows, flats, creek beds and other terrain in the foothills of the Great Smoky Mountains. After the assembled troops left, but before going home, I adjourned to the admin building at Prospect Air Park.

Amelia, four other pilots and their four observers stood around the soda machine in the waiting room.

"We can go up again tomorrow," she said. "Start early and keep up our grid search."

The other people either shrugged or nodded. Everyone looked tired, but no one said they wouldn't try again.

"Daddy'll be home late tonight," she said. "He can take the Cessna, and you and I can use the Red Baron." She was referring to her sexy, crimson biplane.

I sighed. "I hate to put you guys through all this, but it makes a good show for Tommy Lee's parents, and one of us may turn up something."

I heard a chorus of things like, "No problem." "Gotcha covered." And a few laughs after someone said, "That's what we don't get paid for."

The other pilots left, and I stood there with Amelia, hoping she'd break out a bottle of scotch.

"You did one hell of a job today," I said. "I owe you for this."

She closed one eye and squinted at me with the other. "Damn right you do, Bubba." Amelia spoke with no particular regional accent. She was an Air Force brat who never stayed in one place long enough to pick one up.

She wore a gray jumpsuit with the Prospect Aviation logo embroidered above her right breast pocket. She had her long brown hair pulled back into a ponytail, and a small smudge of something dark marked her otherwise flawless face. I took out a clean handkerchief and rubbed her cheek.

"You look like a little kid with dirt on your face," I said.

She smiled. "I'll never see forty again, and it's just my luck my only current boyfriend is married."

I shrugged. "There's someone out there in the wild blue yonder who's the right guy for a hot woman like you."

She laughed silently. "I live in hope."

I smiled. "To show my appreciation and the affection I can't profess, how about I take you to lunch some day? Bring your old man. He's good company, too."

"You've got a deal, Sherlock. I'll think of some place nice...and expensive."

I shook my head. "You better wear something slinky. I'm not spending my hard-earned cash on a girl in overalls."

"It's hard to believe I like you so much. But you've got a deal. I've got this cute little black number you'll like."

I winked at her. "See you tomorrow. Same time?"

She nodded. "Yeah. Maybe we'll have more luck." She looked beautiful, exhausted, but not hopeful.

———

THE SEARCH LASTED TWO MORE DAYS BEFORE MY VOLUNTEERS appeared to lack the enthusiasm for another round.

TV stations continued to broadcast appeals for assistance, but even they began to look at my missing person case as old news. Seemingly, the man and his automobile had dropped off the Tennessee countryside.

Lacking any other avenue to search for possible leads, I revisited Tommy Lee Helton's place of employment, the Prospect Hardware Store.

CHAPTER TWO

IT WAS THE LAST OF A DYING BREED—A REAL OLD-FASHIONED specialty shop not driven out of business by the behemoth home improvement stores that dominate the trade and the country like Russian women dominate the mail-order bride racket.

Located in a fairly large, almost hundred-year-old building on South Main Street below the town square, the Boggs family have owned and operated Prospect Hardware since it would have been appropriate to call them ironmongers.

A trip inside the store was like stepping back in time or into a working folk museum depicting life in the early twentieth century. All the shelving around the store was wooden. The tongue and groove wall paneling had long ago turned the color of maple syrup, the way orange shellac does when it tips the half-century mark.

A low counter spanned half the width of the floor space and sat three quarters of the way back from the entrance. Below the counter, facing the customer, were compartments holding assorted nails sold by the pound, things all grandfathers bought several times a year.

Ervil Boggs stood behind the counter with an unlit pipe between his teeth. He was an odd specimen, short and sort of rotund, almost bald, but with a band of hair just above his ears and a walrus mustache—both too dark not to have been artificially colored by someone akin to Miss Clairol. If you dropped a ten-gallon Stetson on his head, you might mistake him for Boss Hogg.

"Hello, Ervil. How's it going?"

"Hey, Chief. You doin' aw rot t'day?"

"I'm not the chief anymore. I work for the sheriff now."

He nodded, and the pipe wiggled between his teeth. "Well, how 'bout that."

"I need to ask you more about Tommy Lee Helton."

"Why shoot, I already done told John Gallagher all I knew."

"I know you spoke with John, and he looked in Tommy Lee's locker, but I'm at a dead end here, partner. I've got to retrace our steps, looking for a lead."

"Okey dokey, ask away."

I flipped open a folder containing all the notes John and I made for the case book. "You said he worked for you for nineteen months."

Ervil nodded and shifted the pipe from the left side of his mouth to the right.

"During the times when you weren't handling customers, did you guys talk? You know, shoot the breeze, tell each other things or ask questions that weren't business related?"

He frowned and slowly shook his head as if I just asked the $64,000 question. "Nosir, not really."

I tried to make my next statement not sound offensive. "What did you do? No one just stares holes in the walls for eight hours a day."

"Tommy Lee, he'd mostly like ta tidy up. Boy was always dustin' or straightenin' out the shelves. I never had ta do much myse'f 'cept check stock and see if we needed ta reorder. But then again, he kinda kept an eye on that, too. Tommy Lee was a good worker. Knew what needed ta be done."

And Ervil sounded as ambitious as a kamikaze pilot.

"If he was that good, you think someone else offered him more money and he left for another job?"

He shook his head. "Doubt it. I pay as much as them big stores, and them boys with the Ace store in Knoxville got them all the he'p they need."

I looked at my notes again. "His mother said Tommy Lee worked with his father for seven years doing construction. Says Tommy and his old man didn't get along. He ever talk about that?"

"Other than sayin' that his daddy didn't have much patience for him, no. Guess he's still on good terms though. He's still livin' at home, far as I know. And I'll tell ya this, him workin' construction all those years hep'd out when the customers asked questions."

"I'm sure it would. Now help me understand something. His mother said Tommy Lee was a little slow. Yet you say he was a sharp kid. Did you see anything about him that wasn't intelligent?"

"Intelligent?"

"Why would a parent say their kid was dumb if they weren't?"

"Cain't imagine. He seemed pretty reggler ta me."

"Do you know what he did on his off time? He like to hunt or fish or play golf? Or hell, I don't know."

Ervil smiled. "Tommy Lee weren't the golfin' type. Said he didn't like huntin'. Don't know about fishin'."

"How about girls?"

He broke a wolfish grin, "Oh yeah. Tommy Lee, he liked girls jest fine."

That made sense. From the picture we got from his mother, he looked like a real Prince Charming. I needed to know who he chose as Cinderella.

"I'm sure he did. I mean specifically. You told John that a Yardley Abbott stopped in a couple times and seemed interested in him. What's her story?"

He nodded, thinking for a moment. "Nice girl. Good-lookin'. Nice family, I guess. Don't know them well. Think they live jest west o' the Murr-vull line. That's why they come in here 'stead o' goin' ta one o' them big stores ta the west. Father runs a vacuum cleaner shop down south on 129."

"Did you tell John about the vacuum store?"

He shook his head slowly. "Don't think so."

I made a note about the store location as a middle-aged woman stepped up to the counter and asked for three boxes of Mason jar lids. Boggs led her two aisles away where she chose what she needed. As the pair returned to the cash register, the dumpy Ervil moved with the fluid grace of a waddling penguin. After he rang up the sale and thanked the woman for her patronage, she left the store, and Boggs smiled at me, stuck the pipe back between his teeth and asked, "Now, where was we?"

"What did Tommy Lee say about Yardley?"

"Nuthin' much."

Ervil Boggs was beginning to frustrate me. It was like discussing evolution with a backward child. Who works with someone for a year and a half and knows nothing about them?

"Did he ever go out with her?"

"Mebbe. I'm guessin' his momma might know better."

"Mmmm. You think he might have gone over to the casino in Cherokee on the North Carolina side of the mountains and maybe took a girl with him?"

"Never said he liked ta gamble. Cain't see it myse'f. Hate ta lose money. Now, Tommy Lee, he seemed more like the outdoor type."

A spark of hope?

"Like what? Hiking? Playing ball? What did he do outside?"

"Like whatever you do in the environment."

"The environment?"

"Uh-huh. Did say once he was goin' ta meet with an environment group."

"Like environmentalists? Activists? Did they have some kind of cause he supported?"

"Could be, but he never said as much, and I didn't ask. Didn't want ta seem nosey."

I gritted my teeth, spent another fifteen minutes trying to pry information out of Ervil Boggs and left needing a drink.

———

I TAPPED IN JOHN GALLAGHER'S CELL PHONE NUMBER AND GOT him on the second ring.

"You in Maryville?" I asked.

"Just picked up a sandwich and stopped at the office. What do you need?"

"Check around and find a vacuum cleaner store on 129 owned by a guy named Abbott. He's the father of the girl Boggs told you was interested in Tommy Lee. Ask him how you can find daughter Yardley. Maybe she works at the store. Who knows? I had to use a crowbar to get that much out of Ervil. Now's a good time to interview her."

"Yeah, I remember her. Yardley, like the soap. Good lead on the store. That saves me from calling all the Abbotts in the phone book."

"I wish we could find a few real leads. So far working this case is about as easy as landing a 747 on the Long Island Expressway at rush hour. Either this kid is the next best thing to the Phantom of the Opera or someone made him disappear."

"You get anything else from the hardware guy?"

"Unfortunately, no. The man has the IQ of a Brussels sprout."

"Okay. I'll find the Abbotts and let you know. What are you doing now?"

"Looking for Tommy Lee's old man. He's building a house somewhere in Townsend. Oh, don't forget to give our man Sergeant Cullum a check. The rent is due in a couple days."

"Okay, Boss. Soon as I finish my sandwich."

———

JIMMY HELTON BUILT HIGH PRICED HOMES ALL OVER BLOUNT County. He used the most talented subcontractors and the best materials—vinyl-clad, wooden windows, solid wooden doors, real tile and hardwood floors and top of the line carpet and appliances—no cheap contractor grade components for Jimmy.

He had a good business reputation with his customers, but as we came to learn, people said as a husband and father he fell short of the mark.

I found him in the Dry Valley area of Townsend supervising the construction of a rustic 5,000 square foot vacation home for some hotshot from Atlanta.

"I don't know what else ta tell ya." He wouldn't stop walking while I asked questions. "Damn it, Arlie," he shouted at a worker on the roof. "I tol' ya ta use step flashin' against the dormers. Save that roll copper for the roof valleys. Damn stuff costs more 'an gold." He turned to me. "These kids don't remember shit."

"Mr. Helton, I'm trying my best to find your son. How about you stop for a minute, and help me out here?"

"Ya didn't have ta shout. I'm not one of the cops ya can boss around."

Helton was in his late fifties, a few inches shy of six feet tall, stocky and solid, with a good face any woman might consider handsome.

I stared at him for a long moment, remembering he might be distraught over the disappearance of his son and a little short on patience...or not. "I've tried a hell of a lot to find your son, Mr. Helton, but now I need more information than what we've got. Either he's out there doing something with someone..." I hesitated. "Or something's happened to him. Let's work on the first possibility and hope for the best."

He nodded. "All right. I got four houses under construction. I guess I get a little short tempered sometimes. Sorry." He didn't sound particularly contrite.

I nodded and smiled so he thought I understood and harbored no ill feelings. "Let's start with why he no longer works for you. His boss at the hardware store said he was a good employee."

"Then he's luckier than me."

"How so?

Jimmy Helton stared at me with a pair of hard, cold eyes.

"Boy was irresponsible. I know he's a little slow, but he was far from stupid. He can function on a job if he wants ta. He was good with tools and his hands, but he just wouldn't apply himself. I'd have ta tell him something ten times b'fore he remembered. Showed up late sometimes. Didn't show up at all other times. I let it go long as I could."

Tommy Lee didn't sound like a favorite son.

"Why did you keep him around for seven years?"

"For his mother mainly. He started with me right out of high school. He was only eighteen, but even so, didn't show much responsibility. I figgered he'd learn. I figgered wrong."

"You said he showed up late or not at all. He lives at home but didn't drive to work with you?"

"We drove separately. I always need my ve-hickle during the day and might not have been with him at quittin' time."

"You must have talked with him about his attendance problems. He stayed around for seven years," I reiterated. "What did he say?"

"Stupid things, like he was with friends, or he had ta meet someone."

"Like who?"

"Who do you think? Women, that's who. He was a good-lookin' boy, and the girls always liked him. And if ya ask me, Tommy Lee walked around most his life horny as a two petered goat. You find his latest woman, you'll find him."

"Can you give me a few names?"

He pulled out a cell phone. "Don't really pay attention to 'im. I'll ask my wife."

"My partner already did."

He grinned and shook his head. "You don't know Jewel. She thinks that if she gives you a name, she'll get them in some kinda trouble. I'll get you names." He tapped in a phone number with a vengeance and waited for it to ring. "Jewel, I got this detective here. He needs him some names o' Tommy Lee's friends—girls mostly."

He listened with a look on his face that told me he wasn't pleased with what he heard. "Goddamnit, Jewel, that ain't for you ta decide. Gimme a damn name so I can get this man offa my back."

He listened for a long moment. "That's it? That's all ya know. Think, Jewel."

Again he listened and nodded. Then he hung up without a goodbye.

He looked at me again with those cruel, dark eyes. "Sometimes that woman gives new meanin' ta the word *stupid*. She says my son's latest woman was that one fillin' his head full o' nonsense—they wanna make trouble for that paper company over on the North Carolina side. Name's Bernice or Bernadette or somethin'. Tommy called her Bernie."

"You know Bernie's last name?"

"I do not."

"Anyone else?"

"Gettin' that outta her was hard enough, but I'll ask again t'night."

"Will you call me if she remembers someone else?"

He nodded grudgingly.

"How about a name for the people or group dealing with the paper company?"

"I could care less."

"Thanks for your time, Mr. Helton."

———

I called John Gallagher and asked him to meet me at our office when he finished at the vacuum cleaner store.

The rented headquarters for the newly formed Jenkins and Gallagher Private Investigations, LLC came in the form of a one story prefab extension attached to a warehouse-like affair owned by retired Army Sergeant-First-Class Chuck Cullum and used by him for stripping and refinishing furniture. Our digs consisted of a twenty-six by eighteen-foot room broken up into two ten by nine offices separated from the main room by floor to ceiling glass partitions and a pair of flimsy hollow-core doors. John had already set up his room while all I had in mine was an empty desk, an old swivel chair and a battered armless chair that looked like it might have been used when interrogating prisoners at the Lubyanka Prison.

Our building sat on the east side of Home Avenue in the metropolis of Maryville between a computer graphics business and a Triple A wrecker service. A repair shop called Auto Pro was across the street and the Cates Memorial Garden, a place where apartment dwellers could rent an allotment of topsoil and grow fresh vegetables was down the road a' piece.

I parked my truck next to John's old Saturn and walked inside. I found John sitting in his office, nibbling on one portion of a Hardee's fried chicken meal. An unruly pile of scattered French fries and the contents of six envelopes of ketchup lay on a stretched out white paper bag. A plastic cup, large enough to hold enough liquid to hydrate an entire village of desert dwellers for a week, filled with what I assumed to be diet soda, sat only inches from his right arm.

"I thought you ate a sandwich before you went to the vacuum store," I said.

"I did, but I got hungry again on the way back. There wasn't much of a crowd at the place on Calderwood, so I stopped and picked up a snack."

"Your snack looks like Thanksgiving dinner for a homeless person. You're probably detoxing from cholesterol withdrawal."

"Huh?"

I ignored the question. "What did you learn from Mr. Abbott and/or the lovely Yardley?"

"I'm still eatin'. Why don't you tell me what Tommy Lee's old man said?"

"Because you shouldn't be eating again, and I want to hear what you know, which may be a good lead into what I know. Understand?"

"Sounds like a snow job, Boss, but okay, here goes." John licked a smear of ketchup off his right thumb and index finger and dried them with one of the six napkins lying on the desktop. "Yardley was workin' in the store. It's a family business. Father is the manager, mother does the books, and Yardley and her brother help out. She's full time. The other kid works part-time 'cause he's still a student." He paused to take a drink from the vat of soda. Bubbles of air gurgled through the straw.

"Sounds like an American dream come true. But what did Yardley say about Tommy Lee?"

"Have patience. I'm gettin' there. Good-lookin' girl, that Yardley. About twenty-seven and nice, too. But she said that while she and Tommy Lee were friends since school, they never clicked as boyfriend and girlfriend. She said Tommy Lee liked older women."

"Like how old?"

"You know, like older. In their forties."

"Since he was a kid?"

"I don't know for how long, but she said his current girl looks like she's over forty—for him an older woman. See?"

I sighed. "John, your daughter is in her forties."

"I know, I know, but for Tommy Lee, that's *older women*."

"Did Yardley know any more of these *older* women?"

"Gave me a couple names of local girls, but said this newest *older* girlfriend was someone named Bernie something. She ran across them at the Vienna Coffee Shop in Maryville. Tommy Lee introduced them. That's how she knows. But she didn't remember the last name. Said Bernie didn't sound like a local."

"I got Bernice or Bernadette from Mrs. Helton via a phone conversation with the husband, who, by the way, is a first-class pain in the ass. This Bernie is probably part of the environmental group Ervil mentioned, or so says Jimmy Helton, who acted like my presence at his job site was a total inconvenience. I don't see a reason why yet, but maybe he wanted the kid to disappear. He sure doesn't seem to care if we ever get him back."

"If the kid likes older women, maybe he's in competition with his old man. Do we know if Helton senior is a swordsman?"

"Good question, John. I'm proud of you. Let's explore that."

"I have my moments, Boss."

"Now we need a last name for Bernie and a lead on the environmental group. I'd like to talk with Mrs. Helton. The creep husband made her out to be a nitwit. How did she seem when you spoke with her?"

"Upset. I know the kid is twenty-seven, but she acted like her baby went missing. But I figured some people get unglued easier than others. She seemed a little spacey, but normal enough to me."

"Seeing her without the husband breathing down her neck would be good. I'll make an appointment."

"Good idea."

"I have my moments, John."

"Are you, uh, mockin' me?"

"Would I do that?" I didn't give him an opportunity to answer. "Hey, in between sandwiches, vacuum cleaners and fried chicken, did you pay the rent?"

He slapped his forehead with the heel of his left hand. "Damn. I forgot. I'll get it as soon as I finish this." He pointed at the remaining piece of poultry and half dozen fries.

I shook my head. "I'll take care of it. You'd only get chicken fat on the check."

I took our checkbook out of the locked file cabinet and sat at one of the unoccupied desks in the outer office. John had written three new checks but had neglected to deduct the payments from the balance.

We had only been in business a month and hadn't written more than a few other checks, but immediately I spotted two errors in subtraction in the balance column. I turned on the old-fashioned calculator I brought into the office and reworked the figures. That finished, I clenched my teeth and growled.

"John, did you fail sixth grade math when you were a kid?"

"Whassamatter?"

"This checkbook looks like it's being kept by a mentally challenged ten-year-old."

"No."

"Yes. If I write this check to Sergeant Chucky we'll have exactly $3.49 left—as opposed to the $1034.90 you think we have."

"I goofed?"

"You goofed. But at least we're not in the hole. I'll call Bettye and plead for a salary advance so we don't end up homeless private eyes."

"Don't you mean private investigators, Boss?"

I growled again. "I think I'd better take a look at the ledgers."

"They should be in good shape."

And Hitler should have been more tolerant of people without blond hair and blue eyes.

After ten minutes, I shook my head gently so I wouldn't aggravate the onset of a tension headache. "Is it possible you could explain your bookkeeping system, John?" I yelled loud enough for him to hear me in his office.

"It's simple," he said while walking out into the main room, "like my filing system."

"This is not rocket science, buddy. You enter money out and money in. Somewhere at the end of the year, you either made or lost money. You've got notes and phone numbers here. What's next, a grocery list?"

"They're reminders."

"Someday a treasury agent will remind you we'll be going to debtor's prison. I think we need a bookkeeper."

"Can we afford one?"

"Can we afford the interest and penalties those IRS vampires charge if we screw up our tax returns?"

"Hmm, I guess you're right."

"Do I really want to see your filing system?"

"Maybe not."

"Then we need a secretary—no, an office manager, who's also a bookkeeper."

"We can't afford that."

"Of course we can. Sam Spade hired Effie Perrine and Mike Hammer had that hot little item named Velda. Trust me, John, we need a secretary."

———

AT 2:30, I PULLED UP TO A BRICK-FACED, TWO AND A HALF STORY *McMansion* off Mountain View Trail in Prospect. While John was attempting to learn things about Jimmy Helton, I'd try to pry some information out of his wife Jewel without using my rubber hose.

She was expecting me and answered the door less than sixty seconds after Westminster chimes announced my presence. She led me to a living room that adjoined a wrap-around deck that overlooked Chilhowee Mountain.

"Thanks for providing a name for Tommy Lee's friend," I said. "Your husband wasn't sure if it was Bernice or Bernadette."

She smiled shyly, like someone uneasy about being in mixed company. Jewel Helton was past the half-century mark but would have scored a solid nine in anyone's book of attractive women. Dark brown eyes and the dark eyebrows below her blond hair told me the color was her choice, not Mother Nature's. She was about five-five with a trim figure and an expensive-looking outfit of tan slacks and a blue, short sleeve blouse. Having seen her husband in action, I thought the lines at the corner of her eyes came more from stress than smiles.

"It's Bernadette—I think," she said.

"Do you know the last name?"

"I'm not sure."

"Is she a local woman?"

"I don't think so."

"Do you know from where?"

"I think Tommy Lee said originally from Cleveland."

"Ohio or Tennessee?"

"Ohio, I guess."

"Any idea how old?"

"No."

Jewel was a woman of few words.

"How did your son meet her?"

"He said they're interested in conservation."

"Do they belong to an organized group?"

"I think they do."

"Do you know the name?"

27

She made a facial gesture someone would make if they wanted me to assume they were trying to think. "Uh...no."

I tried rewording a previous question. "Does Bernadette live nearby?"

"Maryville, I think. Or maybe Knoxville."

That narrowed it down to only a couple hundred square miles.

"Do they go out often—to dinner, the movies—other than doing things with the conservation group?"

"I think so."

"Did Tommy Lee refer to her as his girlfriend or just a friend?"

"Well, she is a girl—woman actually—and his friend. So, I guess she's his girlfriend."

Screaming at that point would have been unprofessional—but I wanted to.

"Did he ever bring her home to meet you and Mr. Helton?

"No."

If Jewel wasn't so good-looking I would have strangled her.

I tried a stupid but desperate question. "How do I find her?"

"Mmm? I don't have her phone number."

"Would you have any more recent photos of Tommy Lee?"

"I think so. But I'll look to be sure. Excuse me."

At that point, she got up, and I would have sworn Jewel Helton had been born in Chelm, the fabled city of idiots.

———

ON THE WAY BACK TO MARYVILLE, I PULLED OFF JENNINGS Hollow Road and called Sheriff Bettye Lambert.

"Blondie, you owe me for this one."

"What's the matter, darlin'? Not havin' much luck?"

"I just re-interviewed Mrs. Helton, the world's most lovely imbecile."

"How'd that go?"

"Somewhere between brilliant and a bucket of horse manure."

"Uh-oh."

"If I lived among this group of nincompoops like Tommy Lee Helton, I would have run away from home long before I reached puberty. If this guy had any sense, he'd be on a boat with a beautiful woman sailing to Tahiti."

"Can you find that boat for me, Sammy, and get Tommy Lee to phone home?"

I could almost hear her eyelashes fluttering up and down.

"This one's not easy, Betts."

"I know, sugar, but these are the kinds of cases only you can solve. I've seen you in action, and I trust you."

"You play me like a second hand marimba."

"Me?"

"Yes, you, Now, I need three things. First, I put you to work—or one of your trusted minions."

"I have minions?"

"Grrr. Save me a little time and get somebody to find out what environmental group or groups are concerned about pollution of the river system coming out of North Carolina because of a paper company. The newspapers ran a story a few months back. If I remember correctly, it's called the Cataloochee Paper Mill. And that probably involves the Pigeon, Little Pigeon and Little Rivers."

"I kin do that fer ya." She sounded especially bubbly...and local.

"Great, you're my favorite sheriff. Next, I need money. We're desperate. John didn't exactly screw up our books, but we're dangerously close to being broke because of his infantile mathematical skills."

"How much money?" She went from bubbly to suspicious.

"How about a couple weeks advance for both of us. I'll stick my share into the checkbook. The Gallaghers won't eat unless he gets a few bucks."

"What do they do with their money?"

"Besides spend like drunken sailors? My imagination isn't that good."

"Don't you think you should keep the books?"

"Don't go getting supervisory with me. But that brings me to item number three. Do you know anyone with great organizational skills, a fair knowledge of accounting and bookkeeping who'll work for peanuts?"

Bettye remained silent for a long moment; I assumed either thinking of someone or just trying to formulate the words to suggest I was crazy.

"Darlin'," she said, "I've got just the girl for you."

CHAPTER THREE

BETTYE LAMBERT ASSIGNED ONE OF HER NEW DETECTIVES TO handle a little of the tedious work, searching for Tommy Lee Helton's group of environmental activists. With only a few phone calls and short periods of waiting on hold, he found a herd of zealots who called themselves The Smoky Mountain Ecologists. They rented a storefront office on East Broadway Avenue in the Eagleton section of Maryville, a ten-minute drive from our place.

To keep him from writing any rubber checks, I took John Gallagher with me.

"You find any dirt on Jimmy Helton?" I asked.

"Not much. I ran him through the sheriff's office and Prospect PD. Prospect had one old domestic complaint on him. But the kid called and not the wife. Tommy Lee claimed that the old man was verbally abusive to his mother and was afraid things might get physical. No signs of her getting tuned up, though, and Jimmy voluntarily left the house. Harley Flatt handled the call. Terri looked, but there was no recall. Situation resolved."

"That's it?"

"My neighbor works for the lumber yard where Jimmy buys his

31

supplies. I asked him if Jimmy was a ladies' man. He didn't know. Said he might flirt with the cashiers, but nothing that amounted to sexual harassment, and he never saw Jimmy ask anyone out."

"Hard to find out about affairs unless you knew someone who didn't like Jimmy."

"Even if I did a neighborhood investigation, people would never tell me about him screwing around or even coming on to a neighbor's wife. People never want to get involved."

"Until after you independently uncover some major problem with your subject. Then everyone is more than ready to say, 'I could have told you so.' The world is full of Monday morning quarterbacks who wouldn't tell the truth if it saved them from drowning."

"You got that right."

"You check if Jewel ever filed for a separation or divorce?"

"Boss, that hurts. You think I wouldn't?"

"Perish the thought."

I parked my truck in the cramped, poorly maintained blacktop lot next to The Smoky Mountain Ecologist's office. The hand painted sign with colorful impressionistic wildflowers surrounding the business name looked as if it had been created by a former hippie. Flower power all the way.

A horn sounded to our left. Brakes squealed, and we looked around. Someone in a Miata tried to make a quick left turn in front of oncoming traffic and just missed getting creamed by a cablevision truck. I shook my head. John shrugged. The American public bent on killing off each other.

The old door needed a healthy yank to open, but once inside, we found three people sitting behind scarred up desks that had seen better days. I spoke to a bearded young man sitting closest to the door and showed him my badge.

"Hi. We're investigators from the sheriff's office working a missing person's case. We have reason to believe that a Tommy Lee Helton might belong to your group."

He stood and stepped up next to us. "I'm Brad Winstead, one of the volunteers. I heard that Tommy Lee was missing. Yeah, he belongs to the group. How can I help?"

"When was the last time you heard from him?"

"Let me check our login book. Every time a member works, in the office or outside, they get...logged in."

He walked over to a dented, open front metal bookcase that looked like the ecologists purchased it from the same people where I bought our recycled office suite and pulled out a loose-leaf binder. He placed the book on his desk and thumbed through the last few pages.

"Here ya go. A bunch of volunteers were going to Cocke County to set up a demonstration where the Pigeon River crosses into Tennessee. Tommy Lee was part of that group."

He provided a date two weeks before Mrs. Helton reported her son missing.

"And no phone calls or other messages from him since?"

"Nothing logged in, but I can send out a group email asking if anyone has heard from him."

"That would be good. Thanks," John said.

"Did anyone report any problems from the people in Cocke County?"

He shook his head. "No. The average citizen never gives us a hassle. It's only the people at the paper mill who resent what we're doing."

"Was Tommy Lee a very active member?" John asked.

"I'd say he put in more time than most. He liked to do the outside work—handing out flyers, being part of sit-ins and protests. That sort of stuff."

"Was he aggressive?" I asked. "Do things to anger people?"

Brad shook his head again. "We're into peaceful demonstrations. We get permits, and if the police tell us to move, we move. I never saw Tommy confront anyone. Like I said, most people appreciate what we do—except the paper mill, of course. If we accomplish our goal, it will cost them tons of money they're not spending now. We're a threat to their profits."

"You have a member named Bernice or Bernadette?" John asked.

"We have a Bernadette Gavin. I don't think there's a Bernice."

"How do we find her?" I asked.

"Is she in trouble?"

"Don't think so. We've heard that she and Tommy Lee were friends —perhaps a little closer. Do you have her contact information?"

"Sure, hold on."

This time he tapped a name into his computer.

"Here ya go. Phone numbers, home and business address. I'll print it for you."

———

Bernadette Gavin was a case worker for the county's Department of Human Services, Public Assistance Section—otherwise known as our welfare department. Her office was just down the street from our building, next to the Motor Vehicle Bureau. We called first to be sure she'd be in the building.

Bernie was a tall, good-looking brunette with shoulder length 1980s styled hair, a Kate Jackson face and eyes the color of eighteen-year-old scotch. Prior to meeting her, John ran her name through the sheriff's computer system and learned that she was forty-three. She met us in the lobby.

"Ms. Gavin, I'm Sam Jenkins, and this is John Gallagher. We're investigators with the sheriff's office."

She frowned and folded her arms defensively across her breasts, looking a little apprehensive—probably thinking we couldn't find one of her clients and wanted a location. I've never known a welfare worker keen on sharing information about their clients with a cop.

"How can I help you?" she asked.

"We need information on Tommy Lee Helton. We learned that you know him."

Her face lightened up, and she appeared less defensive. She wore a tan cardigan over a white blouse and a pair of chocolate brown slacks, looking more like an executive secretary than someone checking up on welfare recipients.

"Yes, I know Tommy. I hadn't heard from him for a few days and was shocked when I read he had gone missing. Do you have any idea where he is?"

"Not so far. You've probably seen the TV news about our searches." She nodded. "I did."

"Have you spoken to Tommy's parents about him?"

"No. I've never met them and, well, according to Tommy, they didn't seem very interested or receptive to me being his friend."

"We haven't been able to get much information from them...other than Tommy hasn't come home."

She repeated her first question with a look of determined intelligence in her eyes, "So how can *I* help you?"

"I hate to say this, but we're in phase two now—investigating the possibility of a serious accident or possible foul play."

One hand went up and partially covered her mouth. "My God. Do you think those people could have harmed him?"

"What people are *those people*?"

"The people from the paper mill, of course."

"Why do you think they might have done something to Tommy Lee?"

Her open and cooperative look changed to one of moderate impatience. "When Tommy got into it with that security man, the guy didn't even try to hide the threat."

"You're talking over our heads now. No one else has mentioned a threat. Can we go somewhere more private and start from the beginning. We need to know when and where this happened."

"All I have is a cubicle, and it's anything but private. I think we can use the lunchroom. No one should be there now."

We followed her to a typical civil service break room with several Formica topped tables surrounded by chrome-framed, vinyl-covered chairs and a wall full of kitchen cabinets holding a microwave oven and a coffee pot that smelled staler than last year's Christmas cookies. A full-sized refrigerator was plastered with paperwork and photographs attached with assorted fridge-mags. The ubiquitous cork bulletin board, hanging on the opposite wall, held pinned-on inter-office memos, a few three-by-five cards with items for sale and a few personal pictures posted by the co-workers. Bernie pointed us toward one of the tables.

I took a small spiral notebook from my pocket and laid it on the faux marble surface. "Okay, before we get into the date and place of this problem with the security man, I'd like to confirm the information we have on you."

She nodded.

"What's your full name?"

"It's Bernadette Amanda Gavin."

"Spelled like the general, not the Scottish man's name?"

She looked like I said something distasteful. "G-A-V-I-N. I hope there's no general with the same name."

"Jumpin' Jim Gavin. Commander of the 82nd Airborne Division in World War Two. I met him once. Nice man."

She frowned. "I'll take your word for it."

I smiled and decided on not making a clever remark. You've got to know your audience, and so far, Ms. Gavin hadn't exhibited a lavish sense of humor.

Finally, she confirmed all the phone numbers and home address I obtained from Brad Winstead.

"Now, let's talk about this business at the paper mill," I said.

"I'll get the exact date for you, but it happened when we set up a protest outside the actual mill property in Waterville. We blocked the entire entrance when someone tried to enter or leave the property until the police told us to move. Once the vehicle was either in or out of the lot, we stood in the driveway again."

"Did anyone get arrested?" John asked.

She took a moment to brush a few strands of chestnut hair behind her right ear.

"No. The cops were fine. Whatever they asked, we did. It was the security guards and this one...thug or whatever he was who gave us grief. The cops had to speak with them, too."

"So the security guards tried to move you from the driveway?" I said.

"They tried every so often even though there were no cars or trucks trying to get through our picket line. If we didn't conflict with anyone, the cops more often than not just sat in their cars. The mill people just wanted us gone, and often enough, the security guards tried to intimidate us."

"But the police intervened and stopped them?"

"Yes. Because we were on the blacktop road, not on mill property. What we did was legal."

"Did the guards ever get physical with you?"

She shook her head, and her hair swayed back and forth. "They would never touch us while the police were present."

"Tell us about this *thug* you mentioned."

From the corner of my eye, I spotted a wood roach, half the size of a small runabout, hotfooting it toward the bottom of the refrigerator. Maybe I'll write a letter to the Commissioner of Human Services and suggest he buy his caseworkers roach traps.

She half shrugged. "Okay, he wasn't a thug—but he looked like one. He was a security man in plainclothes. He wore a green windbreaker with the company logo on the front and SECURITY in big letters on the back. Don't you people call those things raid jackets?"

I grinned. "Sometimes, but not as often as the TV cops. Did you get a name for this man?"

She shook her head enthusiastically. "No, but he looked like an ex-soldier or Marine. Big man. Really big. Short hair. Had that military look about him. Mid- to late-forties and *nasty*."

John again: "Why did he confront Tommy Lee?"

"Tommy could get loud. Animated, too. He started taunting and making personal remarks about the security people. The big guy didn't like it and came after Tommy. But the police must have sensed something might happen and walked over. A cop got between them before anything got physical. But the big guy said he knew who Tommy was and knew where to find him."

"And you believed him, the big guy?"

She shrugged. "I guess. They could see our vehicles parked on the street, and I know this man took plate numbers."

"How many security officers did you see?"

"Three in uniforms, the big guy in his raid jacket and I assumed one more, although he could have been some other company man. He wore a sport jacket and tie, was older than the big man, maybe mid-fifties, but the same look—military or something like that. Know what I mean? Solid-looking. Crew cut. Serious-looking. And, I don't know, sort of dangerous-looking, like the one with the raid jacket."

"You don't like the military?"

That seemed to take her back. Her eyebrows went up and then down into a frown. She looked at me for a long moment.

"Not especially."

"Have you ever protested against the military?"

"What does that have to do with anything?"

"Nothing. I'm just nosey. And I can check with the FBI. You seem to have your ducks in a row—get the required permits, obey the laws. You have a right to protest almost anything. If you did, be proud of yourself."

Bernie tilted her head and looked unsure if she could trust me. "Okay, yeah. With these Middle Eastern wars going on so long, I've marched in protest of a few things like killing civilians or lack of meaningful help for refugees."

I nodded. "Collateral damage is always a problem. I don't know much about the current policy for civic action projects or refugee assistance."

"I assume you're ex-military?"

I nodded. "I was in the Army. My partner here was Navy. Kinda goes well with our fascist pig personas."

She lowered her eyes in embarrassment. "Hey, I didn't mean... You know, you've been nice. And you're trying to find Tommy. I'm sorry. I guess."

"It's okay. We've been called worse. Did Tommy Lee join in on those protests?"

"No, he wasn't part of that group."

"Okay, let's get back to the security man's threat against Tommy Lee."

She nodded.

"Other than the words you heard, do you have any reason to believe things would have escalated and gone any farther?

"If you had seen the look—the rage—on that big man's face, you might believe he'd want to hurt Tommy."

I shot a look at John who raised his eyebrows.

"Let me change the subject for a moment," I said. "Before you said you hadn't heard from Tommy for a few days and that concerned you. I assume you spoke more often?"

"Almost every day—if we didn't see each other."

"Were you and Tommy Lee more than friends? Were you romantically involved?"

"Why do you need to know that?"

"For one thing, it goes toward how credible your information might be. If you two were intimate, you'd know more than someone who only had a passing acquaintance. I'm not looking for graphic details, and excuse me, but pillow talk gets more serious than just two people standing on a picket line."

"I still don't..."

I cut her short. "Look, you're both of legal age to decide if you want to get romantic. Tommy was a good-looking kid. You're an attractive woman. This is the twenty-first century. What's the problem? You're not married, are you?"

"I'm divorced."

"Uh-huh."

"Tommy was twenty-seven. I'm forty-three."

"Sixteen years. So?"

Her eyebrows went up. "You're something else. Doesn't that age difference bother you?"

"And you're young enough to be my daughter. But I still think you're attractive, and you're old enough to make up your own mind about who you see socially. So, no. I could care less."

"Okay."

"Okay what?"

"Okay, we were having sex."

That was about as straight forward as you can get.

She continued. "I have no problem telling you that. My husband left me for a girl young enough to be his daughter. But I wasn't *doing* Tommy for spite."

"I wouldn't have thought that."

She appeared a little annoyed. "Thank you." But softened up quickly enough.

"Before we wrap this up," I said, "can you tell us exactly why The Smoky Mountain Ecologists have a problem with the Cataloochee Paper Mill?"

She looked at me like I had horns sprouting out of my forehead. "Don't you know about the toxic pollution they're discharging into the Pigeon River? Don't you read the papers?"

She didn't allow me to answer. "In turn, that flows westward and enters the Little Pigeon River and the Little River and all the tributary creeks and streams in the Smokies. My God, they're polluting the entire river system—killing off wildlife, ruining this area for generations to come—unless someone stops them."

"Thank you," I said. "I see you're quite passionate about this. And I haven't done enough homework."

She half shrugged. "You're right. I get twisted out of shape over this. I didn't mean to go off like that."

"No problem. We'll live. Can you think of anything else that might be helpful to us?"

She took a moment to think. "Right now, no, not exactly. But I'm upset. I'll call the people who were with us over there in North Carolina and ask them."

"We'd appreciate that. Could you make a list of those people for us?"

"Of course."

I handed her one of the official cards Bettye had made up for me. "When you're ready, give us a call."

"I will."

"And we're sorry to have upset you." I smiled. "Not all ex-GIs are thugs."

She returned the smile. "I know," touched my forearm and quickly pulled her hand away.

"Thanks for your time, Ms. Gavin."

Out in the car, I spoke to John. "Looks like we've got to take a trip to North Carolina."

He nodded. "Yeah, probably an hour and a half drive."

"How about tomorrow morning? Leave here about eight?"

"Sure."

"Good. Now, let's stop at Bettye's office and pick up a couple of checks, so we can pay the rent? And maybe she'll let us borrow a car for the trip. I'll drive faster if we're using her gas."

CHAPTER FOUR

JOHN AND I HIT THE TRAIL EARLY THE NEXT MORNING DRIVING A
spare, unmarked sheriff's car. Not the best rattletrap in Bettye's parking
lot, but bigger than John's Saturn and more professional looking than my
F-150.

We left his house in Prospect, drove through the Knob Creek
community, and picked up Chapman Highway heading east toward
Sevierville. From there, we took narrow and winding backcountry roads
past English Mountain and that famous baked bean factory in Chestnut
Hill. But we didn't meet Duke the golden retriever. Finally, we reached
the I-40 entrance ramp in Newport. From there it wasn't far to the
North Carolina border and the paper mill in Waterville.

A uniformed security guard at the main gate stepped from a tan
and green kiosk with more coats of paint than a hundred-year-old
rowboat to check our identification and direct us toward the row of
visitor parking. As I pulled away from the guard shack, he picked up a
telephone.

The access road to the mill went relatively straight through simply
landscaped grounds and close to a dark and quickly moving river.
Adrenalin junkies would have loved it. The white water bubbled and

surged over rocks and boulders and would have scared anyone but an Olympic kayaker.

Visitor parking was just on the far side of the double entrance doors, past a row of reserved spots, presumably for the management types.

"Before we leave," I said, "let's get these plate numbers in case we want pedigrees on someone we speak to or the company hierarchy."

"Good idea. I'll grab a few now. Go slow."

Just inside the front door, a middle-aged blonde sat behind a reception desk. I told her about our appointment with Donal Curry, Chief of Security.

In less than ninety seconds a big ex-military-looking guy, whom I assumed might be the man Bernie Gavin described, met us in the lobby.

He stuck out a beefy workman-like hand for me to shake. He wasn't exactly a bone crusher, but I wouldn't want him to get angry and grab me by the neck.

"Hi, I'm Bill Koronkiewicz from company security. I'll take you back to meet Don Curry."

In a room full of average guys, Koronkiewicz would stick out like a bull elephant among a colony of field mice.

I treated him to my visiting dignitary's smile. "I'm Sam Jenkins from the Blount County Sheriff's Office over in Tennessee. This is John Gallagher."

Koronkiewicz smiled at John. "Whaddaya say?"

John responded in typical New York fashion. "Yeah, howz it goin'?" They shook hands, too.

A short walk down a typical hallway in the aging commercial building led us to an open door with SECURITY stenciled on the old-fashioned crinkled glass.

The office wasn't laid out much differently than the one John and I now occupied—an outer room with three desks, file cabinets, a copy machine and all the other minor bells and whistles needed to provide security to corporate America. In the rear, a smaller partitioned-off room occupied the right corner. Everything appeared clean and tidy but looked dreadfully turn of the twentieth century.

"That's Don's office back there," Koronkiewicz said as he continued leading the way.

As we approached the security boss's desk, a barrel-chested man with a salt and pepper—mostly salt—crew cut stood and gave us the slightest indication of a smile humanly possible.

I popped out my badge again. "Morning. Sam Jenkins." I poked a thumb to my right. "John Gallagher from the Blount County Sheriff. Thanks for making time for us."

He extended a hand across his desk. "Donal Curry. Happy to help."

A snazzy Perma-Placque, roughly fourteen by eighteen inches, hanging on the wall to my right, told me that Donal Curry was a Certified Security Professional.

After shaking hands with John and me, Curry pointed toward the two chairs in front of his desk. John and I sat. Bill Koronkiewicz stood against the wall on the left side of the room.

"What can we do for you gentlemen?" Curry spoke with a slight New England accent.

"We're looking into a group, and a couple individuals in particular, that makes Blount County home. I believe you're familiar with The Smoky Mountain Ecologists."

Curry took a deep breath and settled a little further into his large swivel chair. "Are we ever. A constant source of aggravation for the company and for us in security every time they show up. Thanks to them, my overtime budget will be in the red for years."

"Over on our side of the mountains they're quite active, but so far no one has crossed the legal line. They get close sometimes, but when people object to them getting a little too pushy, they back off."

Curry shook his head, not disagreeing with anything I said, but more as if he wanted to indicate they represented an entity he could live without. "They set up out front every so often and block traffic—for what reason I don't know. It's not like this part of Waterville gets pedestrian traffic like the Boston Common. No one sees them but us and occasionally the local news and the police who are taken away from doing more meaningful things than babysitting for them."

"Isn't blocking traffic a violation?" John asked.

"Sure, but the police do their jobs, and the protestors move when asked. They've got sympathy from the courts over all this pollution noise."

"Is it just noise?" I asked.

Curry nodded emphatically. "They've had their own hired lab test the water downstream and haven't come up with anything. They say the company is discharging unacceptable pollutants. This place has been in business since 1922. They've installed new filtering systems as technology progressed. The local department of health tests the water periodically and has published no such findings."

"Uh-huh," I said while thinking, '*And I suppose a local health inspector can't be bought.*' "Could you single out anyone or any number of these protestors who you'd consider more militant...or maybe just more of a genuine pain in the ass?"

Koronkiewicz spoke up, "There's one kid—guy in his late twenties—who's got a real mouth on him. And an attitude. Most of the people who show up with that Tennessee group look like typical leftwing tree-hugger types. Know what I mean? They look like school teachers or artists or other kinds of granola eating liberals. They carry their signs, hold hands and make a human chain sometimes to block the driveway—might even chant some nonsense, but they're not aggressive. A few of them—guys mostly, but a few females—get into the act. They try to goad the uniformed guards. They make personal remarks. You know the type. But only one guy stands out."

I nodded. "I do. Does the name Tommy Lee Helton mean anything to you?"

Koronkiewicz shook his head.

Curry said, "Not by name."

I took a photo from the case folder I held and passed it over the desk to Curry.

"I don't recognize him." He handed the picture to Koronkiewicz. "But I have less contact with them than Bill."

Bill nodded. "That's the guy. Worst of the mouthy ones. But I don't know these people by name."

I came out with a picture of Bernie Gavin. "How about her?" I handed it directly to Koronkiewicz.

Another nod. "Yeah. She's here most of the time. I figure her as one of the organizers or a leader if they have them. She seems to take charge of placing the people and...sort of supervising." He passed the two photos to Curry who placed them on his desk. "I've never seen her cause trouble."

"Do you folks photograph the crowd?"

Curry shook his head. "Not our job. And there might be some kind of a privacy issue the company doesn't want to encounter. If they came onto mill property, we'd detain them and ask the police to effect an arrest. But they always stay just a foot or so off the property."

"Have you seen a police photographer taking pictures?"

"No."

"FBI?"

"Not that we know."

"Have you had any notable acts of vandalism on company property?"

"We're locked up tightly after hours. And we have excellent physical and human security assets twenty-four, seven."

Curry certainly had the lingo of a modern security professional down pat.

"Anyone other than these two stand out as problems? Anyone worth mentioning?" John asked before he stood and picked up the photos from Curry's desk.

"As Bill said, there are a few that like to break balls, but we're not acquainted by name. And at this stage, we probably couldn't give you an adequate description. That group is pretty large."

"Do you know if when these people obtain permits to demonstrate they have to provide a roster of participants?" I asked.

"You'd have to ask the sheriff. He issues those permits."

I nodded. "Now, this is really why we took the ride over here." I paused for a moment to see how they would react to my preparatory statement. Curry raised his eyebrows. Koronkiewicz tilted his head and shifted the weight he had been leaning against the wall. I love body language.

"Did you notice any friction or conflict among the protestors?"

Curry turned his eyes to Koronkiewicz, who took that as his cue to speak.

He shook his head slowly as if he wanted us to think his mind was hard at work. "Not that I noticed. You mean like a heated argument or physical confrontation?"

I shrugged. "Anything that would draw your attention. Specifically concerning Helton. That's the guy in the photograph."

"He and I went nose to nose once over a remark he made. The woman in the picture came right over and hustled him away. I was glad. Sometimes I get my Polish up in the air. I probably wouldn't have hit him, but I wanted to. But I've never seen these people argue among themselves."

I smiled. "I know the feeling. Would you mind passing our questions around to your uniformed guys?"

Curry nodded.

Koronkiewicz said, "Sure."

I handed them business cards. "Please give us a call if you think of anything that will help. We can't locate Helton at the moment and would like to talk to him about something. And if you're ever heading our way and want a recommendation for a good restaurant, give a shout, and we'll help you out."

"We'll do that," Curry said. He stood and extended his hand again. "Nice meeting you."

I shook it and said, "Neither of you sound like locals. How'd you end up here in Southern Appalachia?"

Curry smiled for the first time. I assumed that like any big chief in a small tribe he'd be happy to talk about himself.

"I came here for this position. After twelve years in the Marine Corps and thirteen in Department of State Security, I was ready for a semi-retirement job. Bill's from Pennsylvania and did twenty-five in the Corps. We tied up a couple times during embassy postings. I needed a second-in-command and gave him a call. And here we are."

"Small world, isn't it?"

Curry grinned. "And how about you? I hear northeast when you speak."

"We were on the job in New York together. After years of retirement, we wanted a little extra lunch money, and the sheriff offered the investigator's jobs. Stuff like this keeps life interesting."

"I hear you," Curry said.

"Thanks again, gents," I said. "We appreciate your help."

Curry nodded. "You bet."

Koronkiewicz said, "I'll walk you out."

We followed, shook hands in the lobby and left the building.

"John, I'll screw around in the trunk for a minute after I back out. Get those plate numbers."

"You got it."

I stopped the car in back of the reserved parking spots and popped the trunk, spent a few moments thumbing through the paperwork in my briefcase, took out a half dozen sheets of paper and closed the trunk. Before I got back into the car, I called the weather forecast and spoke to the recording. I didn't care what Mother Nature had in store for us, but those theatrics gave John time to finish his job.

We pulled off I-40 somewhere near Candler, North Carolina to eat lunch at a steakhouse I saw advertised on a billboard.

Inside the commercial log cabin, typical of a chain restaurant that wanted to create a rustic mountain setting, a teenaged hostess escorted us to a booth. Moments later, a waitress with tattoos on her forearms and a silver stud in her nose asked for our drink order. I wanted a pint of Blue Moon, and John took a diet Pepsi. We both ordered salmon marinated in a Jack Daniels' whiskey sauce. Five stars all around, except the appearance of the waitress. During lunch, we observed the Nero Wolfe rule of not discussing business while eating.

Almost an hour later, I headed toward the I-40 exit in Newport where we could pick up US 411 back to the peaceful side of the Smokies. With our official investigative work finished for the time being, I canned the police radio and turned on the last half hour of Phlash Phelps on the satellite radio's 1960s morning show just as Jay and the Americans sang the last few lines about *Bad Man Jose*.

"Nice of the sheriff to give you a company car for the trip," John said.

"It was the least she could do. Pulling up to that potentially hostile camp in my twenty-year-old pickup would look unprofessional. You might even say outré."

"You might. I wouldn't."

I looked over at him grinning like a malevolent leprechaun.

"You know, uh, Sam, back on the old job, some of the younger bosses thought you acted *alooth* when you'd speak all those foreign languages at meetings."

"Some of those *younger bosses*, John, needed wet nurses to help them speak intelligent English. I couldn't care less if they considered me *aloof*. But I do have a flare of tossing out a few apropos foreign phrases, don't I? And I can swear and order a beer in eight languages—so there."

"I'm continually amazed and impressed by you, Boss. And I say that with all due respect. But back to your last remark in English. Did you think those security guys might have been uncooperative?"

"I thought they might have been sensitive about that pollution business and their methods of dealing with protestors. And after Bernie's description of who we now know to be Bill Koronkiewicz, I wondered. But he seemed like a pretty straight forward kind of guy. Typical career NCO would be my guess. Maybe he's got anger management issues?"

"Big guy, huh?"

"You bet. He draws your attention like a nudist playing a trombone." John laughed.

"Tommy Lee's double digit IQ was showing when he went nose to nose with that man."

"Probably have to shoot to stop this Kronk-whatshisname character," John suggested.

"You could put six in Big Bill's ten-ring, and he'd only grab your gun and bite off the barrel."

"He looks like a *Kronkowski*," John said." Good name for him."

"Ko-ron-ka-witz, as he pronounced it. Kor-on-kev-ich, as my Polish in-laws would say."

"You're being *alooth* again."

"I'll stop at Walgreens and see if they sell an over-the-counter remedy for that. But first, when we get back, I'll go see Bettye. While I tell her how we made out and weasel a decent car out of her permanently, you can start getting their Marine Corps records. Koronkiewicz might be big and mean-looking, but it was Curry who gave me the creeps. I wonder what his story is."

"Marine Corps records will be easy, but you think we can get detailed DSS info on Curry?"

"Maybe not through the front door. When I'm back in the office, I'll ask Ralph Oliveri if he can work some FBI magic for us. He may also know someone at the Asheville field office who knows something about those two or the paper mill in general."

CHAPTER FIVE

THE NEXT MORNING, I CHECKED IN WITH MY DAILY PROGRESS report for the sheriff and dropped into her guest chair like yet another sack of Long Island potatoes kicked off a truck at a North Fork farm stand.

"Would you sit down easy? I'd like that chair to last as long as I'm here," Bettye said, while casting an evil eye on me.

I sighed. "I need another you."

"I beg your pardon."

"What's hard to understand? For five years I could hit the road, take John with me sometimes and trust you to take care of all the inside investigating—the telephone work, computer searches, the administrative stuff that takes up too much of my time and drives me nuts."

"Is that your excuse?"

"You may outrank me, Blondie, but..." I wiggled a finger at her.

"That's Sheriff Blondie to you, wise guy. So, what do you want? I can't assign a detective to sit in your office all day doing inside work. The country commission only agreed to my proposal of putting you and John on the part-time payroll because I don't have enough people in CID to invest extra time on these major cases. That, and because you created that 'earthquake' after the Ryan Leary business. They're afraid of you. You're a bully."

"Nonsense. I only eliminated a few bad apples from their incestuous barrel. And I don't want one of your detectives. I've got someone in mind. I'll pay her myself when we need help with a PI case. I can bill her salary to the client then, but now we're working for you. At the wages you pay, we can't afford to pay our rent. So, I certainly can't afford to pay her a decent wage."

"Who is this *her* you have in mind and what does *she* have to do with *me*?"

"Silly question. I want *her* to help *me* solve *your* major cases. I want *you* to pay *her*."

Bettye doesn't often get exasperated—unless I'm the cause. "How can I pay *her* when *she* isn't on the payroll? *You* are impossible. And who is *she*?"

"Terri Donnellson. And you wouldn't have to pay her much. Take it out of petty cash, or say you're buying new bookshelves and fake it. Who cares where you get the money?"

"Terri works for Prospect PD, not you."

"But she gets days off, and she asked me if she could work with John and me part-time. She wants to learn how to be a world-class detective like me." I shrugged. "She'd probably work for food or gas money. But for god sakes, woman, pay her twenty bucks an hour."

"Are you crazy? Our regular deputies don't start at twenty dollars an hour on the budgeted payroll. This isn't New York, you know."

"Pfui. A recruit in New York wouldn't accept twenty an hour. That's peanuts. Okay, how about fifteen? She's sharp and wants to learn. Think of it as investing in the creation of a new Bettye Lambert. You'll get reelected if we knock off all these unsolvable, high profile cases. When John and I get too old to do this anymore, she could be your new star investigator."

"You are so full of..."

"Make it thirteen."

"Twelve-fifty."

"Done."

"Okay, I'll tell the budget director to find some money—somewhere. Just don't make this too much or too often."

"There. Easy, huh? See why I love you?"

She scowled. "You got what you wanted. Now get out. I've got things to do."

"Get out? You've never said that before."

"Darlin' I've got the power now. Out. I have an appointment in fifteen minutes."

I stood up but wouldn't leave. "One more thing. How about this girl you talked about as our office manager-secretary-bookkeeper? Who is she?"

"My cousin Janetta."

"I didn't know you have a cousin Janetta."

"Lots you don't know 'bout me, Sammy. Janetta used to be an accountant for Alcoa. But since she married Dale, who makes oodles of money, and she had a son, she hasn't worked."

"How old is her son? She can't bring a kid to work with her."

"He's twenty and in college."

"Oh. And she wants to start working again?"

"Not sure. She said she'd talk to you."

"Like audition me?"

"Something like that."

"Jeez. Lucky me. When? She hasn't called."

"They're in Bermuda for a couple weeks."

"She'll call when she gets back?"

"I expect so."

"Who spends two weeks in Bermuda? There's not that much to do."

"They like to relax."

"You can do that at home. By the way, what's her last name?"

"Galloway."

"That was your maiden name. Who's your cousin, Janetta or her husband?"

"She's my cousin. She uses her maiden name. Has done since she became a CPA."

I shook my head. "Okay. In less than two weeks then. Please keep up with this and remind her as soon as she's home. We need someone quickly...but don't tell her that. I don't want to sound too anxious."

"Will do, sugar. Now, as I said before, bye."

Whenever she says *bye* and it sounds like a noise a sheep makes, I know the discussion is over.

———

I LEFT THE JUSTICE CENTER, CALLED BERNIE GAVIN AND GAMBLED on finding her at the welfare office.

"I can't just leave here," she said.

"Don't you go on the road to check on your clients? Make sure hubby isn't back at home or that they really have six kids under the age of five?"

"Yes, but today's an inside day for me. I have appointments."

I was getting frustrated with the women of the world.

"It's 11:30. How about lunch or a coffee break? I need to speak with you, and I'll buy."

"I usually take lunch at noon, but okay. I'll tell my supervisor I'm helping you. But I've got to be back here in an hour. I have people to see from one o'clock on."

"Easy. I'll meet you in the parking lot. I've got a dark red pickup."

Five minutes later, she walked out of the Human Services building and climbed into my truck.

Bernie fastened her seatbelt while making an astute observation. "This doesn't look much like a police car."

"It's mine. I put in for mileage. The Sheriff said she'd get her motor pool supervisor to assign us an unmarked county car one day this week. The spare cars all need oil changes or something, so I've got to wait."

We sat face to face, and she had a half smile on hers.

"And this is what you choose to drive?"

I sighed. "My other car is a '67 Austin-Healey. It's too valuable to put on lots of miles. The truck works fine."

She shrugged and turned toward the windshield. "Whatever. Where are we going?"

"How about the Shrimp Dock? It's on the other side of Midland Mall. We'll be there in five minutes."

"Fine. What did you need to ask?"

"First, I wanted to say you were correct about the two plainclothes security men. A pair of ex-Marines."

She turned to face me again. "I thought so. They had that look about them."

"There you go again. You don't like General Gavin and obviously don't like former military men. Were you bitten by a soldier once?"

"Don't be silly. I'm just not enamored by the whole Military-Industrial Complex."

I laughed silently. "You were born too late. You would have made a great hippie."

She chuckled. "You might be right. I take it you didn't burn your draft card and weren't reluctant to serve?"

"Not even close. I'm collecting an Army pension among other money from various levels of government. Double dipping, you might say."

"I should have known."

"You mean I've got *the look*?"

"You could say that. I see you as practical and efficient. I just hope you're not all brain and no heart."

"I'd like to think I've also got good looks and muscle."

She offered a platonic smile. "Well, there's that, too."

She faced front again, and I drove off.

We pulled into the lot of the Shrimp Dock less than a block from where Calderwood changes its name to Cusick Street.

Bernie read the digital sign outside the combination restaurant and fish market. "Oh, good, oysters are on special today. I'll have those."

Still the most expensive item on the menu. I decided to ask Bettye for an expense account.

"Glad to see you've got good taste."

"Ha. Good information costs money."

———

WHILE WE WAITED FOR OUR OYSTERS, CREOLE RICE, COLE SLAW and hush puppies, I made an awkward statement.

"Don't take offense to what I'm going to say, because I'm only basing it on what people have told me. Tommy Lee was...a little slow. And your story about him going toe to toe with a rather large security man at your demonstration doesn't sound like he made a sound decision—in that case anyway. The man's name, by the way, is Koronkiewicz. I'm guessing he's at least six-five and a pretty solid two-fifty. Daring him to throw a punch wasn't too smart. I wouldn't get within an arm's length of that guy to argue over something trivial, and Tommy Lee isn't as big as me. Did he do stuff like that very often?"

She looked like she wanted to toss her iced tea in my face.

"I do take offense—on two counts. Tommy wasn't slow or stupid. He was...uncomplicated and sweet. And how dare you say the wholesale pollution of our rivers and streams is trivial?"

Obviously, it didn't take much to get Bernadette twisted out of shape.

"I didn't mean to imply your cause is trivial or that Tommy was a blithering idiot. It's not, and I'm sure he's not. But he did something foolish, and I'm wondering if he did things like that often. And there is something I don't understand. If you know the pollution is coming from the paper mill and the local health department people aren't doing anything about it, why don't you just take your own samples from downstream more often, get them analyzed and if the levels of toxicity are over the accepted norms, present it the EPA?"

She sighed, no doubt back to thinking of me as an environmental witling. "It's not *that* easy. And, I'll have you know, we have taken samples. The paper mill is supposed to dispose of their waste properly. And they make a production out of having trucks show up, fill up with contaminated waste water and haul it away to be disposed of legally and properly. *But*, that operation is terribly expensive. So, they only dispose of a very small portion of their waste properly. The rest is discharged into the river. And the times that they open the flood gates and empty that poison into the river are more closely guarded than when the government transports nuclear material out of the Oak Ridge National Laboratories."

"I still don't get it. If the toxic chemicals end up in the river, why can't you get samples of the polluted water?"

She turned slightly and tilted her head, giving me a look almost suggesting my stupidity. "You just don't understand, do you?"

"Then help me out."

Another sigh. The woman could easily give me that dreaded inferiority complex all men fear. "Do you have any idea how fast that water is moving?"

I shrugged. "Fast."

"They are class four to five rapids all along that stretch of the river. That's fast. So, let's say they discharge thousands of gallons of waste each Wednesday night at 2 P.M. Of course, they would vary the times, but let's use that for argument's sake. That waste water is mixed with fresh river water and carried away very rapidly. Unless we knew the exact times they dump their poisons, taking inadequate samples is a waste of time."

"If this toxic waste is...emulsified so rapidly, why is there a problem?

"Oh, God, you're just like everyone else."

I tossed my hands in the air. "Come on, I'm trying to understand."

She shrugged. "Okay. Because the effects of the toxicants are cumulative. And as they travel downstream to calmer waters, they lodge in smaller estuaries and coves and who knows where. Over the years, the levels of toxicity have risen high enough to cause problems for the fish and other aquatic creatures and plant life."

"And since the waterway covers so many miles, any evidence that Cataloochee is the culprit is only circumstantial."

"Exactly."

"Okay. Now I understand."

The counterman interrupted our discussion by calling out, "Oysters for Bernie and Sam. Pick 'em up, folks."

"Excuse me," I said and fetched our lunches.

I spread a napkin over my lap and attempted to be diplomatic. "Let's talk about Tommy again. I was only basing my conclusions about his intelligence on the information I've gotten from official sources. Heritage High School tells me Tommy's IQ is eighty-eight. That's a bit below average. And he and Bill Koronkiewicz weren't exactly discussing the correctness of industrial pollution. I was told Koronkiewicz responded to a nasty remark Tommy made. Something like, 'Your mother does gorillas.' That wasn't brilliant, considering several cops could have heard that and the target of his comment had at least seven inches and ninety pounds on him."

She lowered her eyes and picked up a plastic fork. "Okay, I see your point. But forget that IQ business. And a high school would have tested him ten years ago." She paused to collect her thoughts. "As we learn more and new things, we all can score higher on those tests." She shook her head and seemed to grope for a way to make me understand. "You'd have to know Tommy. He has a good heart and a great personality. He was sensitive and..."

She stopped to blot the tear that ran from the outside corner of her right eye with her napkin. "And I'm very afraid of what...may have happened to him."

I took a breath and sat forward. "I understand. I'm sorry I upset you. Look, it seems like we're trying to find Tommy for *you*. His father doesn't appear to care, and his mother hasn't allowed reality to sink in yet or is permanently lost in space. We really need help with this and trying to cram everything into an hour might be a mistake."

She nodded and picked at her rice with a plastic fork.

"I need a ticket inside Tommy's head to find him or learn about what he might have been doing when he met someone who intended to do some harm."

"Oh, God."

Bernie sniffed and dabbed a couple more tears. It seemed as if I couldn't say anything right.

"Do something for me, please," I said. "You're upset now, and we've got less than that hour, and you need to finish eating. This afternoon or tonight, think about him. Close your eyes and think about the things he said when you were together. Write them down. It doesn't matter what. Anything might be important. Especially if you saw him argue with someone or he told you about a confrontation. When you're ready, call me. I'll try to make sense out of what you come up with."

She sighed, took a bite out of a hush puppy and looked like a little girl who just heard her cat got squashed by a garbage truck. She chewed and took a sip from her cup of iced tea. "What if I can't tell you anything that helps?"

CHAPTER SIX

I dropped Bernie Gavin off in front of the welfare building and drove the quarter mile back to our office.

Feeling like I wasted an hour of case time, but pleased, as usual, with the grub at the Shrimp Dock, I walked in, hopeful that John was successful in getting background information on Curry and Koronkiewicz. I found him at his desk, a white paper bag with the red and yellow Hardee's logo on it spread out as a place mat and covered with a cardboard basket of fried chicken tenders, French fries and deep fried onion rings.

"Hey, howz it goin'?" he said.

"You ate the same thing yesterday."

"I know. This chicken is *so* good, I figured I'd get a large order today."

I made a face. "Why don't you just inject 10W-40 oil into your veins?"

"You oughta lighten up. It's not so bad for you. They use *manatchurated* vegetable oil—it's more healthy."

"Ah. That explains it. Aren't those onion rings kind of greasy?" Translucent stains covered fifty percent of the white paper.

"No. They're good. Want one?"

"No, thanks. I ate."

"Yeah, what?"

I told him where I took Bernie for lunch and what we ordered.

"I gotta try that place again, now that they're so close. Bernadette have anything good to say?"

"Not much."

"Hmm. You know, Bernadette reminds me of Frankie Valli."

That threw me for a loop. "Why?"

"He sang that song, *Bernadette*. Used to sing at the Four Seasons."

"The Four Tops sang *Bernadette*. Frankie Valli used to sing *with* the Four Seasons. I doubt he ever sang at the restaurant."

"Oh, yeah? So, how about Bernadette? You didn't learn anything good? You were with her for an hour."

"Nothing new. But I asked her to think about the seemingly inconsequential things Tommy Lee may have said and write them down. Who knows? She may think of something that fits with something we already have. At this point, anything could be important. How'd you make out getting records for Curry and the Kronkster?"

John finished chewing an onion ring and licked his fingers. "Good. Yeah. I called that guy I know at National Personal Records in St. Louis. Retired Navy man."

"Good. What's the story?"

He wiped his fingers on a napkin and picked up a few sheets of scrap paper.

"Curry was an officer. Made captain quick enough but got passed over for promotion to major twice. He's sending me copies of his fitness evaluations to see exactly what his supervisors said about him. But he separated and got an honorable after twelve years and change. He couldn't have been too bad 'cause he got that job with the State Department right after that."

"No court martial or other disciplinary memos?"

"Didn't say so. You know, we should buy a fax machine. We could get this stuff a lot quicker."

"Be patient, John. Let's get a few more paying customers before we try to look like Pinkertons. You try DSS yet?"

"I thought you wanted to talk to Ralph first."

"Yeah, okay. He may have more luck. How about Koronkiewicz?"

"Twenty-five pretty good years. Got out as a gunnery sergeant. An E7. Started out as an infantryman, got to be a member of a sniper-scout team, reenlisted after four years, made sergeant and then got two more promotions. Did a couple tours on board ships and some embassy security work. The ex-navy guy said you had to be pretty sharp to get assigned to an embassy detail. But, he did have one official rep. Got it when he was platoon sergeant in an infantry company. He smacked a PFC for some unspecified reason. He accepted an Article 15 judgment from the company C.O., and the reprimand stayed in his jacket. He's sending that, too."

"That anger management thing again?"

"Could be. But no other *dispatchatory* information. No great acts of heroism noted, but he's got all the common decorations and commendations. Each of them did time in Yugoslavia during the civil wars there. Koronkiewicz was in Iraq for a couple years, too."

"But nothing de-rog-a-tory?"

"That's what I said."

"Mmm. Can you figure out when their embassy duties overlapped?"

"Yeah, sort of. Once I get the exact dates, I can compare duty stations on the paperwork this guy sends. So far I know they were in Saudi Arabia and Kuwait together."

"But nothing noteworthy happened there?"

"I guess not, but can't say for certain."

"I wonder if they tied up after Curry went with DSS?"

"Koronkiewicz did another twelve month embassy tour in Yemen before he got out, but Curry was a civilian by then, so we gotta wait for more paperwork."

"I'd better call Oliveri."

John nodded and picked up another onion ring. "These are good. Sure you don't want one?"

"No, thanks. I'm trying to live to a ripe old age."

He laughed. "Never happen. You drink too much."

"Up yours, John."

———————

Ralph Oliveri answered his cell phone on the third ring.

"You got a few minutes to talk?" I asked.

"I'm driving at the moment. What's up?"

"You have any horsepower to get complete personnel records from State Department Security?

"Maybe. What are you doing?"

I told him about the missing person case and Curry's possible involvement.

"Generally, they'll confirm dates of employment and *maybe* duty stations with a special request. You got anything more than a vague suspicion about this guy?"

"Not much."

"So you're just fishing?"

"I hate to admit it, but yeah. He's just ended up in a quasi-adversarial position at the wrong time with this river pollution business. I'm not sure he's telling us the whole truth. And he's got a shady look about him. I can't articulate much more. You know someone who'd do you a favor a little outside the box?"

"State is a pain in the ass. They think everything from serious stuff to an ambassador's alcohol consumption are matters of national security."

"Great. Everybody thinks they're James Bond."

"I'll get you at least the basics," Ralph said. "Can you get me the dates and places of his embassy postings?"

"Only with the Marines. John has that information coming."

"With them all, I might be able to find names for the resident Bureau agent assigned to those embassies. He...or she...might know the guy by name."

"Good. I'll get back to you with his military information, but who knows what he did with DSS?"

"I'll work on that, but plan on giving me the information you get over the lunch *you* buy at Cheseapeake's"

"You're a mercenary bastard, Ralph."

"Ha. Good information don't come cheap."

"I just heard that from someone else. I need an expense account."

———

"Prospect Police, Officer Donnellson."

"Terri? Sam Jenkins. Got a minute?"

"Oh, hi, boss. Sure. What do you need?"

"Another assistant. Want a part-time job?"

"Are you serious?"

"I only do elaborate jokes on Thursdays. Still interested?"

"Sure. What will I be doing?"

"Since I trust you on the computer more than John, some of that when we need it and telephone work. If that's finished, you can partner up with John or me on the road. We're still coming up with squat on this missing person case. Maybe a fresh pair of eyes will see something we're missing."

"Wow. That's great you'd trust my judgment. You need me to take time off?"

"Let's start with your regular days off, if you can spare the time and that works for you. If we get on a roll and you want to put in for vacation days or comp time, that's good, too."

"Super. Stanley has me on a regular squad rotation so I get a day or two on the road when I catch the weekends. My next RDO is day after tomorrow. Want me there then?"

"Sounds good. Want to know how much the sheriff will pay you?"

"You got me on the payroll?"

"Of course. Can't have you donating your expertise to the county. It's not much, but how's twelve-fifty an hour plus mileage?"

"No kidding? My brother is a carpenter, and he's only getting ten an hour. That's great."

"Good. And don't tell him I said so, but make John buy you lunch if you work with him."

"No problem, boss. I can brown bag it."

"Nonsense. You want to be a great detective, you've got to eat right. See you day after tomorrow."

"I'll be there. Uh, boss, just one question before you go?"

"Shoot."

"I'm the new guy at Prospect PD. Why did you pick me to help?"

"That's easy. You're less than thirty years old, and so far, I've never heard you use the word *awesome*."

She laughed. "Okay. If that's all it takes, you never will."

———

I SAT IN FRONT OF JOHN'S DESK WITH MY FEET UP AND THE GUEST chair tilted precariously back on its two hind legs. "Who are these TV idiots who claim you have to close a case in only forty-eight hours?"

John waved a hand dismissively. "Civilians who never worked in a PD or cops who lie through their asses."

"I'm gonna hate to disappoint Bettye, but it looks like we may never find Tommy Lee."

"Remember working in a precinct squad and carrying thirty-five to forty open cases a month? How many of those never got cleared?"

"More than I'd like to remember. But that's life in a busy PD."

"You think those security guys in North Carolina had anything to do with anything?" he asked.

"According to Bernadette, Tommy Lee could be obnoxious when he was walking a picket line. But are a few nasty words thrown around worth making him disappear?"

"Remember *Kronkowski* was a sniper."

"If we find a body with a .308 between the eyes, we can look at *Koronkiewicz* first."

"How about looking at the uniformed security guards over there, too?"

"If we can build up more than just a desire for a fishing expedition, we can ask the company to ID them for us, but right now, they could tell us to go pound salt, and we'd have no recourse."

"Well, we should have the hard copies of those military records for Curry and Kronko...Whatshisname...in a day or so."

"With luck, Ralph should have something soon. And Bernie might call with a list of meaningful quotations from Tommy Lee at any moment. If she doesn't, I'll call her."

"What do you make of her?" John asked. "I mean she's a good-looking forty-three-year-old woman. What's the attraction to twenty-seven-year-old Tommy Lee who's not the brightest bulb on the Christmas tree?"

I took a second to sit upright before falling backwards and getting my skull crushed. "The other day at lunch she got very protective when I mentioned his low IQ. She told me that was no indication of his personality and common sense. I think she really likes him. Who can figure love?"

John shrugged.

"As far as what makes her tick, she seems quite committed to this environmental thing. Just a guess, but probably other social injustices as well. She is a welfare worker, you know. I told her she would have made a great hippie."

"I'll bet she wants you to say she's a social services worker."

"I'll remember not to be offensive to another civil servant."

"Yeah, right. You know, we haven't looked at her too hard. They say Tommy Lee liked the ladies. You think she might have caught him with a new girlfriend and got pissed enough to whack him?"

"You have to complicate my life?"

"Not for nuthin' but, you know that woman scorned thing."

"Don't remind me."

My reaction seemed to amuse John no end. A grin spanned the

entire bottom half of his face. I'm surprised he was able to ask his next question.

"Hey, you talk to Terri yet?"

"She'll be here day after tomorrow. If we have telephone or computer work, she can do that here. Otherwise, we'll take her on the road. Maybe doing a background on Bernadette would be a good first job for her."

"Yeah, she can handle that. She seems like a good kid."

"She is. Stan is lucky to have her. She'll be a good cop. Already is. She learned a lot in the MPs. Bettye is getting more than twelve and a half bucks an hour worth of private cop."

———

I SAT IN MY OFFICE KILLING TIME, READING JOHN'S COPY OF THE News-Sentinel when Ralph Oliveri called.

"I can't paint a bad picture of your boy Curry," he said, "but I doubt you'd want to work alongside him."

"Oh, this sounds interesting. You've got a real theatrical approach. I'm all ears."

"I hit a jackpot. The woman at State I talked with didn't hide anything. Maybe she just likes guys in the FBI, or she fell in love with my voice."

"That must be it, Ralph. You make Bobby DeNiro sound like nothing but an inarticulate hoodlum."

"I thought he was. Anyways, Curry was around DSS long enough for me to get quite a roster of Bureau people who covered the embassies or missions where he was posted. I'll send you all the notes I took. I'm still waiting for calls from some of those agents. But, bottom line was sort of universal. Everyone thought Curry tried too hard."

"Tried too hard? One might think that diligence would be a good thing."

"Yes, one might, wouldn't one?" Ralph gets sarcastic at the drop of a hat. "But I offer this with a detailed explanation. One agent said it best: For all he tried to accomplish, and the end result he achieved, Curry was more trouble than he was worth."

"Make my life easy and tell me that Curry identified possible security threats and made them disappear."

"Not exactly. But he did get jammed up once in Yemen by kicking in the wrong door."

"Maybe I'm not familiar with the duties of these security officers. Why would he be kicking in doors? Sounds like executing a search warrant or making an arrest."

"Let me back up a bit and explain this *trying too hard* business better."

"It's your dime, partner."

Ralph took an audible deep breath. "Okay, here's the background. Curry worked for Diplomatic Security Services in Overseas Protective Operations. Basically, the job is just what it sounds like—they act the same as a Secret Service Executive Protective Detail—bodyguards. Another branch of DSS would get more into the intelligence and criminal investigative work. But apparently Curry liked hanging out with the dignitaries. Word was he began bucking for recognition and a fast track to being an RSO—Regional Security Officer, or on a par with one of our SACs. In his case, a supervisor of a particular overseas region."

"Makes sense. He got passed over twice for his field grade promotion in the Marines. He probably thought he'd better look like a hard charger for DSS right off the bat if he expected to get above the rank and file."

"Yes, but there's more. Supposedly, he wanted not only to rise above journeyman security officer but make his way into *The Bureau of Diplomatic Security* and catch the attention of the assistant director for international programs."

"What's the difference?"

"A subtle one, fairly technical and something the general population would never know about. They're basically different by budget numbers and spots on the State Department's organizational table. But for career types who want to make the most of internal politics, BDS is the place to be. Having a boss with an assistant director's title as opposed to working for just one of the many RSOs running around the world could be a career maker."

"So Curry was a practicing brown nose or looking for someone with horsepower he could suck up to?"

"That's the simplified version. You wouldn't like to work alongside him because whenever he could, he tried to make himself look like a shining star—even at someone else's expense."

"Okay, he's a jerk. What's the story of the kicked in door?"

"Not too complicated. As you probably know, Yemen is full of jihadists and fundamentalist loonies. Americans are not on their list of favorite people. A couple of guys working the intelligence detail, trying to root out potential threats to the officials of the overseas mission, got word of a small crew of crazies who supposedly wanted to hit the ambassador's car with a rocket propelled grenade. The intelligence section boss made this known to Curry, who was acting as RSO while the actual supervisor was on thirty days leave. So, Curry had temporary control over the embassy's bodyguard contingent.

"Trying to be a bit proactive and get a feather in his cap, Curry coordinated with the intelligence guys, and they mounted an operation to nab these would-be assassins in an apartment building in a pretty decent, upper-class neighborhood. All this would have been totally kosher had not Curry, by mistake, led his troops through the door of a pro-American university professor who, along with his lovely wife, ended up spread-eagle on the Persian carpet while the hit squad tossed the premises for hoods and RPGs. They came up with bupkis. The best Curry could say was, 'Oops.' The professor, on the other hand, personally called the ambassador, claimed to be outraged and made lots of noise."

"Yeah, well, professors have to be able to take a joke in these days of terrorists on every street corner. No big deal. Certainly no feather in Curry's cap, but not the worst black eye either. Unofficially, the ambassador should have thanked him and suggested that the intelligence guys get back on the street looking for the hoods."

"Yeah, in a perfect world. But apparently Yemen is a weird place. Curry almost got banished to the US Consulate in Siberia."

"So when he had his collective twenty-five years of service, someone suggested he retire?"

"Yep," Ralph said. "For the good of the Corps."

"I've known guys in that boat before."

"Haven't we all? If he was an otherwise good guy, I could feel sorry for him."

"Any of your contacts remember Koronkiewicz from Yemen or elsewhere?"

"The Marines are everyday fixtures, but don't necessarily get involved with either DSS or our agents unless the plainclothes guys need warm bodies or cannon fodder. A couple remember him as the NCO in charge of the uniformed guards. He was a big, impressive-looking guy. Not someone you'd easily forget. Competent enough. Never a problem that they knew of. That's about it."

"Neither of these guys ever made much of a splash in their military careers. I wonder if they would stretch the rules to look good for their civilian bosses?" I asked.

"You mean taking out a mouthy protestor because he pissed off the bosses? Sounds a bit extreme, even when you're pushing to be part of the in-crowd."

"Yeah, maybe. Have you heard anything from that guy you know at the Asheville field office?"

"Not yet. He took a few annual leave days."

"With luck, he might have a few words of wisdom for me."

"I'll let you know."

———

SHORTLY AFTER HANGING UP ON MY FAVORITE G-MAN, BETTYE called.

"I think we may have somethin' in Prospect," she said. "Jamey Hawkins called lookin' for you. He got a call over in Orr's Valley. People rentin' a vacation cabin called 9-1-1 sayin' their dog brought home what looks like a human leg bone."

CHAPTER SEVEN

THAT SOUNDED INTERESTING.

"Has a doctor confirmed that the bone is definitely human and not from a deer or...whatever?"

"Not yet, but Jamey said one of the four women at the cabin is a retired nurse and another is a former x-ray technician."

"Hmm. I guess they might know. I'd better get myself over there and stake out a crime scene. Give me Jamey's cell number."

———

JOHN AND I FOLLOWED JAMEY HAWKINS' DIRECTIONS INTO THE remote and sparsely populated Orrs Valley section of Prospect, a place where the universe doesn't always recognize GPS. We found the driveway to the rental cabin by spotting a hand painted sign calling the property Blizzard Hill. I wondered if it had been built around the time of the big storm of 1993, when for the first time in more than a hundred years, East Tennessee got twenty-seven inches of snow at one time.

We found Jamey's Prospect PD cruiser parked near a log cabin at the end of a narrow gravel drive. I called him a few minutes earlier when we turned onto Meissners Station Road where the cabin was located. He met us in the driveway.

"Hey, boss. Good to see you," he said.

We shook hands. Jamey was a tall blond kid who never wore the hat that goes with his khaki over charcoal green PD uniform.

"Howz it goin', John?" Jamey spoke with an unmistakable northern Michigan accent.

"Whaddaya say, Jamey? You keepin' out o' trouble?" John asked.

He shrugged. "No fun that way."

"You convinced this dog brought home a human bone?" I asked.

"Looks like it to me. Norma, one of the women inside, was a nurse. She says it's a fibula—lower leg bone. Holly—she's another one in there —a retired x-ray tech, she agrees."

"Ah. Two experts. Where's the bone now?"

"Inside."

"Where'd this dog find it?"

"Now, that's a good question. It's Holly's dog. She said the girls took a drive over to the outlet malls in Pigeon Forge and left Chamois—that's the dog—on the screened-in porch out back. Only someone didn't close the screen door securely, and the dog got out. So, who knows? She was roaming around for the better part of the day."

"Have they looked around? Or have you? Did this mutt dig a hole or...? That bone could have come from anywhere. How old does this fibula look?"

"Boss, I don't know, but it's not something recent. I doubt it's your missing person. It's been buried a while. I didn't look around. Figured you'd want crime scene to do that. Neither did the women."

"Good. How many women?"

"Four."

"What are they doing here?"

"They're all friends from Connecticut. Renting for seven days."

"No men?"

"No, sir."

"What kind of dog?"

73

"Looks like a yellow lab to me."

I shook my head in frustration. "How the hell are we going to map out a crime scene when only a dog knows where he found the bone?"

"She," Jamey said.

"What?"

"Chamois is a female."

"Whatever."

"Let's ask the dog," John suggested.

"Shut up, John."

"Just trying to be helpful, Boss. Oh, you don't want me to call you that. Sorry. You being grumpy feels like we're back at the PD in New York."

I growled before speaking. "I thought we might be getting our heads above water with this Tommy Lee Helton thing, and now we've got an *old* bone—from who knows whom—tossed into the works. This could be a ten-year-old murder victim or two-hundred-year-old Cherokee."

"That's why you get the big bucks, boss," Jamey said.

"Let's meet this gaggle of women. Are they okay or what?"

"Yeah," Jamey said. "They seem nice."

We stepped onto the covered front porch. The place looked like something created by a Hollywood set designer as the ultimate vacation cottage. The exterior logs were treated with Clear Wood Finish to give them a dark honey color. The metal roof, shutters and window moldings were all forest green. Through the picture window, I saw two lighted lamps in the living room and a deer antler chandelier suspended over a large table in the attached dining room. A chainsaw carved and painted black bear stood guard next to the six-over-six pane, green front door. I knocked, and a dog barked.

A tall middle-aged woman with bangs answered the door. She wore the rest of her dark hair pulled back into a ponytail

"Hello. I'm Sam Jenkins." With my badge in one hand, I poked the opposite thumb behind me and to the right. "And this is John Gallagher. We're investigators from the sheriff's office. You've already met Jamey Hawkins from Prospect PD."

She gave us a big smile. "Hi. I'm Holly Miller. Come in."

Three other women surrounded the dining room table, making a perimeter under the antler chandelier. One kept a hand around the collar of a yellow Labrador retriever who, when she saw us, growled like the MGM lion.

"Your dog doesn't seem happy to see us," I said.

"Oh, don't mind her," Holly said. "She's just a little over protective."

"Yeah. Dogs can get that way." I took a couple steps further into the house and looked at the woman holding the dog. "Let her go. I have to interrogate her and see where she found the bone."

The woman, a short, middle-aged blonde, looked at me as if I was a certified lunatic.

"You want to talk to the dog?" she asked.

I shrugged. "Can anyone else tell me where she found the bone?"

The blonde looked at Holly, the tall girl. Holly nodded. The blonde released the dog. She ran up to me and barked again. I got down on my hands and knees and looked into the dog's eyes. She stopped barking.

"Hi, Chamois. I'm Sam. I like dogs. What do you think about cops?"

She barked again, but only once. I scanned the crowd. The blonde wasn't the only one who thought I might be crazy.

As softly as I could, I said, "Oh, stop your noise. I'm no threat to these ladies."

The dog tilted her head, showing me an expression similar to the blonde's. The dog also thought I was nuts.

"Chamois, I'm going to show you my hand. Very slowly. I'd like you to smell me. I'm your friend. Ready now? Here we go."

I shifted my weight and lifted my right hand slowly, extending it, palm down, toward the dog. She backed up a step and let out a boof.

"Oh, boof yourself. Come closer." She tilted her head the opposite way. "Come on, Chamois. Come here and sniff my hand. I'm not going to hurt your mother or her friends. Come. Come here, girl."

The dog took a step forward. Then another. I wondered if she'd smell my hand or bite it. She sniffed the back.

"That's a girl. Good girl. See, I'm your buddy."

Slowly, I turned my hand over. She smelled the palm.

"Everything okay with you, Chamois?"

The dog didn't move. I touched her chin with my fingers. She didn't object. I scratched her neck. Still no objection.

"Good girl, Chamois." I exaggerated a little as a dog trainer might. "Good girl." I scratched her head with a bit more vigor. She wagged her tail.

"That's my girl. Come here, Chamois. Come here."

She took a step. I lifted my left hand and with both, rubbed her cheeks. Her tail didn't stop wagging. I dropped my hands to the floor and moved a little closer, now only inches from her head. I made gurgling noises, and she slapped my face with her tongue.

"Good dog, Chamois. Good girl. I love puppy kisses. Now I'm gonna make you a police dog."

I slowly returned to my feet, and Chamois came close enough for me to mess around with her head again.

"I guess you two are friends now," Holly said.

"Not hard when you get down to their level," I said.

"I guess so," the blonde said. "Hi, I'm Sue Brown."

"Hi, Sue. You heard who we are." I looked at the other women. "And, ladies, you are?"

The one with frosted hair spoke first. "I'm Norma McTavish."

"A good Scottish girl. Hello, Norma."

She smiled. "My husband was Scottish. I'm sort of a...mixed breed. Nice to meet you."

"Hi, I'm Kathy Doktor," said a woman not quite as tall as Holly with curly brown hair.

"Hi, Norma. Hi, Kathy. Now that we all know each other, let's talk about bones."

————

SEVEN OF US SAT AROUND THE DINING ROOM TABLE. CHAMOIS

returned to the kitchen and began lapping up water from a bowl on the floor.

"I understand that two of you know what a human leg bone looks like," I said.

Norma nodded. "I was an RN. I have no doubt."

Holly spoke next. "I was an X-ray technician in a large hospital for years. I've seen more broken legs than...maybe the number of people you've arrested."

"Don't bet on that," John said. "He was a pretty mean cop back in his day."

I tried to look shy and modest—but not too much. The ladies smiled.

"Jamey told me you ladies are from Connecticut," I said. "But, Holly, I'd bet a pay check you're originally from New York. Am I right?"

She looked a little shy herself. "I guess I never lost my Long Island accent."

"You haven't. John and I are former Long Islanders. You can probably hear that. Where did you live?"

We carried on for a few minutes talking about the old neighborhoods.

"What hospital did you work at?" John asked.

"Nassau County Medical Center, back when it was called Meadowbrook Hospital."

"We know it well," I said. "Okay, ladies, we'll have to get more information from you, but it's getting late, and we lose light fairly early in September. Holly, would it be okay if I took Chamois on a leash and see if we can locate the spot where she found the bone?"

"You think you can?"

"Who knows? It's worth a try."

"Maybe I should come with you?"

"You think Chamois would be more comfortable with you along?"

"Until she met you, I'd say yes. Now, maybe."

"Okay. Just stay next to or behind me. If the dog moves too fast, don't get lost."

She smiled. "I'll put on my hiking shoes."

"Good. Jamey is an ex-Marine who knows his way around the woods. He'll come along with us to make sure I don't get lost. John can keep the rest of you ladies company."

———

I spent ten minutes working with Chamois on a leash before giving the dog her head and taking to the woods. She wasn't a professionally trained dog, but intelligent and immediately understood the snap of a choke collar meant I wanted her attention and focus.

"Were you a police dog handler?" Holly asked.

"No. I had a Scottish terrier for seventeen years. She was a great dog, but a real handful. I hired a professional to train me how to handle her. I just remember how it's done."

"Chamois looks like a good candidate to train."

"Yeah. She's a smart dog." I gave Chamois a friendly scratch on the chin. "You about ready to head into the woods?"

Holly nodded. "Sure."

The air smelled as if autumn wasn't far off. Decomposing summer grass has a unique odor, as does the ragweed that grows to twelve feet tall in the Smokies. The insects were vocal, adding to the natural symphony of the forest, wrestling with the thought that their days were numbered.

"Jamey," I said, "let Chamois smell the bone."

Hawkins took the leg bone from a plastic bag and handed it to me.

"Here ya go, Chamois. Give a sniff. That's the girl. Find more. Go get 'em, girl."

The yellow lab took off pulling me moderately, sniffing the ground, zig-zagging toward the wood line more than a hundred feet away.

"I'm getting a little old to keep up with an excited dog."

"Tell me about it," Holly said.

Thirty-year-old Jamey Hawkins laughed.

We kept up a brisk pace for almost ten minutes, traveling quickly, but not at a run. Chamois seemed tireless and was probably having fun.

"I'm getting a workout here," Holly said.

"Dog ought to be a drill sergeant," Jamey said.

Based on the lead-by-example rule, I kept quiet so I wouldn't sound winded.

After another five minutes of carousing in the woods, we came to an area with only low weeds and a minimum of scrub brush. Chamois began tugging harder, sniffing more frantically. Then I spotted an area perhaps five or six feet across and irregular in shape. Upturned composted leaves created a darker color on the forest floor. Someone or something had spent time digging or rummaging.

I shortened the leash and snapped Chamois' chain collar twice. The dog stopped and looked up at me.

"Good girl, Chamois. Good girl." I bent over to scratch her neck. "Good girl." Then to Holly I said, "Hang on to your daughter. Jamey and I will take a closer look."

I handed her the leash.

"You think this is a...grave?"

"Who knows? But obviously something's been happening here."

With the sun coming through the trees at a low angle, the back-lighting showcased a large cloud of annoying gnats swarming over the area of interest and beyond. I'm really not a fan of hardcore nature.

Wearing protective gloves, Jamey and I carefully moved the old leaves, twigs and other natural litter away from the spot disturbed by man or animal. It didn't take long to uncover a partial skeleton.

———

MUCH OF THE LOWER EXTREMITIES HAD BEEN CARRIED OFF, probably by animals. I doubted that Chamois could have accounted for more than the one fibula she brought back to the cabin. Once we uncovered more of the skeleton, we found what looked like rotten blue denim —probably jeans—and a shirt with pearl snaps. Just above the pelvis, a rotting leather belt with a pewter buckle, shaped like a coiled snake encircled the body. The upper torso and skull, still covered with dirt, appeared to be intact. The area smelled of rotting vegetation and the musty odor of the long ago decomposed body and clothing. I walked twenty feet from the shallow grave to where Holly stood holding Chamois.

"Your hound is quite a detective. No doubt that's an adult-size male with scraps of clothing left. No legitimate reason for him to be here, but there's no way this is our recently missing person."

Holly raised her eyebrows and looked at me with apprehension. "When you drive out of the national park heading this way, isn't there a sign that says, 'Welcome to the peaceful side of the Smokies?'"

I showed her a weak smile. "When you rent a cabin in this neck of the woods, there's always the chance of getting some excitement. I just wish you saw a bear cub rather than a skeleton."

"We would have been happy with the excitement those outlet malls provided."

CHAPTER EIGHT

Bettye Lambert sent two teams of crime scene investigators to deal with the retrieval of the bones and any other physical evidence gathered during the next few days. Investigators Jackie Shuman, David Sparks, Neal Brickman and Neal's partner, Cob Rankin, spent the better part of an hour hauling camera equipment, forensics kits and portable lighting from their two SUVs through the woods to the makeshift gravesite. Half way through the logistics of cordoning off the area and setting up a working crime scene, Deputy Medical Examiner Morris Rappaport and his assistant, Earl Ogle, showed up to ensure that the skeletal remains were handled properly. And in dribs and drabs, a half dozen auxiliary deputies arrived with orders to remain at the incident location overnight until we all returned with the next daylight to search the area beyond the immediate scene for any bones carried off by whatever or whomever.

John Gallagher, Jamey Hawkins and I stood next to Mo Rappaport and Earl Ogle just outside the yellow tape while the evidence technicians photographed and measured the unmolested burial site.

"I feel like an archeologist when we do something like this," Mo said. "Like someone unearthing King Tut."

"A forensic archeologist," I suggested. "From looking at the leg bone, can you guess how long he's been buried? I'm assuming he's not an ancient Egyptian."

"You love to ask impossible questions, boychek. Years. Exactly how many is anyone's guess at this point. We've got lots of work to do on this one, and I'll be asking for help from some of the more archeological minded pathologists at the Body Farm. We should be able to get you into a small ballpark soon enough. But ancient Egypt, no."

"Let Jackie take the scraps of clothing and belt to the TBI lab," I said. "If you need that or just the lab results, tell him to get whatever you want."

"I will."

"This doesn't help us with our current missing person, but I guess it is job security."

"I like job security," John said. "It keeps me out of the poorhouse."

"Don't worry, John," Mo said. "We'll always have a customer."

Jackie Shuman stood a few feet from the disturbed ground and called out, "Hey, Dr. Mo, you and Earl can come in and start doin' yer thing. We're finished with all our prelims."

Morris looked less than enthused with the job ahead. "I had hoped to eat dinner with my wife tonight. God bless her. She made what she calls her fakakta chicken. It's very good, I'll have you know. But, duty calls, Samilah. Dinner will have to wait."

"Give it hell, guys."

As Mo and Earl stepped under the yellow tape, I turned to Jamey Hawkins. "I'm assuming the mayor is still a pain in the ass about overtime."

He nodded. "Sure is. You haven't been gone that long."

From far beyond the gravesite and in the opposite direction from the rental cabin, we heard a dog bark. The barking stopped abruptly, and it turned into a plaintiff howl.

"Jeez," I said. "That sounds like the soundtrack from an old were-wolf movie."

"Oh, man," Jamie said. "Don't say that."

"Yeah, what was I thinking? Let's forget about Lon Chaney Jr. Unless you can talk your way around staying here at time and a half, you'd better head back to the municipal building. John and I will hold down the fort."

"Yeah, I should. I don't want to put Stanley in a bad spot with the big boss. I won't milk the OT. But do me a favor? Don't mention that werewolf thing again."

"You got it, kid. Be sure to leave a little note for his highness about what we found here. Let him put out a press release. I don't do those anymore, and that will make less work for Bettye. Oh, and touch base with Vern Hobbs. This thing is pretty ancient history. Maybe he remembers someone going missing years ago."

"Will do, boss. John, take it easy."

"Thanks for the help, Jamey," I said. "Next time you find a dog with a bone, chase it into Townsend PD's area and let them handle it."

"Sounds like good advice. See you guys."

John and I had time to kill before I gave the ETs their marching orders for the following day and before two of those strong young men helped carry a stretcher full of bones through the woods to the morgue wagon.

"While I was out playing dog handler, John, I hope you got pedigrees on all the ladies in the cabin."

"Of course. It was like interviewing a bunch of former cheerleaders."

"Great, I'm now covered with dirt, and you had yourself a good time."

"Yeah, but you got to take a walk with Holly. She's got a nice smile."

"Yeah, I'll bet she was the star of a few pep rallies. Now, just to satisfy my curiosity, tell me about the other girls."

John took a notebook from his jacket pocket. "Okay. Basic story about the group. They've been friends for thirty or so years. They take a few trips each year, have lunches and dinners regularly, see each other at church and all live in New Milford. Ever been there?"

"Sure, long time ago. Nice little New England town. A real All-American place."

"Well," he continued, "they call themselves *The Guild*. Didn't say why, but who cares?"

"They're not blacksmiths, are they?"

John frowned. "Blacksmiths?"

"Forget it. Do their husbands always stay home during these girl trips?"

"See, that's the thing, they're all single. Three of them—Holly, Sue and Norma are widows. They all knew each other from their kid's schools, church and some other small town stuff. They lost their husbands within a couple years of each other. Kathy, she's divorced. Sad story. Her ex-husband gambled away everything they had. But, she's back on her feet and is the only one still working."

"Sounds like you were busy. Anything else?"

"Yeah, hold your horses. I only got started. Here's the skinny on each one." He flipped a page of his notebook. "Okay, Holly, the one you went into the woods with."

He tried to engineer a lecherous grin.

"Don't make me smack you, John."

"Ha. You're so easy. Okay, back to Holly. She told us she had been an X-ray technician. The other girls told me that after she had two kids and stayed home for a while, she got a job in the personnel department of a big retail store. Got to be manager."

"Sounds like a hardworking woman."

"Yeah. Nice to take a walk with."

I shook my head. "John, you are only inches from death."

"See? What did I say about easy?"

"Keep talkin', you Irish nitwit."

Unfazed, he continued. "Okay, next is Sue. The little blonde. She's originally from Massachusetts. Got divorced young, then met a new guy in college and fell in love. She got a job and helped put him through dental school. Then he opened up a practice. He was the dentist, and she was the office manager. Had three kids. She's a skier.

"Now we come to Norma, the ex-nurse with the frosted hair. She's the only one originally from New Milford. Her husband owned a hardware store. After he passed away, she sold his business and continued to work in a hospital. She's retired now.

"And last is Kathy—like I said, divorced from the gambler. They all have kids and grandchildren. End of the story."

"Good job. I guess they'll never forget their trip to the Smokies."

"Not every day your dog brings back the leg bone of a dead guy."

———

By 8:30 that evening the evidence technicians wrapped up their portion of the job, their last task involved setting out a line of battery powered trail lights marking the way between the clearing beyond the cabin and the burial site. The auxiliaries on guard duty could change shifts throughout the night and not get lost.

Earlier that day—somewhere around 6:30 p.m.—one of the deputies sent to assist us brought in sandwiches made by the cooks at the county jail. But at the end of our day, I was still hungry enough to gnaw the leg off a corpse.

"Let's tell our guild of unmarried women we'll be back tomorrow for another day of frolicking in the woods," I said.

"Man, it's been a long day," John said. "I gotta go home and get something more to eat. That sandwich didn't do it."

"Yeah, me, too."

We mounted the porch. I saluted the chainsaw bear and knocked on the front door. Holly answered holding a classic martini glass.

"Hi," she said, showing her cheerleader smile. "Come in."

We did, and she made an observation. "You guys look beat."

"It's been a long day," I said. "Mother never told me police work would be this hard."

"Aw, poor guys. How 'bout a drink? As you can see, I've got a martini. Norma makes a great Manhattan, and Kathy and Sue are drinking wine."

"Is that a vodka martini?" I asked.

"Is there any other kind?"

"It's September, but still warm out. I could use a summer drink. How about an extra dry one on the rocks? Can you put in a twist?"

"Sure can. And I'll just whisper vermouth over the top of the glass. How about you, John?"

"Uh, have you got a diet soda?"

Everyone laughed.

Sue asked, "Now, why would we have that?"

John shrugged. "Okay, I'll have a Manhattan—with a cherry."

"Norma can make that," Holly said. "And how would you like your martini, Mr. Bond, shaken or stirred?"

"I'm a guest. You're the bartender. But I'll mention something we used to say about vodka in the mysterious Orient—make it muchee cold."

Holly laughed, and something made me think the martini she held wasn't her first of the night.

"Muchee cold with a twist—coming up. Were you in Asia in the service?"

I nodded. "All expenses paid by Uncle Sam's Army."

"You're 'bout the right age for Vietnam."

"Among other places."

"You'll have to tell us about it."

"You'll need to rent the cabin for another week," John said—sarcastic bastard. "He's got lotsa war stories."

I faked a scowl. "Remind me to bury him where Chamois found that bone."

Twenty minutes later, with martinis and Manhattans under our belt, John and I got up to leave.

"There are six deputies watching the crime scene and all around it," I said. "If you ladies see or hear anything that bothers you, call 9-1-1 immediately. The nighttime dispatcher handles the entire county. They'll send a Prospect sector car and notify the guys outside the cabin."

They all agreed.

"Then we'll see you tomorrow. With luck it will be an uneventful night."

CHAPTER NINE

At 8 A.M., John and I were standing outside the rental cabin on Meissners Station Road, waiting for our support troops to arrive. Jackie Shuman called a few minutes earlier to say he and his partner, David Sparks, were on the way from the Justice Center to help supervise. The warm bodies Bettye promised to send consisted of twenty-six veteran cops from departments around the county who were spending a boring week at her academy facility at an in-service training class. The duty officer assured me a bus would be leaving right after the class coordinator took attendance. By 8:30, we should be ready to search for more bones and anything else that might be connected with the body or the killer.

It was partially cloudy, a little cool and very damp. The dew point had gone through the roof that night, and beads of moisture covered the ground.

At 8:15, Shuman and Sparks pulled up in their white, crime scene Explorer. Jackie got out carrying two paper bags.

"Y'all doin' aw right t'day?" he asked but didn't wait for an answer. "Figgered ya might want some extra breakfast." He handed me a Styrofoam coffee cup covered by a plastic lid. "A black no sugar fer yew, and a reggler fer yew, John."

"Thanks, young feller." I said, removing the lid.

"Brought ya some goodies, too," David said, as Jackie opened the second bag and held it out.

"I'll have one of those," John said.

"I thought ya might," Jackie said.

"They know you, John," I said.

"What have you got?" There could have been an angry Gila monster in the bag, but John reached in anyway.

He came out with a blueberry muffin large enough to choke a Beluga whale.

"How 'bout you, boss," Jackie asked.

I shook my head. "Thanks. I'll save mine until lunchtime in case we get more of that scrumptious jailhouse chow."

Jackie laughed. "I hear that."

As I sipped the hot coffee, a Prospect PD sector car pulled into the driveway.

"Aha," I said. "Vernon has arrived."

PO Vern Hobbs, the guy I call the shortest cop alive, exited the vehicle, tugged his gun belt up an inch and with a slightly bowlegged gait, swaggered toward us.

He stuck out a hand. "Whatcha say, boss?"

We shook hands, and I said hello.

Vern continued. "John, you doin' aw right t'day?"

"Howz it goin', *Vermin*?" John said.

Vern shifted his ever-present toothpick from the left side of his mouth to the right. "I see you got yerse'f this worthless deputy and Young Sparks he'pin' ya t'day."

Jackie laughed and couldn't let that go. "You ain't heard, Vern? Prospect PD got them a mandatory retirement age. You're so old, they oughta put ya out ta pasture with the rest o' them gray-haired hosses."

Vern snorted. "Man calls hisse'f an evidence technician. Couldn't find a pitchfork in a haystack."

I interrupted. "I'm guessing this conversation could go on for hours, so I'll thank you two," I pointed at Shuman and Sparks, "for the coffee and John's second breakfast, and talk to you," now looking at Vern Hobbs, "about our skeleton."

"Okay, boss," Jackie said. "Me an' Sparky got us a few things ta do first, and then we'll start working out with our metal detectors. Jest might find us a bullet or spent shell or something good."

"Great. Let us know what turns up."

Vern pushed the soggy toothpick back to the left. "Last night Jamey Hawkins called and told me what ya'll found. After that, Jackie showed me a pitcher he took o' that belt buckle. Be my guess that's more'n likely Jake the Snake."

"Jake the Snake? I can't wait to learn more about him."

Vern pulled a couple of folded papers from his back pocket and handed them to me. "I printed these out fer ya. Jake went missin' back in 2002. His ex-wife reported 'im gone when she wasn't gettin' no child support, and nobody could find 'im. Place he was livin' at looked like he didn't take nuthin' with 'im. Everybody figgered sumthin' happened or he jest took off, but there weren't a trace o' the man."

I scanned the PPD missing person report on Jacob Alford Quarles who, if alive, would have been fifty-five. His ex, Alva Janine Quarles, stated that she had no idea where he might have disappeared to. "And you assume no one else in the area wore a belt buckle like that?"

"Was sorta Jake's trademark. Never figgered out what came first, the buckle or the name. Anyways, I never seen nobody else with one like it."

"If he died around the time he was reported missing, that would put him in the ground more than nine years."

Vern nodded. "Got any idea how this body ya found got killed?"

"Not yet. Dr. Mo and his cohorts at the Body Farm plan to work on that. But now that we've got a possible ID and child support was mentioned, we can come up with some offspring DNA to compare with the remains."

"Uh-huh," Vern said. "Jest a wild guess now, but I'll bet they'll find some evidence o' him gettin' shot—if'n the bullet didn't go clean through. Shot or stabbed, one."

"I have a feeling the nickname Snake has something to do with that."

"'Course it has. Ol' Jake was one horny booger. More'n one husband wanted ta put him in a pine box. Jake messed with a lot o' women."

I rolled my eyes. "Dangerous when they're married women. Seems like someone skipped the box and put him directly in the cold ground and none too deep."

"Cain't argue with that."

"Can you get together with the guys who worked at Prospect PD back in '02 and come up with some names of possible suspects?"

"Yep," Vern said. "Lemme see. Back then there was Lenny, Harlan, Bobby Crockett was new and Bettye. Mebbe somebody else who's still livin' 'round here if they's not at the PD no more. Might be one or two. I'll check and ask around."

"Good. I'll ask Bettye what she remembers. You hit the others. Thanks for your help."

———

ASSUMING JAKE "THE SNAKE" QUARLES WAS OUR SKELETON—THE one killed and buried in the neighborhood of nine-and-a-half years ago, old Jake wasn't in danger of getting any deader and could be put on the back burner while we focused on Tommy Lee Helton. Making a second assumption that Sheriff Bettye Lambert might want to keep her detectives from rummaging through a cold case while they caught new and exciting assignments each day, she'd probably ask John and me to work on that one after we finished with Tommy Lee. Jake the Snake would keep John out of financial trouble for a while and provide Terri Donnellson, our apprentice detective, with some extra spending money and good training. I, on the other hand, would make myself scarce after clearing or scrapping the Tommy Lee Helton affair.

. . .

At around ten o'clock that morning, two cops from the in-service class found a decomposing cowboy boot, complete with left foot and ankle bones, in the thicket, not far from the main gravesite. More for the pathologists to play with, but not something that could point the finger at a specific killer.

Shortly after that, David Sparks found what looked like a partially mangled .30 caliber, soft nose rifle bullet under the composted soil, buried beneath the surface of the former grave.

At 12:15, while most of the searchers were taking a lunch break, enjoying the current collection of sandwiches from the county slammer's kitchen, I hobbled off toward Jackie Shuman's SUV to retrieve one of those mammoth blueberry muffins.

Then, as I plucked a pint bottle of water from the cooler in the back of my truck, Holly Miller walked out from the cabin.

"Hi," I said. "I thought you all went out for the day."

"The other girls were going to Dollywood. I wasn't in a country music mood. Actually, I wanted to see if you turned up anything interesting."

"We've got some experienced guys working today. They've already found more bones, a bullet and an old boot, and no one is making noise about abandoning ship before quitting time. They may find more."

"Any ideas yet?"

"A Prospect cop thinks it may be a missing person from 2002. We've got some avenues to explore, but there's nothing urgent here. Tomorrow I've got to get back to looking for our current missing guy."

Holly shook her head. "I never thought you'd get this much crime around here."

I shrugged. "We're no Detroit, but we have our moments."

"You look pretty hot and tired. Can I get you something proper to eat?"

"The day is turning out to be beautiful but traipsing around in the woods has me pretty sticky. I must smell like a goat. Thanks for the lunch offer, but it wouldn't look good to the guys if the boss took his meal break in a cozy cabin while they're eating jail food among the poison ivy. And Chamois' canine nose wouldn't want to smell me. That might undo the friendship we made yesterday"

She laughed.

"I'm good with this muffin until dinnertime."

"Okay, but if you want to stop in for a martini before you leave, I'll have the vodka good and cold. Your posse should be on their way home by then."

I smiled. "I could manage that. By quitting time, I'll have a full report ready for you ladies."

———

At 2:30, we had two additional bones showing that some woodland creature had taken a turn gnawing on. The troops looked at our meager progress as good luck omens and continued to scour the woods, viewing the search as a challenge or contest—who could find the most productive clue.

Fifteen minutes later, as I was poking around some brush with a four-foot dowel, my cell phone sounded off.

The caller said, "This is Special Agent Clint Reading, FBI Asheville. Ralph Oliveri from the Knoxville office asked me to call you."

My first thought and unasked question was: Is anyone really named Clint Reading? It sounded like the hero of a soap opera or romance novel. Only an FBI agent.

"Yeah, thanks for calling," I said. "Ralph told me you might have some information about the people at the Cataloochee Paper Mill over on your side of the Smokies. Specifically, I'm looking closely at the men in security, but I'll take anything you've got if it pertains to a missing person's case I'm working."

"He explained all that. We've got something going over there—sort of unusual. It's more of an EPA matter, but because this industrial pollution business involves two states and there's a possibility of bribery of one or more public officials, we got involved."

"You think the mill owner paid off local health inspectors?"

"Basically, yes. I've got no doubt about that. And maybe a local cop or two. But we need more to put together a good case for the AUSA to prosecute."

"Do any of the mill security people have a role in this?"

"Don't repeat anything I say, but we believe that not only are the county health department people involved, but a few sheriff's deputies—guys with some rank—are also on the payroll, so to speak. Donal Curry, the security chief, has close ties with the sheriff's department. We think that through Curry, the deputies made the introductions to the health department employees, and the mill management personnel took it from there. That's all circumstantial, so we just have to prove it. I would also imagine that Curry's assistant, Bill Koronkiewicz, at least knows what's going on."

"I'm on a pretty thin wire here," I said. "But I'm trying to see if either of those security men or even their uniformed guys may be involved with my missing person, one of the environmental activists who periodically set up shop and harassed the mill owner. The MP is Tommy Lee Helton, and no one disputes the fact that he got into Koronkiewicz's face with a few inflammatory statements. Koronkiewicz has documented anger management problems. It's not much, but no one else is volunteering to jump into my handcuffs and confess to snuffing Tommy Lee and dumping his body on some lonely mountain."

"I wish I could be more help, but the best I can do is take a look through the photos one of our guys took during a couple of those demonstrations. Ralph said I can trust you. But remember all this is confidential. If the case breaks and we get a statement that helps you, I'll let you know."

"Good. I'd appreciate that. And as far as I'm concerned, we never had this conversation. If you think you've got something interesting, I'll send someone over to take a look."

"No problem. I'll call you again."

———

I've been doing police work for a long time and can categorically state an investigation full of dead ends stinks.

Tommy Lee's parents weren't much better than useless. His employer and girlfriend tried but fell well short of providing beneficial information. So far, the only individual who contributed to the whole cockamamie operation was a Labrador retriever who found the body of an unrelated man, presumably killed by who knows whom almost a decade ago.

———

The next day, I sat across from Bettye Lambert on a burgundy, leather-covered seat in a booth at Sullivan's Restaurant in Maryville. The aged brick wall behind her extended two stories above us in the one-time furniture store that someone turned into a chi-chi eatery with a few down-home meals on the menu.

"Darlin', I'll help you anyway I can, but this new body is yours—yours and John's, that is. *It's all yours.* The weather's still good. The tourists are still around. And my detectives are catching new cases each day. This old murder is just perfect for you two private eyes."

I took a long sip of Blue Moon before kvetching. "That's private investigators, if you please. And thanks a bunch for the new case. Now, Missy, yew might jest start pre-parin' yerse'f fer the e-ventual reality that we jest ain't a'gonna find ol' Tommy Lee Helton dead or alive."

"Oh, I doubt that." She smiled like a wicked cat eyeing up a wounded bird. "You're Sam Jenkins, sugar, world's greatest detective. You do the impossible."

"Pfui. That's flummery. How much are you paying me?"

"Twenty dollars an hour."

"I made more than twice that much twenty years ago. Peanuts. I repeat, pfui."

Bettye fluttered her eyelashes like some Hollywood femme fatale.

"Don't pull that act on me, Blondie. If John Boy didn't need the cash to live, I'd abandon ship and weed my garden."

"Surely you don't mean that, darlin'." She did the flutter act again and sipped imperceptibly from a tall glass of chardonnay.

"Don't bet your panty hose on that one, sweetheart."

"Who wears panty hose nowadays?"

I raised my eyebrows twice. "Wanna elaborate on that?"

"No!"

"Then tell me about this guy Jake Quarles."

"Not much to tell. Are you also askin' the other cops from Prospect?"

"Of course, you're not dealing with an amateur. Vernon is handling that. John and Terri are checking with your records section and all the surrounding PDs, and as soon as we track them down, one of us will interview the ex and son. But you were there in Jake's hometown, and you have an excellent memory. So, speak, woman. I need data."

She sighed and sipped again before beginning her story. "Well, as you already know, he was married to a woman named Alva. They had a son named Jacob Junior. Jake worked at Alcoa and by all accounts was nothing more than a randy ol' Billy goat—he picked up women at all the local bars and roadhouses and got into lots of the usual minor troubles. He kept cattin' around, and Alva kept takin' him back 'til one time he just moved out. She had no choice but to take him to court so he'd pay child support. After that, Prospect PD and the county deputies kept lockin' him up on family court warrants for not payin' his child support. Then one day, he just ups and disappears."

"Ups and disappears?"

"That's what I said."

The background music in the restaurant reminded me of the FM radio stations of forty years ago—Ray Conniff, Paul Mauriat and the ever popular Montovani.

"Any investigation?" I asked.

"We didn't have any concrete reason to suspect someone wanted to do him harm. He left some personal belongings in his apartment, but not much. It didn't look like he ever owned a lot, so what was there didn't amount to much. There was another outstandin' warrant, so we figured he was just another fugitive who moved on. And remember that was durin' Buck Webbster's time as chief. If that old fool could kiss off a case, he would. The DA's investigators might have opened a case on him. I'll ask. Prospect didn't do much more than take Alva's report of not gettin' her child support and bein' unable to find Jake so she could take somethin' back to court and then to the welfare people if she qualified. I'll check and see if the sheriff's office has anything on it."

"And I just happen to have an in with welfare. I'll ask her to run the name through their files."

"Good idea."

"And now, according to Vern Hobbs, the telltale signature slitherin' serpent belt buckle tends ta indicate that Jake the Snake done got hisse'f kilt."

"Sammy, I believe if you live here much longer, you're gonna sound downright local."

————

My lunch with Sheriff Bettye provided me with three things: A little more background on Jake the Snake which Mo Rappaport promised to enhance and fill in some blanks after his archeological —or is it more properly anthropological—autopsy? News that her cousin Janetta was back home and would call John or me soon. And I devoured a wonderful plate of Low Country shrimp and grits courtesy of the sheriff's expense account.

CHAPTER TEN

The next morning Terri Donnellson met John and me at our office ready for her first day as a private investigator in training. She walked in carrying a Wendy's coffee cup, wearing a lightweight navy blue pantsuit over a white shell blouse. Her dark hair was pulled up on the sides and fastened at the back with some sort of rubberized thingie. If looks alone counted, the woman was born to be a detective.

John did most of the talking, bringing her up to speed on what we did and how much we had or had not accomplished. I felt that we were at a dead end and couldn't justify her working with us, but being a life-long civil servant not opposed to spending taxpayer money, I wanted Bettye to invest her twelve bucks an hour to give us a fresh pair of eyes looking at the case.

At quarter after nine, my cell phone sounded off. Sue Brown, one of the women renting the cabin near where Jake "the Snake" Quarles' body had been found sounded almost breathless.

"Can you get over here?" she asked. "We've got big troubles. Chamois got out again and took off into the woods to the right of the cabin. She chased a pair of coyotes into that heavy brush and mixed it up with them. Chamois got hurt badly. Holly and Norma took the dog to an emergency vet in Prospect."

"I'm sorry about the dog, but how can I help you?"

"When we found Chamois lying in the woods, we also found another grave."

———

I asked John to check with Bernie Gavin for any old information on Jake or Alma Quarles and after grabbing a pair of green rubber Wellies from my truck, Terri and I took off toward Prospect in her Mini Cooper. John immediately phoned Prospect PD to get at least one sector car to the cabin. His second call went to county CID, alerting them that we'd probably need a team of crime scene investigators shortly. We would confirm the presence of a body before screaming for the medical examiner.

We pulled up to the cabin on Meissners Station Road and met PO Billy Puckett standing in the driveway with Sue Brown and Karen Doktor.

It was a pretty morning. The thermometer on the dashboard of the Mini read sixty-four degrees. The dogwoods had already started to redden up, and a few other trees were beginning to turn partially yellow. The rains of August might have prepped the trees to give us a colorful autumn.

I introduced Terri to the women and followed Sue behind the house as she answered my question of how the dog got out again.

"Holly was sitting on the porch this morning having a second cup of coffee when a coyote loped through the backyard. Chamois started going crazy. When a second coyote showed up, the dog just put her head down and rammed through the screen at the bottom of the door and took off after them."

The screened-in porch was an old-fashioned affair having simple four foot wide roll screening fastened to the 4x4 uprights, with the seams covered by thin battens. The lower screen portion of the lightweight door had been torn away from the wood frame and was literally flapping in the breeze.

"Sixty pound dog versus stapled in screening. No contest," I said.

"Those coyotes really cranked her up," Sue said.

"Are you sure they were coyotes, ma'am?" Terri asked.

"Yeah. I lived in Texas when my husband was in the Air Force. I know what a coyote looks like."

"Give us an idea where to look for this new grave," I said.

"That's easy. Just walk straight back ninety degrees to the driveway." Sue paused for a moment to clarify her statement. "I shouldn't say it's easy. It looks pretty thick in places, but it's basically a straight walk."

There was almost a hundred feet of driveway, a gravel parking area and clear land between the exterior side wall of the cabin and the wood line—beyond that, forest.

To Officer Puckett I said, "Give me a minute, Billy. I want to put on a pair of boots before heading in."

"Glad I got me a uniform allowance," he said. "I figger we might get cut up some in there."

Billy is only about five-eight and stocky. Two Marine Corps tattoos showed on his forearms, not covered by a short sleeve uniform shirt.

I shrugged. "I don't get that allowance anymore, but I'll plead with Bettye to replace whatever I ruin in there playing tin soldier."

Billy snickered. "Good luck there."

"Terri, even though you've got on sensible shoes, why don't you stay here, your clothes will get ruined."

She smiled. "I came prepared, boss. I'll be right behind you."

"Okay then, let's get our boots on."

I pulled on my Wellingtons and tucked my pants legs into the tops. Terri took off her jacket and flipped up the hatchback of her Mini. From a cardboard box, she took out a pair of Army camouflage field pants and put them on over her slacks.

"You weren't kidding. You're ready for battle."

Her smile from before turned into a wide grin. "An MP is ready for anything twenty-four hours a day."

She sat on the tailgate of the little car and laced up a pair of tan, rough-out combat boots and bloused the cuffs of her battle dress trousers over the boot tops.

"How do you spit shine those Hush Puppies?" I asked.

"Spit shine?" It sounded as if she heard me ask her to perform a lobotomy on an angry rhinoceros. "You must have been in the 'brown shoe army'."

"Not exactly, youngster, but close enough. No starch, no polish nowadays, huh?"

"You're just jealous." She put on a fatigue jacket that matched her pants over a silky white blouse. "Now I'm ready."

"Then let's take Puckett, the ex-jarhead, with us and hit the bush."

Billy smiled. "Be my pleasure, boss. Once a Marine, always a Marine. Lemme show you Army types how it's done."

The area wasn't as difficult to navigate through as we originally thought. Areas of thick brush we could walk around gave way to relatively clear spots with old growth trees everywhere. About a hundred yards into the woods, we found the spot where the two coyotes had savaged Chamois. Spattered blood covered the low brush marking the spot where the three animals mixed it up. But a larger, more concentrated blood spill showed us where Chamois got the short end of the stick and lay until Holly and Norma found her. Not far from that spot, we found a shallow grave recently disturbed by animals. A hand and forearm protruded from the dirt less than two feet below ground level. The leaves that covered the spot had been scattered haphazardly.

I looked closely at the exposed hand. "Been here a little while, but this is no old grave."

Puckett and Terri shook their heads. The smell in the woods from the early putrefaction of the corpse caused them to wrinkle their noses.

"Hell of a coincidence," I said. "Two makeshift graves this close. Terri, first thing I want you to do when we get out of here is check with the Register of Deeds for the owner of this land."

She nodded. "Sure thing."

"Billy, let's get a full complement of troops to process the scene. The county should have a pair of evidence technicians standing by. May as well start the ME rolling, too. And see if the duty officer can spare a couple of deputies."

"You got it, boss."

I flipped open my phone. "I'll get John out here. Might as well tell the sheriff what we've got. I'm guessing this may be Tommy Lee."

"You think so?" Terri asked.

"Just a guess, but we don't have any other recent missing persons on file and this guy's only been in the ground a week or so. I haven't got a crystal ball in my back pocket, but it's a man's hand." I stood up and stretched my back. "Before disturbing the grave any more, I want some real detailed photos of the area. After that, we'll let the ME tell us how he wants to extricate the body."

She nodded. A few moments later, Billy Puckett returned.

"Everybody's rollin'," he said. "Got two deps comin' and another man from Prospect PD. Ever'body should be gettin' here directly. And the DO said he'd see if he could scare us up some more he'p."

Just after I nodded, a loud shot rang out, and a bullet struck the trunk of a Virginia pine less than a foot from my head.

The two combat veterans and I dropped simultaneously, and we all redundantly shouted the same thing, "Get down!"

After hitting the dirt, we each scrambled for the cover of the largest tree close to our relative positions. The sound of a high caliber, center-fire rifle is unmistakable in an open field. In the close quarters of the woods, it sounded like a howitzer fired no more than thirty or forty yards away.

I drew my revolver and peeked from behind the sweet gum that afforded me a little cover and limited concealment. "You two stay down. I'm going to move up a bit and take a look."

Billy said, "You ain't got a helmet, boss. Keep yer head down, and we'll watch yer back."

I low crawled twenty feet to a spot that gave me an advantage to look almost a hundred and fifty degrees over the wooded area. I saw and heard nothing.

Talking softly, but loud enough so Billy and Terri could hear me, I said, "I have no idea if they're still out there. Move up a little but stay far apart. Go low and slow."

My partners did exactly as I suggested. Their military training showed by their cautious but efficient movement. A slight breeze pushed the Cordite smell of an expended round toward us. The shooter couldn't have been very far away when he pulled the trigger. But I didn't see a trace of him.

Once they came parallel to my position, I began crawling farther forward. When next I stopped, they followed, both approximately fifteen feet to my sides. After we covered another twenty yards and with no additional shots fired, I called for them to stop. Using an old Ponderosa pine for cover, I stood upright and surveyed the forest. I saw nothing but more trees.

"I'm going to take a quick look around," I said. "Stay down and watch for a muzzle flash. You see one, empty half your magazine in that direction. Let's see what happens."

"Be careful," Terri said.

"Sure ya want ta do that, boss?" Billy added.

"Can't camp out here until dark," I said. "Just be ready for anything. I don't want this guy getting away if he's close. If you hear gunfire, shoot back, but remember that I'm going to prone out and scramble, so give me three feet of leeway overhead."

I stayed low enough to only offer a minimal target, but high enough to see over the low scrub brush. After only two minutes of skulking around, my thigh muscles began to tire. I stood again behind the closest and biggest tree. Nothing happened.

"I can't see a damned thing," I said. "I'm guessing I'm a big enough target if this guy is any kind of a marksman. Must be gone. Let's back-track and find the tree the bullet struck. Billy, cover the rear in case he's playing 'possum."

"Got it," he said.

Only minutes later, Terri found the tree. I marked the spot by jamming my pocket knife into the bark above the bullet hole and tying a handkerchief around the handle.

"The crime scene guys can cut a chunk of pine and free up the bullet when they get back to their office. I want to see what that guy used to shoot at us."

"I think he was shootin' at *you*, boss," Billy said.

———

LESS THAN AN HOUR LATER, MEISSNERS STATION ROAD WAS crawling with cops. PO Joey Gillespie, working the desk at Prospect PD, received approval to call in off-duty officers. Four more men responded. Bettye sent me two teams of crime scene investigators, four uniformed deputies and ten auxiliaries. And four state troopers graced us with their presence. A fresh grave of an obvious victim of foul play and a shot from what sounded like a big bore rifle aimed somewhere at or between three cops tends to cause a commotion in the local law enforcement community.

The two ladies in the rental cabin heard the shot. After a period of patient waiting behind the front steps of the cabin, they met Terri, Billy and me as we emerged from the woods. Later, Billy Puckett led a platoon of cops toward the spot where we had been fired upon. Terri remained behind with me to regroup and speak to the girls from Connecticut.

"I'm glad no one was hurt," Sue Brown said.

"Just a few ruffled feathers," I said.

"I'll bet," Kathy said.

"Did either of you see a vehicle around," Terri asked.

"We were looking in your direction since you walked into the woods," Sue said. "Honestly, I didn't pay any attention before or after the shot. How about you, Kathy?"

She shook her head.

"Understandable," I said. "It would have been nice if you saw a vehicle hotfooting it away from here after the shot, but life's never that easy."

"That is another body in the woods, isn't it?" Sue asked.

"Oh, yeah. And I'm just guessing, but it's probably the young missing person we've been looking for all these days. We have to wait until the ME exhumes the body to get a positive ID."

Kathy shook her head and sighed. "This is a vacation none of us will ever forget."

I nodded. "And I need another dead body like the world needs another Elvis impersonator."

———

We were standing around outside the cabin waiting for additional reinforcements to arrive when my cell phone sounded off. The Rolling Stones began playing *Paint it Black* in my jacket pocket, and I looked at the caller ID.

"Excuse me. The boss is calling."

I walked a few feet, answered the phone and stuck a finger into my left ear to hear better. "How's my favorite sheriff this morning?"

No greeting for me. Bettye got right down to business. "And just when in hell were you goin' to call me, Sam Jenkins? What's this about gettin' shot at?"

"Shot? Oh, yes, the shot. I really don't know. But, as you can imagine, we're looking into that at this very moment. Thank your duty officer, by the way. He scrambled the troops to come and assist. But I guess I should remember he's not exactly good at keeping secrets."

"Are you okay? Forget that. I know you're okay, I'm talkin' to you. Oh, Lord have mercy. Actually, I don't really know you're okay because you wouldn't complain if an ax was stickin' out o' your back."

"Come now, that's not true."

"Why do I have to hear about this from someone else?"

"My phone needed charging?"

"Stop that. When something like this happens, I would think you'd call me."

"Yes, ma'am, Miss Bettye. I done wrong, and I apologize. Kin ya ever forgive me?"

Finally, she laughed. "Maybe. Maybe not. But if you want that paycheck, you better come in here and say you're sorry."

"It'll be my pleasure. But right now, I hear the sound of reinforcements approaching. I gotta go and lead our troops to victory. Talk to you soon."

———

WITH JACKIE SHUMAN AND JOHN GALLAGHER ARRIVING AND jointly shouldering responsibility for the new crime scene, Terri and I cleaned up and took a ride to the emergency veterinary clinic in Prospect. We found Holly Miller and Norma McTavish in the waiting room. Chamois was in surgery.

"How's she doing?" I asked.

Norma answered. "She lost plenty of blood, but she was awake and relatively alert when we found her."

Holly looked as if she had been crying, and her eyes looked tired. "She wagged her tail when we found her. Those...things bit into her neck. Can't someone kill those wild animals?"

Before I could formulate a satisfactory answer to Holly's question, Norma rescued me and elaborated on the dog's condition. "She's got cuts on her neck and a nasty gash on her hind quarter." She shrugged. "The vet sounded optimistic. She'll wind up with a bunch of stitches, but I'm guessing she'll be as good as new in a while."

"Oh, I hope so," Holly said.

"She's a big dog," I said. "How did you get her out of the woods?"

"We each took an end of a blanket," Holly said, "and used it like a stretcher."

I nodded. "Smart. I'm sure you saved the dog's life."

"I really hope so. I'd hate to lose her."

The vet's clinic was relatively new with a spotless and comfortable waiting room. Several people sat in the padded chairs while their dogs stood nervously alongside their owners, and cats made noises from within their plastic carriers.

In a back room a dog barked three times and stopped, the last noise sounded more like a gurgle. That made a few dogs in the waiting room uneasy. They began to whimper and fidget, their nails clicking on the tile floor. One of the cats cried loudly from within a carrier.

I asked if the women had seen anything more than the two coyotes, either that morning or any time prior to Chamois finding the new grave. Like the others, neither of them had. No strange vehicles, no hikers, bicyclists or even noises in the forest.

So, we had a new grave, another dead body and only a foot between my head and a rapidly moving chunk of copper jacketed lead, but no good suspects.

———

"Remember what I asked you to do first?" I said to Terri.

"Sure. Find who owns the land where we found the second grave."

"Good. When you drop me off, take care of that. But now I was just thinking. There are three possibilities here. Tell me if you can see another."

"Okay."

"The most unlikely scenario is the shot was an accident."

Terri nodded. "I agree."

"So, supposing the shot wasn't just a fluke and unrelated to anything we've been doing, and it wasn't just a careless hunter or someone practicing with his new rifle. Let's suppose the shot was intentional, and the shooter wanted to hit me and missed? That's the second possibility. But then, suppose the shooter didn't want to hit any of us? Suppose he wanted to hit that tree and send a message—keep away. Foolish to think we'd just leave, but maybe the shooter was that good with a rifle and could pick his target from a distance."

"All possible," she said. "But why do you automatically think the shooter was a him?"

"Why do you women always complicate my life?"

"Just saying. And you asked for another opinion."

I made a sour lemon face. "Yeah. I think it's important to find out where our ex-sniper, Bill Koronkiewicz, was this morning."

————

TERRI DROPPED ME OFF AT THE OFFICE BEFORE HEADING TO THE Prospect Municipal Building to check with the register of deeds. To keep me from forgetting, I left a note for John to think about finding Alma and Jake Quarles Jr. after Bernie Gavin provided us with whatever information Human Services had squirreled away in their archives. Then, I drove my truck to the Justice Center looking for some creative legal advice.

————

MOIRA MENZIES' NEW OFFICE OCCUPIED A CORNER OF THE THIRD floor with windows facing north and west. She had a bird's eye view of the busy intersection of US 321 and Washington Street and most of the hospital. I sat in a russet brown, leather-covered guest chair in front of a reproduction Early American desk. Moira stood behind the desk with her left fist nestled atop her hip while she tapped a rousing tattoo on her blotter with a pencil she held in her right hand.

"I thought I'd never see you again after you left Prospect PD," she said. "Now I've got Blount County's newest private eye sitting in my office."

It looked as if she'd just gotten a haircut, but her wavy blond locks still touched the shoulders of her merlot-colored suit top.

I gave her an insincere smile. "Private *investigator*. It's nice to see you, too."

If I didn't know better, I would have thought she caught a whiff of the elephant enclosure at the Knoxville Zoo two hours after a big dinner. She unwrinkled her nose before commenting. "Why did you and Gallagher ever start that business?"

I shrugged, knowing she had caught me with a difficult question. "John can use the money. I have no good answer for myself."

"Probably wanted to be Maryville's answer to Jim Rockford."

I sneered. "Maybe not. I don't live by the beach in a single-wide. Philip Marlowe is more my speed."

That seemed to go in one ear and out the other.

"I can't figure it out either, and believe me, I tried. But I'm even more surprised that you would ever come in asking for legal advice. I never thought Sam Jenkins would ask for *anyone's* opinion."

"That's just not true and a little harsh. Besides, you should be flattered I came to you first. Since my problem has interstate ramifications, I could have asked some AUSA for Justice Department help."

"Yeah, you get along great with Heidi Piper. I'm sure she'd *love* to help you."

I gave that a quick and dismissive wave. "You know how those Feds are. Make an inquiry and they want to take over an investigation. By the way, have I said that wine-colored suit is a good color for you? Goes great with your blond waves."

"Oh, stop. You don't have to butter me up any more. I didn't say I won't help you. I'm implying that I'm surprised your enormous ego is allowing you to seek assistance."

"Pfui. Look at it academically—a test question, if you will. I'll give you the circumstances and see if you can find what I need. So far all I see is a basic suspicion and want more."

"Suspicion gets you nothing—but frustrated, maybe."

"Right. Okay. I've got a missing person to find—who I'm guessing is, as we speak, being exhumed from a makeshift grave in the hinterlands of Prospect. This missing person has been occasionally harassing the entire Cataloochee Paper Mill staff and the assistant chief of security in particular—rather vehemently at times. That assistant chief is a retired Marine Corps sniper. This morning someone with exceptional skills with a rifle took a shot at yours truly—which, I think, was designed to scare me off the case. How do I get the legal leverage to put the arm on him and get him here from North Carolina?"

"That's it?" Moira sounded flabbergasted and blinked her light brown eyes several times. "That's all you've got?"

I raised my eyebrows. "I would have told you more if there was more."

She shook her head. "Calling it a simple suspicion is even a stretch. You've got nothing."

I nodded reluctantly. "I know that. I can usually get creative with manipulating the law, but this time I'm at a loss. If I was this guy Koronkiewicz and I asked him to account for his time this morning, I'd laugh at me and tell me to go pound salt."

"I can't say any more than that. Hey, I'm pleased with my ability to understand the criminal procedure laws, but you want a miracle from a few flimsy elements that *may* be connected and would lead only the most suspicious person to see them as any more than that."

"Hmmph. I guess I can ask a Carolina trooper to find out where Koronkiewicz was today."

"And tip your hand completely?"

"But if he was at the paper mill, I wouldn't waste any more time looking at him. Sooner or later, we'll have to ask."

"There is that."

"So we're baffled, stumped, stonewalled."

"What do you mean 'we,' gumshoe?"

"You're a big help."

"I'm not a magician."

I shrugged and decided to change the subject. "Yeah, I know. Hey, I liked your old office better than this one. The view of the jail was sort of comforting."

"The jail is one of the ugliest buildings on earth."

"But they always have a customer and consistently a higher rate of occupancy than most hotels."

She shook her head. "I hate to throw you out, but since I became the interim DA, I do have things to do."

I refused to be rejected offhandedly. "Are you going to run for election when the time comes?"

"I guess I'm getting to like the top job here, but I don't have the money—or chance of raising it—to run a political campaign."

I shook my head. "You don't use your own cash. You solicit fat cats who want to say they backed a winner. Ask the party for help. You deserve this job."

"Thanks, but I'm not exactly endowed with an abundance of political clout."

"I may be running out of favors from high places, but I might be able to help you with that."

"Then I'd owe you a big favor."

"Yes, you would. Be nice to me, and I might help you get elected."

She smiled. "I don't know if the job is worth that much."

———

Before leaving the Justice Center, I called John to see what was shaking at the gravesite.

"Doctor Mo and Earl are doing their thing with Jackie's help. Sparkie is doing all the photography, and the cops here are looking around the immediate area for anything relating to the one who dumped the body and took a shot, assuming they're the same person."

"Sounds like I'd be as useful as antlers on a frog."

"It's gonna be a while. They're uncovering the body using little garden trowels and whiskbrooms. I checked when they uncovered the face. Looks like Tommy Lee to me. Mo figures the day he was reported missing is a good guess for a time of death."

"You're sure it's Tommy Lee?"

"Yeah. He's not such a good-lookin' kid any more, but he's recognizable."

"Know what killed him?"

"Took a round in the chest. If it wasn't a heart shot, it was pretty close."

"Something a sniper might do."

"Good shot. Entry wound looks a little small for a .38 or nine millimeter. Probably a .30 caliber. Everybody thinks a rifle. No exit wound, so Mo will be able to retrieve a slug."

"Good. TBI can give us a positive ID on the bullet and a ballpark on the gun."

"Uh-huh."

"If you're certain it's Tommy Lee, I'll break the news to Bernie and see how she takes it. Then, let's get mom and dad in one spot and see their reaction. We can do that together."

"Okay. Need anything from here?"

"Did you speak with Bernie this morning about Jake the Snake's family?"

"She wasn't in. I left a message."

"Under the circumstances, it won't be a good time for me to ask for an unrelated favor. We'll have to work it another way."

"Yeah, no problem. I'll handle it or give it to Terri. Need anything else?"

"Ask one of the girls in the cabin for the rental agreement and get all the information on their place. Terri is checking on the surrounding property. When I finish with Bernie, I'll call Jimmy Helton and make an appointment to see him and his wife."

"Give me a call when you're ready."

———

A CLERK AT THE WELFARE OFFICE TOLD ME THAT BERNADETTE Gavin was on the road visiting her clients. A call to Bernie's cell phone caught her between stops.

"I'm on Harper Avenue about a block from the Broadway traffic circle," she said.

"I've got some news. Want to meet me in the café at Southland Books on the circle? I can be there in ten minutes. I'll buy you coffee."

"Good news?"

She would have to ask.

I tried not to sound overly pessimistic. "Not exactly. I'll explain."

"Do they have more than coffee? I haven't eaten lunch yet."

"Jeez. You women wrap me around your little fingers. Okay, I'll buy you lunch."

"I wasn't asking. I'm just hungry and don't have much free time."

"Don't worry. I can't refuse a diligent civil servant."

"Okay. That's nice of you." She paused for a moment. "I've never been inside. I'll meet you in the parking lot."

"Parking is kind of tight in front. Use the lower lot behind the store."

"Okay. I'm almost there."

A few moments later, I pulled into a spot next to Bernie's light green Prius. It wasn't exactly sage green, nor was it lime. Ecologically appropriate for her, but it was a color I wouldn't want to look at for more than three days. She got out and locked the car door before my foot hit the blacktop. Wearing white slacks, a pale blue blouse, she looked more suited for lunch at the yacht club than making the rounds looking for deadbeat clients.

"Want to tell me what's new?" she asked.

I wasn't looking forward to this. "Let's go inside and sit down."

A pair of cardinals landed in a tall bush at the rear entrance of the parking lot and began chattering away. She looked toward them for a long moment, almost as if she wanted to avoid my response.

"The last time I met you for lunch," Bernie said, "I ended up becoming unglued. I don't want to cry in my soup. Tell me what happened."

I hesitated a little too long. "I sometimes have that effect on women."

She frowned. "You found him, didn't you?"

Bernie must have been expecting the worst. Her once bright, amber-colored eyes appeared sad and flat.

I took a breath before handling one of the most difficult parts of a cop's job. "There's no easy way to tell you. I'm sorry."

Everyone understands that.

"You found his body?" She blinked, and her eyes began to leak.

I nodded and repeated my last line. "I'm so sorry."

"An accident?"

I shook my head. "He was murdered."

"No." It came out as almost a whisper. Tears ran down both her cheeks.

Foolishly, I said, "It's okay."

She shook her head vehemently. "No. No, it's not." Her eyes widened, and she raised her eyebrows. "I'm not handling this well."

Bernie took a step closer and reached out to put her arms around me. She pushed her head against my chest.

Normally, when an attractive woman puts her arms around you, a man's thoughts might wander toward the romantic. But death notifications don't even come close. And women who hear that one of their loved ones just bought the farm usually seek a little platonic comfort where they can get it. Having found myself providing that bit of manly comfort often enough, I can't count the number of times I've experienced that awkward feeling. Even with my experience, knowing the right things to say or doing the right things with my hands *did not* come naturally.

I settled for the tired old line, "I'm really sorry for your loss," and a gentle pat on the back.

"How did he die?" she asked between sniffs.

A good detective doesn't immediately disclose those details.

"We have to wait for the doctor."

"How do you know he was murdered?"

"We uncovered a shallow grave."

That brought on additional tears and a tighter hug, perhaps even a vision of what I didn't describe.

"Oh, God. Why Tommy?"

"When we know more, I'll let you know."

She released me, took a step back and wiped the tears with the back of her hand. "I'm sorry. I should be able to control myself."

"No need to apologize. Crying is okay."

"Look at me." She rummaged in an extra large handbag for a tissue. "This is not acceptable."

"I'm really sorry. I wish I could have brought you better news."

She frowned, with an intense look in her eyes. "Who did this?"

"We're working on that."

Her shoulders dropped. "You have no idea, do you?"

Hang around with her more often and I'd develop an inferiority complex.

"Nothing yet."

"Poor Tommy."

Still feeling awkward, and for the lack of anything else to say, I asked, "Can I get you anything?"

Typical cop. Fix an emotional problem with coffee or food.

"I couldn't eat." She shrugged. "Actually, I need a drink. A *big* glass of wine. But I refuse to go into a public place looking like this. My eyes must be a mess."

"Will you take the rest of the day off?"

The look on her face told me she clearly thought there was such a thing as a stupid question. "I have to. I can't talk to my clients like this."

"Follow me back to my office. It's very private. Just us and maybe my assistant if she finished a job I gave her. She'll understand. You can call your job, and I have a bottle of scotch."

She tilted her head and sighed. "Scotch will do."

"We're just a block up from your office. Follow me."

———

As we pulled into the parking lot in front of Jenkins & Gallagher, Terri Donnellson was opening the office door. She walked in, and Bernie and I followed. I made the introductions.

"I'm so sorry, Ms. Gavin," Terri said. "And I know this is no consolation, but if anyone can find who did this to your friend, Mr. Jenkins can. I work for the Prospect Police Department, but I'm helping him and Mr. Gallagher with Tommy Lee's case."

"Thank you, Ms. Donnellson." Bernie sighed as if she had done something wrong. "I'm sorry, Officer Donnellson."

Terri nodded. "Call me Terri. And please sit down. You must be exhausted."

Women are so much better at this than me. Terri could be the new Bettye at Prospect PD.

"I'll get you that drink," I said. "Would you like water and ice?"

"Both please."

"Terri, are you drinking?"

She frowned and shook her head. Why, I don't know. She'll learn.

I brought Bernie a glass with two fingers of Glenfiddich, a splash of spring water and two cubes. She took a long sip.

"Thank you. This will help."

"If you want more, just whistle." I looked at Terri. "How'd you make out at the Register's office?"

"Very well. They gave me a plat of the immediate area with names and contact info for the owners."

"Good."

"The acreage where we found Tommy Lee is owned by a company that calls itself Foothills Land Development Corporation. They have a Prospect address." She raised her eyebrows making an unspoken gesture implying, 'Wait until you hear more.'

But Bernie spoke first, clarifying something about the land company. "Tommy's father owns that business."

CHAPTER ELEVEN

***

After opening the bottle of Columbia Valley dry Riesling Kate had put in the fridge an hour earlier, allowing it to "breathe" a little, I fixed myself a vodka and tonic with a healthy chunk of lime. My wife's drink was still three-quarters full.

"Where did you get this recipe?" I asked, looking at a baking pan sitting on the kitchen counter and a small dish containing a multi-colored pile of assembled condiments.

"One of your fishing magazines."

"That halibut must have cost an arm and a leg."

"Don't ask."

"What else goes in?"

"Some of the black mission figs you picked this morning, onion, fennel seeds, New Mexico chili, garlic and all the usual seasonings. A little grated cheese on top and voila!"

"And you just happened to be reading my copy of *Saltwater Sportsman?*"

"Why do you think I always catch the first and biggest fish?"

"Remind me to hide my reading material."

"Speaking of a reminder, when did you plan to tell me someone took a shot at you this morning?"

"Ah. Yeah, I forgot to call. Sorry 'bout that, but John and I were running all over the place."

After crushing and mincing two elephantine cloves of garlic with what appeared to be more vengeance than usual, Kate said, "At least the TV news people were quick to say no one got hurt, and the source of the shot was still unknown. How much is still unknown to the county's chief investigator?"

"It's a long story."

"We've got time. Tell me."

"As you no doubt heard, we found Tommy Lee Helton's body."

"Yes. The women in the cabin again and their dog. The news was all over that."

"Yeah. Poor dog got mauled by a couple of coyotes. Anyway, the dog or the coyotes or both found a new grave. When Billy, Terri and I were in the woods, someone took a shot. But listen, I don't know if it was more than someone trying out his new rifle and not taking proper precautions."

"Billy Puckett and Terri, your new protégé from Prospect PD?"

"Right. The former MP. After the shot hit a tree we sounded like a bunch of soldiers taking tactical action and made enough noise that the shooter might have gotten scared and took off thinking he'd get into serious trouble."

"But you didn't think it was oddly coincidental that someone took a pot shot at you right after you began looking at the shallow grave of another murder victim?"

I chuckled. "Pot shot? This is not an old cowboy movie."

"Oh, pa-leeze."

"Nuts. If someone wanted to kill me, they could just drive by the office and do it from a moving car."

She didn't look convinced. "Sure."

"Anyway, now we've got two bodies, dead years apart, but within a couple hundred yards of each other. We've got to get back into the woods and scour the place for some evidence of another person being there."

"A capital idea, Holmes."

I sneered. "Thank you, my dear Watson."

"Putting this *Snake* person aside for the moment, what did the victim's parents say about finding your missing man?"

After setting aside several drawn and quartered figs, Kate attacked a Vidalia onion, mincing it. I thought she still may be using her blade with a little too much vehemence, but maybe that was just me.

"I told the girlfriend first."

"Your friend Bernadette."

"The victim's friend. John says her name reminds her of a Four Season's song."

"Four Tops, Samuel."

"I know that. But you know John."

"Uh-huh."

"The girlfriend took it pretty hard. Obviously, they were more than just environmentally friendly."

"Very clever."

I thought it was downright laughable.

"Then John and I talked with the parents."

"And?"

"The father looked like he just learned someone's dog peed on his flowers—more annoyed than grief stricken. And the mother—what a space cadet. She looks like she sits home popping chocolate covered Valium all day. Zero. Flat effect. The best she could come up with was, '*Oh, my.*' She sounded like George Takei."

"Also clever. Do you think they had anything to do with the boy's death?"

"Their behavior is definitely strange, but I see nothing that points to them being involved. They just seem about as troubled as if their pet goldfish died."

"That is odd."

"And even more strange, the grave was on land owned by the father's corporation."

"You knew this before you talked to him?"

"Sure. He shrugged it off. Said he inherited the land long before the big real estate crash. Before that, his father sold off a few five acres lots to private individuals. Jimmy wanted to use his free land to build spec homes or rental cabins for investors. Now he wants to wait for the property values to go back up before he does that and can't get top dollar. He claims that he hasn't set foot on the property in more than a year."

"It sounds like he's more worried about his business prospects than his dead son."

"I know. The guy is a real coldblooded hump. Talk to him for ten minutes about his son and you'd think he'd just as soon punch the kid's ticket as smash home a ten penny nail."

"Must have been fun growing up with him."

"Oh, yeah. Not exactly a *Leave it to Beaver* childhood." Before sliding Kate's halibut concoction into the oven, I made one final observation. "My big question is if the killer or someone involved with Tommy Lee's death took that shot, why was he in the woods at that particular time? Nobody kills someone and stakes out the grave for more than a week afterwards."

———

THE NEXT MORNING JOHN WALKED INTO THE OFFICE ON HOME Avenue carrying a white paper bag with a Taco Bell logo.

"Morning, Boss, uh, I mean, Sam."

He sat at one of the desks in the outer office next to where I had been reading a copy of *The Maryville Daily Times*.

I frowned at him. "Don't you ever eat breakfast at home?"

"Barbara doesn't get up early, and I don't know what to make."

"You're having a Mexican breakfast?"

"A breakfast burrito. Ever have one?"

"Not while I'm east of the Mississippi."

He took a fat cylinder wrapped in opaque waxed paper from the bag.

"That looks big enough to be a rolled up bath towel, for chrissakes."

Unfazed, John smiled and explained. "They call it the Super Grande Burrito. It was only a buck and a half more than the regular size."

"Looks like it could feed six hungry vaqueros *and* their horses. What's in it?"

"Uh, scrambled eggs, bacon, beef, beans, tomatoes, cheese, and uh... other stuff."

"Hmmm."

"You make coffee?" he asked.

"Just finished dripping."

"Good. Whattaya wanna do today?"

"Other than call Bill Werner at TBI firearms ID, I don't know. After talking with the Heltons yesterday, my head wanted to explode."

"I know what you mean. Couple of oddball parents. You think Werner will have the ballistics work finished yet?"

"He said he'd put a rush on it." I looked at my watch. "It's 9:15. He's had time to settle in. Let's rattle his cage."

"Good. I'll eat while you talk."

———

"Like I told you, Sam," Werner said. "I put a rush on the work you sent. You're my favorite local cop. I was going to call right after I finished my coffee, but here you are. Okay, I processed the older round first, the one from the first corpse. A Remington 180 grain Core-Lokt soft point .308."

"Hunting round."

"Yeah. They've been around for seventy-five years. Sold almost everywhere. The rifling looks like a one in twelve twist. From the type of lands and grooves, I'd say a Remington 700."

"Like a Marine Corps B-40 sniper rifle?"

"Could be."

"Interesting."

"Yeah, but it gets better."

"Billy, I need better now. So far we've got squat on these cases."

"This could help. Or it could just complicate your life. The second round, the one fired at you that Shuman removed from the tree and I got late yesterday, was a bit more exotic. I think you'll love this. How about a Lapoua 185 grain boat tail, D-46 bullet? Also out of a one in twelve twist barrel. Also from a..." He paused for dramatic effect "...Remington 700."

"Why do I think there's more?"

"Hang on now. Under the microscope, both bullets match. They were fired from the same weapon."

"Son of a gun. Only a serious shooter would use Lapua ammo. Last I heard that ran around two bucks a round."

"With sales tax, more like three."

"Sportsmen and casual target shooters don't get that specialized, but snipers would."

"Pretty good guess."

"Same gun, years apart. Hot damn."

"You bet."

"Two down and one to go. You'll get a third bullet to deal with after the autopsy on our second corpse. With luck it'll be another match, and we get a trifecta."

———

I TOLD JOHN WHAT THE FIREARMS EXAMINER SAID. BASED ON THE specialty ammunition fired at me, I renewed my interest in Bill Koronkiewicz, the ex-sniper.

"You want to pull him in and question him?" The look on John's face told me he might not see that as a good idea.

"I'd love to, but what happens if he says we're crazy and walks out?"

"We're up Shit Creek."

"Exactly. I know we may have to sooner or later, but he's no dummy. And even if we ask a trooper in North Carolina to see if they can place his whereabouts on the day someone shot at me, what's he gonna find out? If Koronkiewicz is innocent, he'll come up with a story putting him at work. If he's guilty, he'll lie and clam up and ditch the rifle. Curry won't give up his own man if they wanted to whack Tommy Lee—for personal or professional reasons. And if Koronkiewicz just did it to get back at the kid for having a big mouth, Curry would still cover for his old comrade. Marines are like Masons and cops, they stick together."

"And," John grinned like he had just come up with the most unique thought of the century, "who says Curry might not have taken the shot? All Marines learn how to use a rifle."

"Right. I wasn't a sniper but, modestly speaking, I could put a .308 up a gnat's ass at 400 meters using a B-40 and Lapua ammo."

"So, we're gonna lay off *Kronkowski* for now?"

"Yeah. Koronkiewicz can rest easy for the time being, but I'm not sure how long we can flounder around. It's possible we'll never get more evidence linking him to a crime. Then we have to shoot craps and hope for the best."

"I know. So what do we do now? I'm running out of ideas."

"Let's forget North Carolina and look at the Kronkster from a different angle." I picked up the phone. "I'll see what Ned the Fed can tell us."

Edward "Ned" Greznik was a senior special agent at the Bureau of Alcohol, Tobacco, and Firearms in Knoxville. My call caught him in the office at 710 Locust Street.

"Can you do a quick search on a person and see if he's got a specific firearm on paper? I don't know where he might have bought it."

"Sure, but only if he filled out a 4473 Form for a dealer. If he bought whatever you're looking for privately, we'd never know. And I should be ashamed to tell you this, but if the 4473 was filled out long, long ago, those records may not be on the computer yet. If you had a serial number, I could back-trace it."

"I understand. No number, just a suspicion and a subject. But this guy should be easy to locate. He did a couple of tours at embassy secu-rity with the Marines. He should have plenty of fingerprints on file and at least a secret clearance revalidated throughout the years."

"Okay, gimme his vital statistics."

I spelled Koronkiewicz and provided the other information Greznik would need. "I'm interested to know if he bought a Remington 700 in .308 caliber or if he was around any Marine Corps base where a B-40 7.62mm sniper rifle went missing."

"The last one may take a while, but I'll get back to ya."

———

"What did you learn from the guy who owns the property where the 'Guild' girls are staying?" I asked John Gallagher.

"He bought the five acres from Jimmy Helton's old man before the land company was in existence."

"So he knows about Jimmy Helton."

"Right. And he told me that Jimmy's father, Young Robert Helton, owned the whole shebang along Meissners Station Road for years. Before that, Jimmy's grandfather, Old Robert, owned it. Land's been in the family for a long time."

"The guy you spoke to is a local?"

"Born and raised. Family's been here since Davy Crockett or one of those guys."

"Then he should know."

"Yep."

"Yet Jimmy never elaborated about the land being in his family for so long."

"Yeah. That's stupid. He's gotta know we'd find out."

"Nothing here makes sense. We have to drag everything out of him and the wife with a tractor. Jimmy's a cold bastard, and the wife acts like she's the original dumb blonde. Lying comes as easily to them as falling off a log. John, I'm telling you, this whole thing is giving me brain fever.

I'm starting to feel like Frankie. Remember how he'd get frustrated and claim his head was going to explode?"

"Boss, you don't usually get so twisted out of shape over a case."

"I know. I'm too old for this mess. I never should have let you talk me into starting this business."

"It was the sheriff who talked you into being her investigator. She never has much trouble getting you to do things." He grinned like the village idiot after saying that.

"Then I hate you *and* her."

"No, you don't. We just need a good break. We'll keep looking. Something 'ill turn up."

"You think Jimmy Helton could have killed the kid?" I asked.

"He's being pretty evasive. But why would he kill his own son? And why would his dimwitted wife go along with it?"

"Hard to believe a mother would protect the guy who killed her child. You see why I want to scream?"

"I know," John said. "You hear if the dog from the cabin is doing okay?"

"I haven't spoken to any of the 'Guild' women since Terri and I stopped at the vet's office while the dog was in surgery. But it sounded like she was going to be okay."

"That's good."

"Yeah, nice dog."

"They only have two more days left before they're scheduled to leave."

"I wonder if the dog can be moved?"

"I can check," he said.

"Good idea."

It was 9:30. The sun was shining. I put on clean clothes that morning. The weather forecast couldn't have been better, but we were no closer to finding our killer than solving world hunger. Then Terri Donnellson walked in, again dressed like a TV detective, so I assumed she wasn't working at Prospect PD today.

"What are you doing here?" I asked. "I thought you were working days at the PD this week."

She shrugged. "Are you kidding, boss? Some half-crazed sharp-shooter pops a cap at us, we've got two unexplained corpses in the morgue, and you want me to answer the phones and dispatch cars? No way."

"So you're moving in with us? For how long?"

"Well, I've got three personal leave days coming. Harley Flatt is in charge until Stanley comes back from California. I told Harley what happened and asked for the time off."

"And he's okay with that?"

"Sure. When I told him someone took a shot at you, he said if you want, *he'd* take time off and help out."

"Good old Harley."

"Yeah, he's a standup guy. Everyone thinks he and Lenny Alcock will get the stripes if the city council approves refilling the sergeant's slots."

I nodded. "Good choices."

"So," Terri said, "What can I do for you?"

"We've still got to do a background on Bernadette Gavin, but based on her reaction to Tommy Lee's death, she's probably clean as a whistle. But don't lose the note. Then, I wish you could tell me who killed these guys. John and I have been wracking our brains. I really don't know."

"Can I look over everything we've got so far?"

"Sure. I'd love for you to find the missing link."

John went to a file cabinet and pulled out a thick accordion folder with the case notes and the loose-leaf binder holding the more official documents.

"Here ya go, kid," John said. "Find something good, and I'll get the Boss to buy you lunch."

———

FOR THE NEXT HOUR, TERRI DEVOURED THE NOTES JOHN AND I HAD

compiled, read and reread the crime scene and medical examiner's reports and spread out all the photos we'd collected over the course of the investigation on the desk John vacated.

While she worked on that, Gallagher and I began running down a background history on Jake "the Snake" Quarles, trying to learn his connection with the Heltons.

A little after 10:00 A.M. an attractive woman with honey blond hair, a nice tan and a head full of sun-bleached highlights walked into the office. She looked like she was forty-something, but wore a pair of tight fitting, washed off jeans and a UT Chattanooga polo shirt that gave her a bouncy younger appearance.

Being closest to the entrance, Terri greeted her. "Hi, can I help you?"

The blonde smiled. "I'm lookin' for Sam Jenkins."

I looked up from the pad I'd been writing on. At first glance, she reminded me of someone. "That's me."

She nodded at Terri, repeated the polite smile for me and stepped over to the desk I was using. I stood, and she extended a hand.

"I'm Janetta Galloway," she said. "My cousin, Bettye Lambert, said y'all are lookin' for an office manager."

"Yes, I am. Uh, we are. Let me get my partner out here, and we can talk about it."

After a round of introductions, we dragged an extra chair to the back of the room and adjourned to my office. We spoke for twenty minutes about the basic job, what we needed and ideally where the business was headed. Then Janetta insisted on bringing up the topic of salary.

She looked at me as if I had just turned green and started croaking. "You want me to be your office manager for ten dollars an hour?"

I nodded. "That's what we can afford."

"An established company would pay me thirty plus benefits for what you need, and the responsibility involved."

I shrugged and showed her my most sincere civil servant's smile. "We're currently working for your cousin—as extensions—if you will—of her criminal investigation division. At the moment, we're responsible for two of the highest profile cases in the region, and your cousin only pays us twenty bucks an hour plus expenses. No benefits. Not much considering that collectively John and I have almost sixty years of police experience. Terri, the young lady you met up front, is a veteran police officer working for Prospect PD and part time here. She only gets twelve-fifty—and someone shot at us yesterday. Tennessee cops are not famous for getting fabulous salaries."

Her frustration began to show. Why, I'm not sure. "But I'm not a cop."

I shrugged. "If you worked here, you would, in effect, sort of be one. You wouldn't have powers of arrest, nor would you be able to carry a gun unless you obtained a special permit. And no one would shoot at you. But ask Bettye. What you'd do here would parallel the job she had at Prospect PD. She loved working there."

Janetta started to say something, but I persisted.

"Depending who we're working for, we're all cops—private or public. Right, John?"

"Right."

"Yeah, but—"

I cut her off. "If you want to start a new career with some structured company—a company with strict rules and, pardon the expression, a bunch of chicken-shit policies, I'm sure you could go to Knoxville—only twenty-five miles away—forty minutes or so in traffic—and get a good job." I shrugged again, thinking Janetta might see me as only partially interested in hiring her. "Bettye told me you were a good accountant once. You have all the skills we need, but you've been out of the work force a long time. That doesn't matter one bit to us. Right, John?"

John quickly woke up and blinked a couple times. "You bet."

I nodded. "They say there shouldn't be age discrimination in the work force nowadays, but I don't know if I could get a private sector job at my age. And," I emphasized, "I'm not even close to being sure I could work for some thirty-year-old who thinks in a different atmosphere than me. Maybe you feel the same."

She opened her mouth again, but I was on a roll and wouldn't give her a minute to think. "Look, we need someone to oversee the technical and administrative stuff John and I aren't exactly savvy on. For your expertise, we'll pay ten bucks an hour. I know you're worth more, but so are we, and we take what your cousin can afford.

"If you don't want to work five days a week, that's okay. Bettye said you have a boat, and you like to spend days out on Tellico Lake. Sounds like fun. A real company expects you to be at your desk five days a week and eight hours a day. If everything here is up to date, we don't want you to polish a clean counter. Go out on the water with your husband or son. An answering machine can take care of any emergencies."

From her expression, I thought the boat and lake thing might have hit a nerve.

"If you want to make your own hours—within reason—that's okay. For ten bucks an hour, you'll have more flexibility than most any other place on earth. I've always said this, so I don't plan on changing my story now. When all the necessary work is done, you can screw off. We don't care. Sit here and wait for a customer. Do your nails. Look pretty. Read a book. *Who cares?* Go home if you're bored. Go shopping. You'll be just like John and me. If you work, you get paid. You'll always have a job waiting. If you're not here and we need you, we'll call. It couldn't be easier."

She frowned, rubbed two fingers of her left hand across her forehead. "Flexible hours, huh?"

I treated her to my irresistible grin. "Once the logistics are squared away, this is only a maintenance job."

"Hmm. Bettye did say y'all were easy to get along with."

"The easiest. Right, John?"

"That's us, Boss."

"Just what did you mean I could sit here and look pretty?"

"Simple. You're a good-looking woman. It's something that would just happen. You got a problem with me saying you're attractive?"

She hesitated. "Uh, no. And...thank you."

"Don't mention it. You want the job?"

Her eyebrows went up. "I don't know. That is, I guess so. Do I have to let you know right now?"

I frowned. "Of course you do. We've got dozens of other candidates to interview."

She smiled and looked unmistakably like Bettye. "No, you don't."

I returned the smile. "No, we don't. We need the help. And if you're anything like your cousin, we'd like you to work with us. Ask her. You'll end up loving the job."

She shook her head, but her expression said she was prepared to agree with me. "Okay. What do I have to lose?"

"You have nothing to lose, but you can't imagine what you have to gain by getting involved with us."

"Oh, man, where'd ya get a line like that?"

"Comes with my po-leece training."

"Hmm. Do I have to work holidays?"

"John and I might. You don't have to."

"Do I get any *paid* holidays?"

I flicked my hands out to the sides. "I'll buy you a Christmas present and flowers on Valentine's Day."

"Remind me to talk to my cousin. She really owes me for this."

———

"Let's go back outside," I said, "let you pick a desk and see what Terri's up to. She likes working here. I'm guessing she'll be around for a while."

Terri welcomed and congratulated Janetta on her new job. Then she quickly changed the subject.

"You know, boss, John, I've been looking at these pictures until my eyes crossed, and I finally realized why I thought something is wrong."

"Wrong?" John said.

"Yeah. I'm talking about Tommy Lee and his parents. He's got these crazy-cool blue eyes, and they don't."

"So?" I said. "Couldn't that be from a recessive gene or something?"

Terri shook her head. "From what I've learned, that might be pretty rare. Supposedly, there's only a twenty-five percent chance of two brown-eyed parents having a blue-eyed child. And another thing. Tommy Lee looks nothing like Jimmy. They're all good-looking, and he's got his mother's nose and cheek bones, maybe, but nothing from Daddy."

"Hmmm." I said.

"If y'all don't mind me buttin' in," Janetta said, "I've been readin' about the case in the papers. I know this family. I remember Jewel from high school and know Jimmy. That man's got a reputation of bein' a real lady's man. A weddin' ring never stopped him from playin' the field. And I hear Tommy Lee did his share of romancin' the ladies, too."

"We kind of knew Tommy Lee liked the girls and heard the rumors about Jimmy," I said.

She shook her head. "They're not rumors. I've seen Jimmy in action. Came on to me more than once when we met them at a party."

"You go to parties?"

She looked surprised. "Everybody goes to parties."

John said, "He doesn't," and poked a finger at me. "He's anti-social."

I frowned. "When you say he played the field—and flirted around—was he blatant about it?"

"I know a lot about him, and I'm no detective. Most of the people I know knew about Jimmy, too."

"Let's talk *more* about what you know. Start with how Jewel reacted to Jimmy's wandering eye."

"Wasn't just his eyes that wandered. He never groped me, but I know a few girls who had to push him away."

"And Jewel knew about this?"

"Be deaf, dumb and blind not to know. And he didn't exactly treat her like a gentleman."

"You think he was abusive?"

"Verbally, for sure. Embarrassed her in front of people more'n once that I know of."

"Jewel seems like something of an airhead. Did you ever see that these rumors had an effect on her?"

Janetta shook her head and grinned. "Jewel Helton is about as stupid as a fox. If you think she's good-lookin' now, you should have seen her twenty, twenty-five years ago. She's always been something of a flirt. I wouldn't be surprised if Terri's idea of Jimmy not bein' Tommy Lee's father wasn't a real good one."

CHAPTER TWELVE

Janetta left us, promising to come back the next day to begin organizing the office.

John and I drove out to see what progress the county troops were making with a search of the area surrounding the spot where we found Tommy Lee's body.

When we pulled up to the cabin on Meissners Station Road, we found a white and blue Prospect PD sector car parked in the driveway. Other sheriff's vehicles were scattered along the two-lane blacktop. Seeing unit 501 on the Prospect car's rear quarter told me PO Junior Huskey was there.

I knocked on the screen door. The front door was already open. Junior and the four women were sitting at the dining room table. Chamois was lying on the couch.

Holly Miller unhooked the screen door and ushered us in.

"Are you okay?" she asked me. "We didn't see you after the shooting thing."

"Yeah. No one got hurt."

"We watched the news, but they didn't give much information."

"They told you about as much as we know. My father and I," I poked a thumb in John's direction, "stopped by to see how the searchers were doing and check on Chamois."

"I don't know about the guys in the woods," Holly said, "but you can visit with Chamois yourself."

I waved to the other women. To Junior I said, "Hey, kid, how's tricks?"

"Whaddaya say, boss. You doin' aw right t'day?"

John and I walked over to the couch, which someone had covered with a large maroon bed sheet. Holly followed. Chamois fluttered her tail. A four-inch row of stitches ran diagonally across a shaved portion of her neck. More than twice that number ran over her right rear flank. The sutures were not bandaged, and what looked like petroleum jelly covered the wounds.

I slowly bent down and touched the dog's face.

"You poor old girl. Couple of four-legged thugs ganged up on you, didn't they?"

Chamois' tail went back into motion, a little faster this time.

"You were protecting your mom and her friends. You're a genuine heroine."

"My *heroine* is doing okay compared to the last time we saw you. The vet asked me to bring her in for a post op visit in three days."

"I thought you were leaving in two," John said.

"We checked with Mr. Gregory, the cabin owner. He doesn't have other renters due in until mid-October. We're going to hang around and pay on a day to day basis."

"That's probably best for Chamois," I said.

"We think so."

I stood up and felt a pain shoot through my troublesome left leg.

I pointed at Junior. "What's my former son doing here?"

"We called 9-1-1. He pulled up a couple of minutes ago. Something funny happened."

———

Now, ALL SEVEN OF US WERE SITTING AT THE BIG DINING room table.

"I guess it's kinda early for martinis or Manhattans," Norma said. "But would anyone like a soft drink?"

Junior tried to look shocked. "Martinis and Manhattans? What are y'all gettin' inta, boss?"

I frowned. "Shut up, kid. Nobody likes an inquisitive cop."

He drew his head back an inch or two and frowned. "Do what?"

"If you want some sweet tea or Mountain Dew or one of the other god-awful things I've seen you drink, tell the lady. Otherwise, I want to hear about this *funny* thing that happened."

Junior showed me how much he'd grown up since I left Prospect PD a month ago. "Since my one-time *father*, the *former* chief at Prospect PD, wants ta hear about this new incident, why don't I let you ladies tell 'im? And, ma'am," he now spoke to Norma, "I'm fine, thanks."

I raised my eyebrows, and Sue Brown spoke up. "A little more than an hour ago someone knocked on the door, and I answered. A young man, maybe in his early thirties, said he was from Tucka-something utilities."

"Tuckaleechee?" I prompted.

"I'll take your word for that. Anyway, he asked if we were having any problems with the electric service."

I shot a look at John who frowned.

Sue continued. "He asked if he could come in and check the meter. I had seen a meter on the outside wall and thought that was somewhat odd. So, I told him to contact Mr. Gregory because we weren't having any problems."

"What did he do then?" John asked.

"He asked what all the police personnel were doing on the road and in the woods."

"What did you tell him?" John asked.

"Just that they were investigating why someone had been shooting near the houses. I didn't elaborate. I wanted to get the door closed and locked as quickly as possible."

"Good idea," I said. "Did this man speak with an accent?"

"Sounded local to me, but I wouldn't know the difference between a Tennessee and North Carolina accent."

"I understand. Can you describe him?"

"Like I said, thirty-something. Early thirties, I guess. Not as tall as you, maybe two inches shorter. And he was strong-looking, very fit. Not bulky like a weightlifter, but like an athlete. He had short dark hair and dark eyes. Very dark. It looked like he hadn't shaved in a few days."

"What was he wearing?" John asked.

"That's another thing I thought funny. He wore jeans and a dark green plaid shirt. No uniform and no ID card hanging around his neck. At home, all the workers from the utility companies have to wear ID cards whether they're in uniform or not."

I nodded. "You did the right thing. Alcoa Utilities provides electric to this area, not Tuckaleechee. They pick up about a half mile away off the main road. They handle the water and natural gas in places, maybe here, but not the electric. I wonder what this guy wanted. He could be the shooter." Then I started thinking out loud. "Could also be a reporter, but why would one try a scam? Who knows? Why would the gunman return to the area with all those cops walking around? Did you see a vehicle?"

"There were a lot of cars and trucks parked on the road. He didn't park in the driveway, and I didn't see anything with utility company markings anywhere else."

"You gave a pretty good description, but will you do something for me? I want you to think again of the important small things by envisioning this guy. Start at the top of his head, and slowly work your way down. Sometimes closing your eyes helps. Ready to go?"

"Sure." Sue closed her eyes and appeared at ease.

"Did he wear a hat?"

"No."

"Any scars, marks or moles on his face?"

She shook her head. "Uh-uh."

"Did he wear an earring?"

"No."

"Travelling south now, how about anything unique about the shirt?"

"Just a plaid long sleeve shirt. Blue and green and black. Like a Scottish plaid."

Thinking about Jake the Snake, I asked another good question. "Did he wear a unique belt buckle?"

"I think it might have been a black cloth belt—canvas or webbing. I'm not sure. The buckle was black too, a simple, square thing."

"Could be military issue."

"I wouldn't know."

"Okay, good. Now picture his hands. Anything special there? Did he wear a wristwatch? Any unique rings?"

"Yes. Wait. He had his shirtsleeves turned up. I saw part of a tattoo on his forearm. He had muscular forearms, and the tattoo looked like a pair of wings on something."

"A bird? A dragon?"

"No, a stylized thing. More like angel wings turned up on the ends."

"So, not a living thing? Some kind of winged object?"

"Right."

I took a small spiral notebook from my pocket. "Open your eyes for a minute and look at what I'm going to draw."

I quickly sketched the Army version of a basic parachutist's wing. "Sometimes guys who are or were in the military get tattoos of paratrooper wings, flyer's wings or other qualification badges. Of course, motorcycle enthusiasts might get Harley-Davidson wings tattooed on themselves. Did his tattoo look like this? Should we change the shape?"

Sue frowned as she looked at my crude drawing.

"The shape of the wings looks right, but I didn't see it all. I don't think it was the bottom of a parachute that I saw. There was something else in the middle."

"Good. That's a start. I'll get pictures of other possibilities for you to look at. For now, let's go back to our visitor. Close your eyes again. You're doing great."

Sue nodded and closed her eyes.

"Notice anything special about his hands? Any rings?"

"No rings. I think he chewed his nails. They were too short."

I nodded, thinking her attention to detail was extraordinary.

"His watch?"

"All black. Pretty large and with a complicated face."

"We're doing good. Anything special about the jeans?"

"No, just blue denim. Sort of washed off."

"How about his shoes?"

"I didn't really see them because of the door, and when he walked away, I was too busy locking up."

"Doesn't matter. You're probably one of the best eye witnesses I've ever met."

"Unbelievable detail," John said.

"You bet," Junior added.

"Thanks. I guess I developed a way to remember people over the years. If I didn't recognize all my husband's patients, I'd make them feel bad."

"We wish all witnesses were half as good as you," I told her.

"What do we do if he comes back?" Holly asked.

"He probably won't," I said. "But we'll post someone here to keep an eye on you." I looked at Junior. "Can you guys get approval for overtime while Stanley is off taking care of family business?"

"I'll ask Harley, but I guess I could work some."

"I can pick up the overnight time," John said. "Long as it's okay with the sheriff."

"Junior, you're off at four o'clock, right?"

"Uh-huh."

"How about four hours?"

"Works for me."

"Ladies, can John camp out on your couch tonight?"

We heard a chorus of affirmative answers.

"Don't let him drink too many Manhattans," I suggested.

Holly winked. "We'll take good care of him."

"Eight to eight work for you, partner?"

"Sure, I can use the money."

"I thought you could. This may put you in a higher tax bracket. I'll be here at 8:00 A.M. to see what's up. Everyone okay with that?"

———

JUNIOR MADE ARRANGEMENTS TO RETURN AFTER 4:00 P.M. JOHN and I headed toward the spot where we might find the supervisor of Bettye's county troops scouring the woodland and where Jackie Shuman and David Sparks were again in attendance to handle any recovered physical evidence.

"Whaddaya think? Our guy military?" John asked.

"Current or former would be my guess. Of course, he could also be a phony who just got the tattoo to make people think he's a vet."

"That stolen valor thing."

"Yeah, but that might be a long shot."

"Everything about this seems like a long shot."

"You got that right, buddy."

"The guy who stopped at the cabin was probably the shooter," John said. "But why the hell did he come back to the crime scene?"

I felt a twinge of irony at my thought but said it anyway. "We'll have to ask him."

We found a detective sergeant named Hugh Bledsoe standing at the edge of the woods with a portable radio in his hand. Like any of the regular deputies assigned to potentially dirty 'fatigue' duty, he wore a black, tactical utility shirt with subdued patches and a pair of matching pants with large cargo pockets on the thighs.

"Standby, team 4," he said into the radio. "I'll come in and take a look. Crime scene 351, you copy team 4's transmission?'

"10-4. We'll see if we can locate 'em and meetcha there."

"10-4, 3-5-1. Team 4, see if you can talk him toward you."

"Roger, that."

Bledsoe turned to us. "Hey, Chief, Detective Gallagher. You boys doin' all right t'day?"

"How's it goin', Sarge? Sounds like you've got something."

"Yessir, mebbe. We covered a lot o' territory t'day, tried to hit every bush and tree between the first grave site and where you thought that shot came from, but came up with a lot of nuthin'. Team 4 jest found what they think is a spot where somebody camped out. I's jest goin' in ta take a look. Wanna come?"

"Sure. We've got nothing else to do, and I put on a pair of clean pants this morning. May as well get them dirty."

We picked our way through the thicket for almost ten minutes, Bledsoe taking the lead and me bringing up the rear. After getting smacked in the face a second time by a branch Gallagher let snap back, I decided to rebel.

"John, if you do that one more time, I'm gonna stick a sixty-foot pine tree up your ass."

"What? What did I do?"

"When you push a branch out of the way, you Irish nincompoop, don't let it snap back and hit me in the face. You did it twice."

"No." He sounded surprised.

"Yes. You don't know how close you come to death at times."

"Me? Why?"

"Think about it, John."

I heard Bledsoe snicker.

"You sure I did that?"

"I can't believe we're having this conversation. I should just kill you and blame it on the madman running around these woods."

"You wouldn't do that, would you, Boss?"

"Count on it."

"You get so volatile over little things, Boss. Watch your blood pressure."

I wouldn't dignify that with a remark. In another couple of minutes, we walked up on three deputies standing around a small clearing. In the center, an area roughly eight by ten feet had been flattened down, in the center of which, a smaller rectangle, was even flatter.

"Hey, Sarge," one of the cops said.

"What've ya got, Marty?" Bledsoe asked.

"You see it. Looks like some ol' boy done camped out here. Probably our shooter. Cain't see no other reason for a body ta make a camp in the middle o' nuthin'."

"You boys know Sam Jenkins and John Gallagher?" Bledsoe asked.

"Gents," I said.

"Howz it goin'?" John asked.

The three deputies nodded and offered us a few variants of the classic regional greeting.

I took a closer look at the area in question, getting down on my hands and knees.

After only a few seconds of scanning the ground, I spoke to the man named Marty. "Don't move your foot."

"Do what?"

"Nice and easy now, step backwards with your left foot first. Then back away from the flattened leaves."

He had been too close to begin with and dangerously close to what I hoped was a crucial piece of evidence.

"Everybody stay clear of this camp site. Sarge, where are the evidence technicians?"

"I'll check."

Bledsoe spoke into the handheld radio. A moment later, Jackie Shuman's voice came back with an answer.

"Best I can figger," Shuman said, "'bout a minute or two away. Kinda thick brush 'tween us and you."

I nodded. "Ask if he's got a camera."

Bledsoe did.

Jackie's voice again: "David got his. We see all y'all now. Comin' up on yer backs."

Moments later, John and the deputies stepped back further from the flattened campsite. The two evidence technicians and I looked at the roughly eighty square feet of ground.

"See that V-shaped hole with the point away from the flattened patch?" I asked.

"Uh-huh," Jackie said.

"Looks like what an army tent peg would do to fasten down this side of a shelter half."

"See whatcha mean," Jackie said.

"Move a couple o' them leaves, Jackie," David said, "and lemme git a quick shot o' that."

David bent forward, getting closer to the hole. After a moment to zoom in his lens on the spot in question, the autofocus made a slight humming sound, and a flash went off. A moment later, a second blast of light from a follow-up shot caused me to blink.

"Got 'em," David said.

"There should be four holes—or slots—on each side," I said, "and one on each end to hold down the guy ropes. If this is an army two-man pup tent, they're about seven feet long and five wide."

"We'll check real good," Jackie said.

I looked at John, the former sailor, who stood next to Hugh Bledsoe. "In the Army, each guy carries a shelter half, three short tent pole sections, five pegs and a section of rope. You pair off with another soldier, snap your shelter halves together and use the rest of the gear to erect your two-man tent."

"You think there were two people involved?" John asked.

"Damned if I know. Could be. Are you thinking about our two former Marines?"

"They came to mind."

"Or one ex-GI with a tattoo, familiar with the equipment, carried two sets of everything."

"Easy ta get," one deputy said. "I bought jest what yer talkin' about for my kids from Amazon. $39.95. They put it up in the backyard, nice an' easy-like."

"$39.95 by mail order or swipe one from a military supply room," I suggested.

WHILE JACKIE AND DAVID COMBED THE AREA WITH—AS JOHN Gallagher would say—a *five-tooth comb*, Hugh Bledsoe mustered a few more members of his search party to work the area immediately surrounding the campsite.

"John, I'm rapidly losing enthusiasm for traipsing all over the woods, getting dirty and sweaty," I said.

"I hear ya."

Before I could make another disparaging remark, my cell phone sounded off. Terri Donnellson's number showed up on caller ID.

"Doctor Rappaport called to say he was sending us the autopsy report on the new body. He'll get a courier to hand deliver it here. He also wanted you to know he recovered a rifle bullet. Earl is already on the way to Knoxville so the TBI can get to work on it."

"Great. Anything other than the bullet worth knowing about?"

"Didn't sound like it," she said. "He figures another .30 caliber soft point slug. It mushroomed a lot."

"Another hunting round. Our rifleman is busy at work. I'll bet it came from the same gun as the other two."

"We'll see."

"From a few things we learned today, I'm getting the idea that we might have a third Marine involved, or we're looking at an unrelated person, maybe a former 'eleven bravo'." I used the Army's military occupational specialty number with which Terri would be familiar.

"Light weapons infantry," she said. "I can't wait to hear about this."

"Someone showed up at the cabin who's probably connected to this. I'll tell you more later. If you get a few spare minutes, call North Carolina, and ask them to send a detective to the mill looking for ID card photos of their uniformed guards. I want Sue Brown to see if one of the guards looks familiar."

"I'll make time, boss."

————

I CAUGHT TBI FIREARMS EXAMINER BILL WERNER ONLY MINUTES

after Earl Ogle handed him the bullet recovered from Tommy Lee Helton's body.

"Sam, you are one impatient man. Earl only left a few minutes ago. Hang in there. Your vic isn't going to get any deader."

"Do you have the bullet in your hand, smartass?"

"Right here on the desk."

"What do you think?"

"It's mushroomed out perfectly. It's a lump of copper and lead."

"A non-expert could tell me that."

"Okay. After a quick glance—no microscope—it's probably another .308 Winchester round, but because it's a bit different from most bullets, I'll speculate that it's a Nosler Partition bullet head. There are two chambers of cast lead encased in the copper jacket. The soft point tip blossoms back but stops where a second copper barrier blocks the lead base. Very efficient round. Because the base stays intact, it keeps pushing everything with all those foot-pounds of energy."

"Nosler just makes the bullet heads, right?"

"Correct."

"So, this is a hand load?"

"Not necessarily. Federal makes a .308 Winchester round called their Premium Vital-Shok. They come in 150 and 180-grain versions. I'd say this is a 180."

"You're showing off, Willie."

"I've seen a few of these. What can I tell you?"

"Tell me what rifle fired it."

"I need the microscope for that. This thing is a twisted-up mess, but I see enough land and groove marks for me to work with."

"Is this an exotic round, or do they sell them anywhere?"

"Not a hunter, are you?"

"Never been hungry enough to shoot Bambi."

"This is a great round for Bambi. A .308 would probably drop a moose or elk, too, but I'd want a gun with a bit more oomph—a .300 magnum maybe. But back to your question. They may not carry these in Walmart, but any good sporting goods store sells them."

"So, if it's top notch to use against a 200 pound deer, I guess it would massacre a 160 pound man."

"Guaranteed. I'll call you as soon as I get finished."

———

BEFORE JOHN AND I COULD LEAVE THE MEISSNERS STATION ROAD area, a deputy stepped out of the woods and waved at us. I shut down the car, and we walked to meet him and see what he wanted.

"Sergeant jest radioed me ta git you two. Someone found a trail leadin' away from the blacktop and stretchin' way back."

"Just a trail?" I asked.

He shrugged. "Lemme let ya talk with the sergeant."

He keyed the transmit button and called Bledsoe.

"Here." He handed me the portable. "Ya don't need you a middleman."

"What have you got, Sarge?"

"One o' the men picked up a trail leadin' due south away from the road and the house."

"Is this a proper path going somewhere?"

"Jest a makeshift trail, not used much, but it leads inta the area that's platted, but where no roads have been cut. Not far from the campsite— less than 150 yards or so—then there's a creek."

"How big is the creek?"

"Not wide. Mebbe twenty feet at most. But looks deep enough."

Deep enough for what? What did he have in mind?

"Stand by one."

I looked at John. "You heard that. I wonder if Tommy's killer would have brought the body in by water and carried it up here? Sounds like a lot of work."

"Why not bury it somewhere closer to the actual murder scene? Why lug a corpse a hundred and fifty yards?"

"I wish I knew. We need to see this area from the air."

———

THE STATE POLICE HELICOPTER MET US ON THE HELIPAD AT Blount Memorial Hospital. Moments later, we were airborne heading in the general direction of the woodland between Meissners Station Road and the narrow waterway called Cricket Branch.

As we hovered over the immediate area, I radioed Sergeant Bledsoe, who popped a purple smoke canister. Billows of the colorful smoke rose above the forest canopy, marking the exact spot where the newly discovered trail met the creek. The pilot came about and descended in a nose-down attitude until we were little more than two hundred feet over the trees.

After a few low altitude passes over the entire length of the creek, we located a stretch of relatively flat and clear meadowland that, by four wheel drive vehicle, would connect a secondary road with the creek.

The pilot followed that small gravel track to a larger one with a few homes scattered and spaced far enough apart that you wouldn't have to worry about your neighbors hearing you snore. That road, in turn, connected with the main thoroughfare, Ellejoy Road, in the northeast section of Prospect.

The pilot said finding it on the ground would be a snap. He assisted me by marking my map. Perhaps he assumed my sense of direction was more suited to urban areas.

This discovery opened up a whole new world of exploration—one that Sheriff Bettye Lambert needed to coordinate.

———

I DROPPED JOHN OFF AT OUR OFFICE, AND I HEADED TO THE Justice Center.

"Oh, Lord have mercy!" she said, shaking her extremely attractive head. "My overtime budget is going to be so far in the red, the county commission will want to crucify me."

I shrugged and tried to downplay the scope of the monumental search effort I proposed. "You must have a battalion of auxiliary deputies just itchin' to get their boots dirty doing some real po-leece work. They love this stuff—and they're free."

"And just how long do you envision this search is goin' to last?"

"Who knows? We're looking for one, maybe two people with an unknown vehicle, who obviously know the terrain and how to operate in the bush, not an entire North Vietnamese regiment that's been harassing the local villagers and can't hide too well."

She took a deep breath and filled out her pale pink blouse. "That's not very encouragin'. Now I see why some of these county people have gotten to hate you. You don't consider expenses."

"Pfui. What do you want to do, solve crime or pinch pennies? What can I tell you? Ask TWRA to lend you a few of their wildlife officers to work the backcountry. Get the troopers to do more by air. Now that we've got an area mapped out, the Civil Air Patrol can do some more flyovers. I'll ask Charley and Amelia Goodhardt to help again."

She wrinkled up her nose and looked annoyed. "I'm sure you'd like Miss Goodhardt to help. Will she take you up in her little red plane?"

The heady fragrance of her perfume reached me from across her desk.

I frowned anyway. "I don't know, maybe. And maybe we can get the Army Reserve aviation unit to invest some of their training hours combing the area with their choppers."

Bettye let out another long breath. "Do you really think the killer will stick around very long? Couldn't all this be a fool's errand?"

"If it was me, no. I'd be out of here lickety split. I'm amazed he hung around long enough to take that shot at us. I mean, why come back? It's like stealing a rowboat and getting caught when you come back to pick up the oars. I can't figure out why he did that—and why, if it's the same guy, did he try to get into that rental cabin?"

"Could this person be working with or for the people at the paper mill?"

"Your guess is as good as mine. But if you send a composite artist over the see Sue Brown at the rental cabin, he should be able to come away with something almost as good as a photograph. That woman is one great witness. Years ago, I met an autistic kid who described the man that stuck up his father's liquor store so well, he swore the man's eyes set apart 2 and 9/16th of an inch, pupil to pupil. He was right. Next to him, this woman is the best."

"With a good likeness, you can see if any of the security guards are your man," Bettye suggested.

"We know what Curry and Koronkiewicz look like. I asked Terri to get a North Carolina detective to see if Curry would give up ID photos of the security guards. I hope he cooperates. Once they know we're looking at one of them as a suspect, they'll probably clam up. I can't think of a good way to finesse our way around that. These guys are not stupid, but we have to confront them sooner or later—evidence or not."

"You're not making this any easier for me, Sam Jenkins."

"That's why you're now making the big bucks, Blondie."

"Thanks a lot."

"Look, this guy, the shooter, isn't foolproof. We found a few leads today thanks to your searchers. Maybe we can find the spot where he launched a boat or canoe or raft to reach his spot by water. If we find that or where he parked his vehicle, maybe we'll find more clues—tire tracks, gum wrappers, cigarette butts, who knows what. I can't guarantee anything, but we can look. The big problem is nothing makes sense here. We've got two bodies close together, but years apart. So far, nothing connects them. I can't start investigating this Jake the Snake thing while the more recent murder is still open. No one, and I mean no one, can even point me toward something productive. Some people say Tommy Lee was slow upstairs." I pointed to my temple. "Others say he was as sharp as a tack. I've heard he chased the ladies just like his old man, but from what I've seen, he's been faithful to his current girlfriend. His father acts like the kid's disappearance and murder is a major inconvenience. The mother could pass for a spaced out mental patient without much effort. I admit being baffled, but we're still doing something."

Bettye sighed and looked mostly resigned to making the best of a bad situation. "Okay, I'll keep those same men on the detail and get someone to enlist as many auxiliaries as possible. Will you take charge of the search?"

I let Humphrey Bogart answer for me. "Not on your life, doll-face. The bugs like me too much. In the last couple days I've been bitten so many times, I've got more lumps and bumps on me than when I used to sail the African Queen up and down those jungle rivers. Hugh Bledsoe is doin' just peachy."

"He's got other duties, you know."

"Sure, but what's more important than a couple of connected homicides—eight years apart?"

She gave me the evil eye.

I ignored that. "Another thing, Jackie Shuman's cousin runs a river trip company. He's helped out before. I'll get the kid to ask about letting us borrow a couple of canoes to cruise the creek looking for..." I shrugged, not really knowing what we'd be looking for, "something."

Bettye shook her head. "Go get 'em, Sammy."

WHEN I GOT BACK TO THE OFFICE, TERRI DONNELLSON LOOKED excited. I assumed that John told her and Janetta everything that transpired since early that morning, so I prompted her to spill her beans first.

"You look like you might pop a gasket. What's up?"

"Well, first thing this morning I called North Carolina. I found out that their state detectives work directly for the attorney general. They're called the SBI—State Bureau of Investigation."

As she took a breath I thought that this excitement made her seem more like a young girl and less like the no-nonsense former MP sergeant I hired at Prospect PD. Terri is a very attractive young woman, but so far, I had seen her as all business and fairly unemotional —until now.

"I talked to a senior agent from Asheville," she said. "He promised to send someone to the Cataloochee Paper Mill. I figured maybe later today or even tomorrow. But, guess what?"

I shrugged. "They confronted Bill Koronkiewicz, and he confessed to both murders?"

She shook her head. "Nooo." She drew the word out for all it was worth. "But the investigator, his name is Steve Gatliff, already called back."

I raised my eyebrows. "And what did Steve say?"

"He talked with Koronkiewicz and Curry. At the time someone took the shot at us, they were busy with another environmental group protesting in front of the mill. An Asheville group. All local people. The county sheriff confirms that."

"How did Steve finesse his way into the conversation?"

"Just came straight out. He told them they were persons of interest in the Helton murder, and he wanted photos of everyone working in security."

"Really no way we or another detective could pussyfoot around it much longer. He used us as the bad cops. That works. Did they offer any other voluntary information or lawyer up?"

"Said they had nothing to hide and barely knew Helton."

I sighed. "I never thought they'd break down and confess."

"Maybe they're not involved," Terri suggested.

John said, "That's always been a possibility."

I nodded.

Terri continued. "Steve is faxing the pictures to the sheriff and said if we needed anymore help, I should call him directly. He sounded nice."

I frowned. "Nice?"

"Yeah, nice."

"You sound nice, too. Maybe he thought so. Did Steve sound young?"

She began to blush.

John gave her a devilish grin and stuck in his two cents, "Nice and your age?"

"Hey, give me a break, guys. I thought I did pretty good getting quick cooperation that got us the photos and established an alibi for Koronkiewicz."

"From a *nice* guy at NCSBI," I said.

"Oh, stop."

Janetta decided to chime in and stick up for her female colleague. "Twelve-fifty an hour doesn't entitle you to harass the girl."

I chuckled. "I'm the boss. I'm authorized."

"Wait a minute," John said. "You told me not to call you boss anymore."

"Shut up, John. See why I hate you?"

John again: "Calm down and tell us what the sheriff said."

I presented all the facts and what we could expect to happen starting tomorrow.

Terri asked, "When we have a sketch of this person who might be the shooter, and if it looks something like one of the security guards, want me to ask *Steve* to explore the possibility that one of these guards at the paper mill might have an Army tattoo?"

"That seems like a good reason for you to call again. Go for it. Sue Brown gave us a dynamite description."

She smiled. "I'll call tomorrow—or tonight."

"I thought you might. Will tomorrow be your last day with us for a while?"

She nodded. "I have to get back to Prospect PD."

"I know."

Then Janetta innocently shocked us all.

"If you think this guy might be a soldier, maybe Tommy Lee's brother could help somehow. Last I heard he's still in the Army."

That almost knocked me on the floor. "What brother? No one's told us anything about a brother."

CHAPTER THIRTEEN

I MUST HAVE SAID THAT WAY TOO LOUD. HER EYES WIDENED.

I repeated the question with lower volume. "What brother?"

"They call him J.J., for Jimmy Junior. Although he's really not a junior. His middle name is Lee. His father's is not. Both young Jimmy and Tommy got middle names after Jewel's father, Lee Vern Samples."

"And Jimmy Lee or J.J. or whatever we're going to call him is in the Army?"

"I think he still is. I'm sure he doesn't live around here. If I remember correctly, he went in right after high school."

"Is he older or younger than Tommy?"

"Older. I'm guessing five to six years older."

Rhetorically, I asked. "And why didn't the parents tell us about the brother?"

Janetta must have thought I wanted an answer. "Did you ask them?"

Normally, I would have growled at a question like that. But for some reason, I answered rationally. "Standard missing person question—could he have gone to stay with a brother, sister, cousin, aunt or uncle? And have you called your relatives? I remember Jewel the nitwit saying, 'He doesn't keep up with his cousins.' She said nothing about a brother."

"What does the brother look like?" John asked.

"Haven't seen him since he was a teenager. Dark hair. Nice-looking boy. Sort of quiet. Looked like he could be Jimmy's son. Of course, Jewel had dark hair, too—once."

Spoken like a true natural blonde.

"John, when you did a group search to get driver's license information on all the Heltons, do you remember seeing a Jimmy Lee?"

"There were a bunch of Heltons in the county, but no others with a Prospect address. I'll run him alone and see what I get."

He walked back to his desk and computer.

"If he's still in the Army," Terri said, "and has been since he was eighteen, he probably enlisted and began his time as a private. If he's thirty-two or thirty-three now, that would give him as much as fifteen years in. If he's an NCO and hasn't gotten commissioned, with the regimental system, he could have spent a lot of time at his home station and may have gotten an out of state driver's license."

John came back out to the big room. "No Jimmy L. or Jimmy Lee or J.J. listed at the Department of Safety, either with a license or registration."

I shook my head in frustration. "Someone call the county clerk's office and get a DOB off his birth certificate. Then call a military locator and find out where this guy is."

"I'll do that." Terri looked at her watch. "First thing tomorrow. People are going home now. I'll ask Harley for another day off. And if I can get on your computer, John, I'll start on the background for Bernadette Gavin. If she lived in Cleveland, I'll need NCIC to go nationwide."

"Go for it," John said.

"Okay," I said. "Sounds good."

"Want me to do anything?" Janetta asked.

"Hang on a bit. If we can establish where the hell J.J. hangs his helmet, we can get a photo of him from either his military ID or whatever state issued his driver's license."

153

"You think he might have been the guy who went to the cabin?" John asked.

"I can't imagine why. Unless he's doing his own investigation into his brother's death...but that's stupid. Looking at it from the opposite end, if he hasn't been around here for years, why would he want to kill Tommy Lee?"

"Why did Cain kill Abel?" Janetta asked.

"I don't remember much about the Bible, but after all these years and all the translations, it's mostly fable." I smiled. "I mean, really, why did Abraham tie his ass to a tree and walk twenty miles?"

Janetta looked as if she might strangle me. "*That* is an old joke...And it's blasphemy."

For once John came to my rescue by diverting her attention. "Nothing here makes any sense."

"We keep saying that," I said. "If we don't make any headway soon, I'm gonna develop a nervous twitch."

———

The next morning at quarter to ten, Terri let out a cry of triumph. "Aha!"

"You're getting to sound like a proper detective," I said.

"The game's afoot, huh, kid?" John added.

"Found him," she said. "I can't believe the woman at the county clerk's office was so nice. She got me the birth certificate info right away. Then the military locator came up with a personal history just as quick."

Then John did one of his goofball voices. "Don't keep us in suspense, Terri. The Boss might wet his pants."

"Can't have that, can we?" she said, with more smile than necessary.

"You're learning the wrong things from Gallagher, Mizz Donnell-son," I said.

"Who, me? Anyway, Jimmy Lee Helton is a staff sergeant with the 1st of the 327th Infantry at my old home—when I was with the 716th MPs at Fort Campbell, that is. As part of the 101st Airborne Division's

1st Brigade Combat Team, he's been deployed overseas for eight of his fifteen years—to places like Kosovo, Iraq and Afghanistan."

"More time out of the country in pretty tough places," John said. "That's not a good job."

"The 101st isn't on jump status any longer. They're air assault," I said.

"Correct," Terri said. "Been that way for years."

"So J.J. probably isn't parachute qualified, but should be air assault trained. Different kind of wings. If J.J. was the guy who showed up at the cabin, the tattoo Sue Brown saw could have been air assault wings."

"Yeah, *if* J.J. was the guy." John sounded doubtful.

"Don't rain on our parade, John. Terri, did you speak with anyone at the 101st about him?"

"I called CID at Fort Campbell. One of the agents agreed to follow up for me because of all the stops necessary. He'll go to G1 and get more info from J.J.'s 201 File *and* a photo. Then he told me he'd find out what company J.J. belongs to, see the first sergeant and CO *and* see if J.J. is on duty there."

"That's a lot easier than a drive out west to the Tennessee/Kentucky border."

She smiled. "I thought you'd be pleased."

"I am. You get a three-day pass so you can work at Prospect PD."

She rolled her eyes. "Wow, thanks."

"Or would you rather tie up with Steve?"

"Boss, you've got to give me immunity with that Steve business."

"Maybe."

"You people speak a strange language," Janetta said. "For a start, what's G1?"

"Personnel section on a regimental level," I said. "It's where Jimmy Lee's full-service record would be. S1, personnel at the battalion level has an abbreviated file, as does his company orderly room—which some very special agent from Army CID will check out for us because Terri has a voice that mesmerizes the male cops she talks to."

Terri mildly protested my assessment. "Oh, boss, come on."

"Do I have to learn all this?" Janetta asked.

I grinned. "Only I know *everything*."

She shook her head. "Bettye said you were like this."

"You're fitting in here just great. Did your cousin send you because she's mad at me?"

"Stop whining. For ten dollars an hour I can talk back."

"Women!"

While I was feeling abused, John asked, "When Terri gets that picture of J.J., want us to run a six-pack over to the cabin for Sue to look at?"

"Yeah. You guys do that. And when you get a chance, John, do a full background on Jimmy Lee. See what the locals know about him. Terri, when you get to Bernadette, show Janetta how we do a background investigation. I'll call Bettye and have her shake up her artist. And somewhere along the line, we've got to find Alma and Jake Quarles Jr."

"Gotcha," John said. "Not enough hours in a day, huh?"

"Yeah. For now," I said, "I need to ask Jewel Helton why she never mentioned a second son."

"Good idea," John said.

————

JEWEL HELTON WORE HER HAIR UP ON THE SIDES, TIED IN A TAIL high at the back, but with a few loose strands hanging at the sides to give her a casual and incredibly attractive look. Her pink tank top and faded blue jeans didn't look too bad either. If I didn't want to smack her in the head with a 2x4, I would have been impressed.

Jewel knew she was a good-looking girl, and I wondered if she thought her dumb blonde act was what the boys wanted to see.

I wanted to speak to her alone, figuring if Jimmy Senior heard my pointed questions, he might assume I was no longer one of their sympathetic fans. So, I didn't call ahead and got lucky finding her at home alone.

We sat in their living room—me in an upholstered chair big enough to hold Haystacks Calhoun, the professional wrestler and she on a sofa looking like Catherine the Great's dimwitted sister.

"I heard from the medical examiner and assume he'll allow people from a funeral home to pick up Tommy Lee now. When will you have the services?" I asked just to break the ice.

She smiled her faraway smile and wiggled slightly to get comfortable on the sofa. "Jimmy will handle all that. I'm not sure."

"Will you have a traditional three-day wake before the burial?"

She kicked off her flats and tucked her bare feet under her backside, wiggling just a bit more. "I suspect so."

I felt like I was talking to someone not quite as smart as a camel.

"I know I've said this before, but I'm very sorry for your loss."

Her smile looked anything but friendly. "Mmm. Thank you."

"In working on Tommy Lee's case, as a missing person and now as a victim of violence, I believe I've gotten to know him very well. People think he was a good young man."

She showed me a more motherly smile. "Yes, he was."

"I didn't know he had an older brother—your other son."

The foggy, almost hypnotic look that she let occupy her face quickly changed. Her eyes narrowed, and her brow furrowed. "That's not a secret."

"I never thought it was. I only wondered why neither you nor your husband mentioned him and suggested we check with Tommy Lee's older brother—to see if he paid him a visit. Did you call him?"

"J.J.?"

"Yes, J.J. Do you have any other children?"

"No."

"Where is J.J. now?"

"I'm sorry. Where are my manners? Would you like something to drink? Sweet tea? Water? Something else?"

"No, thank you."

She smiled again and allowed her face to soften.

"J.J.," I said. "Where is he?"

"Oh. I just assumed you already knew."

"Why don't you tell me?"

"That army base near Clarksville...Clarksville, Tennessee."

"Have you called him recently?"

"Jimmy may have called."

"Were Tommy Lee and J.J. close?"

"I don't know what you mean by close. They were brothers. Brother are brothers."

"Were Tommy Lee and J.J. best buddies? Would Tommy Lee confide in J.J. if someone was giving him a hard time? Did J.J. usually stick up for his little brother if Tommy Lee had a problem? Would he tell J.J. if he considered someone an enemy?"

She tilted her head up and to the left, staring into space. "That would be a question for Tommy Lee. But not one you could ask anymore."

Jewel was not the one with whom I wanted to have an existential conversation.

"Then, I'll have to ask J.J. Is he coming home for the funeral?"

"J.J. travels a lot."

"And personally, you haven't spoken to him since Tommy Lee disappeared?"

"J.J. is difficult to contact. Soldiers often go on secret missions, you know."

Secret missions?

"So you have not?"

"I tried."

I wanted to strangle her.

She smiled another faraway smile. It made me think she was on Quaaludes.

"Thanks for your time, Mrs. Helton."

"You're quite welcome. Would you mind showin' yourself out?"

———

BACK IN THE OFFICE, I SLAPPED DOWN THE YELLOW LEGAL PAD I'D

been carrying on the desk Terri was using. She flinched. I pulled off my jacket, tossed it at her guest chair and missed.

"Will you stop throwing your clothing around," she said. It didn't sound like a question.

"You sound like Bettye."

"Then she had the right idea."

Terri picked up my jacket and hung it on the back of the chair.

"I'm not going to do this every time you get pissed at something or someone."

I growled.

"Did you growl at me?"

"No! At the world in general. You spend more than five minutes with Jewel Helton and tell me your mental health isn't in jeopardy."

"That bad? What happened?"

"The woman has the intelligence of a bed bug and the common sense of a lemming."

"Don't underestimate her," Janetta said.

"Then she's got one hell of an act."

John walked out from his office to see why I was ranting.

"How'd you make out with the weird mother?" he asked.

"Get me the zip code of Uranus. I'll send her a postcard. The woman is gone with the wind. I wanted to kill her."

"Then at least we could clear one homicide."

"I'll take it. After enough time with her I could get off with a defense of extreme emotional distress."

"You get *anything*?"

"Nothing. Absolutely nothing. She doesn't know if or when there will be a funeral for her son. She doesn't know if her other son will come back for his brother's funeral—because he may be on a *secret* mission. I've spoken to people on LSD who made more sense. I want to kill her. Really. No kidding. She needs killin'."

"Can I get you a cup of coffee?" Janetta asked.

I sighed. "You could get me a pitcher of vodka martinis—extra dry. Shaken, not stirred."

"Sounds like a better idea. You don't need any caffeine right now."

"Wanna hear what we did?" John asked.

"After a half dozen martinis, John."

"No vodka, Boss. Suck it up. We got good news."

"Okay, tell me." I tried to relax in the chair next to Terri's desk.

"The sheriff sent over the composite drawing her guy made from Sue Brown's description. We're on the county's inter-departmental courier route now, I'll have you know. He dropped off a box of chain envelopes to save postage. New ones."

"Wow. Lucky us."

"Yeah, right. The drawing's just one thing. Then Terri's CID guy emailed us Jimmy Lee's military ID photo from Army Personnel. Guess what?"

"20 Questions has been off TV for sixty years. Tell me, or I'll kill you instead of goofy Jewel."

Janetta interrupted. "Why are you so mean to John?"

"Just wait. You'll see. This overweight leprechaun gets in his digs whenever he can. You've only known him for a couple days. I'll give you two weeks, and you'll want to kill him, too."

John showed me his village idiot grin. "Boss, how can you say that? I'm shocked. Anyways, you'll wanna hear what else we got."

I took a deep breath. "Before I forget again, tell me how things went overnight."

"Oh, yeah. Good. Nothing happened. I snoozed a few times but was awake a lot. I kept the outside security lights on all night so no one could sneak up on the house in the dark. But nothing happened.

"Around seven o'clock Holly woke me up. She already made coffee and then gave me breakfast."

"Tough duty, huh?" I said. "Don't tell Bettye what you're doing for your overtime wages."

He gestured like he was turning a key in his mouth. "Don't worry, Boss. My lips are sealed."

"Okay, now we can get back to what you found out while I was talking with the world's most aggravating woman."

"Okay. I called everywhere. I mean everywhere. And when I got to family court, I learned that Jimmy Lee wasn't the perfect child."

"How many of us are?"

"Yeah, right. Anyways, the court clerk said J.J. had problems with his mother. She, the dopey mother, said she couldn't do anything with him and wanted him declared a PINS." He paused for Janetta's benefit. "That's a person in need of supervision. After that, the weird mother took the kid to a county shrink because he went after his little brother."

"Went after?"

"Aside from the minor fights all brothers have, she caught him trying to strangle little Tommy Lee."

"That takes sibling rivalry to a higher level."

"You bet. Jimmy Lee was fifteen, and Tommy was only ten. Big difference there. The shrink's report said Jimmy Lee's behavior was *within the normal parameters of adolescent brotherly conflict.* But that's not where it stopped."

"How so?"

"When Jimmy Lee was sixteen, he wanted to quit school, but the parents wouldn't sign off on that. So, his grandparents took him to family court where he petitioned to become an *emastipated* minor. He wanted to officially make his own decisions and leave home to live with the grandparents, who seemed in tune with the idea."

"Which grandparents?"

"The father's parents."

"The grandparents who are no longer alive?"

He smiled. "Nobody lives forever."

I rolled my eyes. "What happened?"

Janetta interrupted, needing a translation. "Emastipated?"

I nodded. "It's a word in the Galagheese language. Sounds like a cross between emancipated and masticated."

Terri couldn't resist a dig. "You might throw in a little constipated."

"You guys are ganging up on me. It's not *emastipated?*"

I shook my head. "No, John. E-man-ci-pated. See why everyone hates you."

"Not true."

"Come on, tell us what happened with this *emastipated* minor ordeal."

"Got denied. It's kinda complicated, but Jimmy Lee didn't have good grades or an overall good record in school. The teachers called him a loner who was *socially awkward*. So, the judge said he stays at home under the supervision of his parents."

"What were the grounds for emancipation that the kid's petition cited?"

"Lack of affection and personal alienation."

"Sounds like that deserves a better look."

"Yeah, I made arrangements to go there and have them pull the petition and ruling for me."

"Did the clerk say who prepared the paperwork and represented the kid?"

"Payne and Sutton, family law practice."

Terri let out a little laugh. "I've heard guys at FOP meetings call them Pain and Sufferin'."

"Cops tend to get screwed by lawyers like that in divorce cases," John said.

"We've seen more than our share of guys flushed into the big cesspool of life after getting caught catting around, haven't we, John?"

"You ain't just whistlin' Dixie, Boss."

"But these guys are top shelf shysters," I said. "Jimmy Lee couldn't pay their freight out of his lunch money. See if you can get the name of who signed the checks."

"Probably privileged information," John said. "But I'll ask if anyone else had their names on the record of attending the hearing. The clerk said the kid wanted to live with Robert and Nannie Mae Helton."

I looked at Janetta. "Did the elder Heltons have enough disposable cash to front the money for this kind of law suit?"

"You better believe it. That acreage where you're digging up dead bodies isn't all Robert owned. He's been buyin' and sellin' property in Blount County since before I was born. But I'll tell you, not far from that rental cabin on Meissners Station Road, just past the big stretch of wild blackberries, is an old white farmhouse. That's where Robert and Nannie Mae lived. He gave some land adjoining that to Jimmy when he married Jewel. They built their first house there."

"Is either place still in the family?"

"Sold them long ago."

"I wonder why J.J. picked the paternal grandparents to live with? Were they a lot wealthier than Jewel's parents?"

She laughed. "Shoot, Lee Vern and Monetta Samples have plenty of cash. And they're both still alive."

"Hmmm. I wonder if the petition elaborates on what *lack of affection* and *alienation* meant to J.J."

"I'll try to find out," John said.

"But when the kid's request was denied, he had to stay at home with Jewel, Jimmy and his younger brother. What did that do to family relations? A sixteen-year-old can be pretty vindictive."

"Until he graduated," John added. "Then he joined the Army right away."

"Exactly."

I looked over at Terri. "Besides the photo, what else did our CID man send us?"

"Mostly everything. Besides the photo and personnel summary, he sent names and numbers at C Company, 1st of the 327th in case you want to speak to the company commander or first sergeant. He spoke with them but figured you might have specific questions."

"Great. What was everyone's impression of Jimmy Lee?"

"Basically, good soldier."

"Then why is he still an E-6 after fifteen years? If he was such a good soldier with no disciplinary strikes against him, he could be a sergeant first class running a platoon or an operations sergeant at battalion level."

"The agent must have thought the same thing," she said. "The CO told him Jimmy lacked leadership qualities. He'd rather do the job than push troops."

"That sounds absolutely un-army-like."

She smiled. "One more thing that sounded important, under the circumstances. The first sergeant told him that J.J. was the best shot in the battalion. Back when he was a Spec-4, he applied for sniper school, but didn't make it through the selection process."

"Jeez, he must have failed the psych evaluation. They're looking for a killing machine, not a master's candidate in military science."

"Maybe J.J. is nuts," John said.

"You and I are nuts, John. If this guy was rejected from sniper training, maybe he's dangerous nuts. After you get more information from the family court, I'll call the first shirt at Charlie Company and see if I can schmooze him out of a few unit secrets."

"You got it."

"Terri, did the agent say if J.J. was on base when he checked? Did he interview him?"

"J.J. is on thirty days accrued leave. Has been for two weeks."

I let out a long breath. "That could put him here around the time Tommy Lee was shot."

Everybody nodded, but Janetta asked a good question. "Do you think *lack of affection* and *personal alienation* of J.J. takes the Helton brothers back to that old Cain and Abel story?"

"Since we're not coming up with any better ideas, you may have the key to this mystery."

Janetta gave me a look that could only have meant she wished she wasn't correct.

"What do you want me to do now, boss," Terri asked.

"Get on the computer to the US Institute of Heraldry and print out pictures of all the qualification wings for the Army, Air Force and Navy and Marines. As soon as you and John finish at Family Court, head out to the rental cabin and show Sue Brown J.J.'s photo and see if she can ID the air assault wings. That's a unique design—a head-on look at the front of a chopper superimposed on the wings."

She nodded, making a few notes.

"While John is getting his act together, call the girls in the cabin and make sure they stay there. Oh, yeah, call someone at the sheriff's ID section to find five more mug shots of guys who look something like J.J. to make an acceptable photo array."

"Easy."

"I hope so."

———

WHEN JOHN AND TERRI LEFT THE OFFICE, I ASKED JANETTA, "So tell me, why *did* Cain kill Abel?"

"Have you never been to church?"

"Not recently, but don't worry about my religious training or saving my mortal soul. Why did Adam and Eve's kids not get along?"

"I'll tell you the real story, but somewhere along the line, things reverse from what we're seein' here. But, I'll get inta that later. Basically, Cain, the older brother, slew Abel. Cain represented evil while Abel was a better person. Get it?"

"Uh-huh. I knew that."

"Sure you did. Well, Abel was the actual son of Adam and Eve. And he never failed to impress upon Cain that Adam was not *his* father. That's where our little drama differs. J.J. looks like Jimmy, and Tommy Lee does not. See where I'm goin'?"

"Sure."

"Well then, because of bein' envious that Abel got more attention, Cain killed his younger half-brother and left Eden for The Land of Nod —in J.J.'s case, he left Prospect for the Army."

"But J.J. enlisted in the Army fifteen years ago."

"I said things are a little different, but still the same."

"And this is evidence?"

"It's my theory."

"Yikes."

"What do you mean, Yikes?"

"Let me rephrase—if I can. J.J., who's older, like Cain, resented Tommy Lee, who's younger, like Abel, because he got more attention."

Her face lit up. "Exactly."

"Most younger kids get more attention."

"Doesn't matter. Keep going."

"Okay. You're saying J.J.—Cain—somehow knew that Tommy Lee—Abel—wasn't Jimmy's son?"

"Could be."

"And Cain—I mean J.J.—finally decided to whack Tommy Lee because he thinks Jewel had an affair with someone who was Tommy Lee's real father?"

"Could be."

I shook my head. "Yikes."

"Stop that."

"Since the same rifle was used to kill Jake Quarles and take a shot at me near Tommy Lee's grave, could Jake Quarles be Tommy Lee's real father?"

"I've never heard that rumor, but it kinda goes along with my theory."

"You may be right, but I can't take the Bible into court and claim it's a credible basis for a prosecution."

"I'm just tryin' ta help."

"I need more information on the third bullet. And I wish DNA test results could get processed quicker. If Mo Rappaport confirms Tommy was Jakes' son, we'd be able to narrow our focus."

"It's startin' to look like that's possible."

I shook my head, not exactly knowing where this new theory might take me. "Contrary to popular belief, Eden sounds like a tough neighborhood. I'm going to get your cousin to put out an alarm to pick up J.J. For one thing or another, we need him to answer a few questions."

———

JOHN CALLED ME AS SOON AS HE AND TERRI FINISHED EXAMINING the paperwork at Family Court. Unfortunately, they didn't learn much more than we already knew.

Wanting more information on Jimmy Lee, I called the orderly room at C Company, 1st Battalion, 327th Infantry Regiment at Fort Campbell, Kentucky. The company clerk connected me with the first shirt.

"First Sergeant Sizemore speaking, sir."

"Hello, Top." I used the old Army tag for a first sergeant. "My name is Sam Jenkins, special investigator for the Blount County Sheriff in East Tennessee. Have you got a few minutes to talk about one of your soldiers?"

"You talkin' about Staff Sergeant Helton, sir?"

"That's the one."

"Figgered as much, sir. He's the man Mr. Fowler from CID came here about. What's he done?"

"I'm not sure that he's done anything. His brother was murdered, and we're trying to get as much information as possible on the brother. Only, so far, pickings have been pretty slim, and I can't locate Sergeant Helton. How well do you know him?"

"Man's been around. Good soldier, sir. I've known him a few years now."

The first sergeant still sounded a little stiff. I needed to warm him up a bit more.

"Top, let me switch gears for a minute and ask you a personal question."

"Sir?"

"I'm just curious. You ever do any time with the 82nd?"

"No, sir, but my father did."

"He a first sergeant, too?"

"Yes, sir, surely was. Long time ago."

"I knew a first sergeant named Spurgeon O. Sizemore when I was with the 1st of the 508th Infantry—back when Stormin' Norman Schwarzkopf was a major, and I was just a PFC."

"Lord have mercy. That's my daddy. Small world, sir. Damn sure is. Small world."

"Your father was a good man. I liked him."

"Well, sir, ain't that somethin'?"

"Lots of people in it, Top, but the Army *is* a small world."

"You spend much time in service, sir?"

"Counting active and reserve time, twenty-one years."

"Then maybe you got to be a first sergeant, too."

I chuckled. "They never gave me that much power. I only made it to lieutenant colonel."

He laughed like crazy. "Well, I'll be damned. What'd ya say yer name was, sir?"

"Sam Jenkins."

"Well, sir, twenty-one years is a long time. Where'd ya go after the 508th?"

I told him, and after shooting the breeze for almost ten minutes, we got back to Jimmy Lee Helton.

"Helton is a good soldier, sir. Jest didn't want ta get himself a platoon or go any higher than assistant platoon sergeant. But a damn good soldier though. Just no ambition to make rank. Kind of a loner, if ya know what I mean. Volunteered for everything. Damn good in the field. Loved the trainin', too. Sum'bitch could shoot the eyes out of a hummin' bird. Jest didn't want command responsibility."

"I'm guessing he got passed over for E-7 a few times."

"Yes, sir. He did."

"Why didn't he get cashiered out?"

"Times are different in the all-volunteer army, sir. Helton was physically fit, able to do the job and committed ta the mission. We don't get rid o' men like that."

Even if, deep down, they're an unleashed shithouse rat?

"Even though he wasn't psychologically fit to be a sniper?"

"I ain't no psy-chologist, sir. I guess they had their reasons ta deny him the trainin', but far as I'm concerned, Helton was combat ready."

"Hmm. Mr. Fowler told us Helton was on thirty days leave. Do you have the destination he put down?"

"Hold one, sir. I'll ask the company clerk."

In the background, I heard, "Runcyman, pull Helton's leave request, and gimme the place he said he's goin'." A long moment later, "Runcyman, goddamnit, the man on the phone ain't got all day."

Then Runcyman sounded off. "Got it, Top. Gave his HOR. Parents place in Prospect, Tennessee."

"You hear that, sir?"

"Sure did."

"You got that address?"

"I do. Thanks. While you've got the company clerk's attention, can you tell me Helton's local address near Fort Campbell?"

"He's lives on post. Got him an unmarried NCO's billet."

"Okay. Before the clerk digs that out, how about his personally owned vehicle and the information from the on-post registration?'

"Yes, sir. Hold on again. Runcyman!"

A few moments later the first sergeant gave me the physical location of J.J.'s quarters and told me that he owned a green 1992 Ford Econoline van with Kentucky plates.

"Top, I appreciate all your help."

"Yes, sir, no sweat. Glad ta he'p." He paused for a long moment. "Sir, lemme tell ya one more thing about young Helton. Our motto is 'Above the Rest'. He fits in."

CHAPTER FOURTEEN

I walked out front, slipped on my jacket, and dropped into the chair behind what we began to call Terri's desk.

"This case is a nightmare," I told Janetta." One contradiction after another. And so much plod work is unfinished because we keep getting interrupted by other things."

The words weren't out of my mouth when her eyes widened. From the parking lot, we heard a car door slam loud enough to have awoken a hibernating Eskimo. Moments later the door burst open, and Bill Koronkiewicz filled most of the frame. He never waited for a greeting or invitation to enter.

He stepped inside and showed us a look that would have frightened the defensive line of the Tennessee Titans. "You got something to say to me?"

Not wanting to appear impressed, I shrugged like a problem teenager staring up at an ineffectual teacher. "Sounds like you're waiting for me to ask you a question. Okay, did you kill Tommy Lee Helton and take a shot at me?"

He shook his head. "No to the first and if I took a shot at you, you wouldn't be sitting here."

"Unless you wanted to miss."

He started to turn red and look even more frustrated. "What's your problem? You can't ask me questions? Gotta send a North Carolina detective?"

I shook my head as if he was nothing more than an annoying insect. "Why should I spend three hours of travel time when I can get a local cop to help out?"

He percolated, and his jaw muscles worked frantically as he listened to me. "Now that I'm here I ought to—"

I didn't allow him to finish. "No, you shouldn't. Do you think I'd slug it out with you? Come down to earth, sport. That would make as much sense as wrestling a Lowland Gorilla."

He turned his head to the right and snorted while a half smile crossed his face. Then he leaned over, rested his hands aggressively on the desktop and balanced on straight arms. "I ought to kick your ass."

Janetta picked up her telephone. I looked toward her and shook my head.

"I didn't think your bosses at the mill hired you and Curry as mindless muscle. But it seems you're a security man who doesn't know squat about the law."

He backed off an inch and frowned. "Whaddaya mean?"

"I mean I have no obligation to take a beating from a guy your size to satisfy your explosive anger. If I reasonably believe you'll cause me serious physical injury, I can just kill you to prevent that. I might even enjoy doing it."

"Oh, yeah?"

I rolled my swivel chair back three feet and showed him the Smith and Wesson pointed at his stomach. His eyes popped open, and he straightened up.

"Yeah. I guess you think you're pretty good with a rifle. Well, a lot of people *know* I'm just as good with one of these. So, why don't you sit down and cool off. Ms. Galloway won't call the local cops, and I won't put three shots into your tummy. Sound like a plan?"

He let out a long breath. "You have any idea how pissed off I am?"

"I really don't care. Sit."

He pulled the guest chair way from the desk and planted his bulk on it.

I slid my revolver back into its holster and snapped the thumb-break safety.

"Before I answer your last question, Bill, let me ask you something. You were a supervisor in the Marines for a long time. Did you ever have to do something that caused a subordinate to look at you as other than his buddy?"

"I see where you're going, but I never accused anyone of murder."

"If I was ready to accuse you of a crime, my friend, you'd already be in cuffs. I had questions because you are what we in the *real* police business call a person of interest."

"Why? Why would I kill that kid?"

"Based on your documented volatile nature—the one that got you an Article 15 in the Marines and the one you put on display right here. And your altercation with Helton at the mill. You may not have looked guilty enough to arrest, but you occupied a big spot on our list of possible suspects."

"Hey, I've cooperated with you all along. I told you I had a quick argument with him. That was it. You had no reason to look at me anymore."

I shook my head. "That concept went out with stick shift and wooden boats."

He wasn't calming down. "Hey, I told you the truth then. You should have believed me."

I smiled and shook my head again. "And no killer has ever lied to me or appeared to be outwardly cooperative?"

In turn, he closed his eyes and shook his head in frustration. "What do I gotta do to convince you?"

I asked him to account for his whereabouts on the estimated date of Tommy Lee's death. I ended with, "Feel free to check a calendar."

His face lightened up. "I don't need a calendar. That's my wife's birthday. We both took the day off and went to lunch at a place in Waynesville, Frog's Leap Public House. Ask the bartender. His name's Greg. He'll remember me. And ask him who our waitress was. I don't know her name, but obviously he will."

"You're doing fine. Thanks to that North Carolina detective, we've established that you were busy with a group of local protestors outside the mill at the time someone shot at me and two other cops."

"Wasn't me."

"Are you a hunter?"

"No, why?"

"Do you own a Remington 700? Something like your old B-40?"

"No, why?"

"You sure about that?"

"Yeah, I'm sure. Got no use for a weapon like that."

"If BATF comes back with information that you do, I may ask that North Carolina detective and a couple of his friends to pick you up."

"Jesus, I'm telling you the truth."

"Okay."

"Hey look, other than getting into a shouting match with that kid, I had nothing to do with any of this. I swear."

"It looks that way. Easy to resolve when we do it like gentlemen. You think?"

His body relaxed a little. "Yeah, I guess."

"I've got nothing more to question you about, but since you're here, don't go away. I want to show you something."

I walked back to my office and got the original composite sketch Bettye's artist drew based on Sue Brown's description.

"Have you ever seen this person before? Look like anyone who now works or used to work security at the mill?"

Koronkiewicz took a long enough look at the likeness before answering to make me think he made a sincere effort. He shook his head and passed the drawing back across the desk.

"No. I don't know anyone who looks like this."

"These drawings aren't always one hundred percent accurate. How about someone who *remotely* looks like this?"

Another shake of the head. "No."

I pulled J.J. Helton's military ID photo from the case folder on the desk. "How about this man?"

He gave the picture a once over. "No again. Looks like the same guy. Who is he?"

"Someone seen near the place where those two cops and I took fire."

"Sorry. Can't help you."

"Okay. Thanks for looking." I paused, choosing my words carefully. "Look, I'm not in the habit of apologizing for doing my job, but I can tell you that unless you and Curry have been blatantly lying to us, you're off the hook and won't be hearing from us again."

He nodded and took a moment to answer. "Okay."

"But here's a true story for you. Sooner or later, someone is going to grab a sample of the toxic waste from your mill right after they discharge it into the river. Then, all hell will break loose, and the place will at least be closed down."

He pushed his hands out to the sides—the universal signal that he couldn't help what fate tossed at us. "I help supervise security guards. That's got nothing to do with me."

"Then you'll just be out of a job. But if you see that place going down the tubes, I suggest you don't get involved in a criminal conspiracy with your bosses and some local officials who are part of an under-the-table payroll. It's easier to get yourself a good deal after being arrested for an armed robbery than to get a break on a felony stemming from a major environmental law violation."

Without much emotion, he said, "I'll keep that in mind."

"Uh-huh."

"Am I in some kind of trouble for coming here?"

"No. I didn't get hit, and you didn't get shot."

He gave a half shrug. "Okay then...I better get back."

"Have a safe trip."

———

"Would you have shot him?" Janetta asked.

"If he was stomping me into the linoleum and you didn't do anything to stop him?"

"Me? What could I have done?"

I shrugged. "Then I would have shot him. Nothing personal. I just bruise easily and don't like coming to work black and blue."

"Lord have mercy."

"That's what Bettye used to say."

———

It was too late to dig Jimmy Helton out of a woodpile and ask him about his older son's current visit to Blount County, so I figured I'd kill the rest of my day bothering Bettye Lambert before heading home.

Since becoming an officially employed minion of the county sheriff, I no longer needed a visitor's pass to wander through the non-public areas of the Justice Center unmolested. So, I hung my special investigator's badge from the top pocket of my sport jacket and trudged up to the second floor. No one questioned my reason for being there.

Bettye's secretary, Cynthia, was no less officious than Trudy Connor who protected Mayor Ronnie Shields from me for the five years I worked at Prospect PD. After signing away my life and that of my first-born child, should I ever have one, to the sheriff's general fund, and satisfying Cynthia that I had honorable intentions, I entered Bettye's wood paneled office. She wiggled her fingers at me as a form of hello while she continued with a telephone conversation. U.S. and Tennessee flags on polished wooden staffs stood behind her impressive polished walnut desk. I dropped into one of her guest chairs and crossed my legs.

Less than two minutes later, Bettye cradled her phone. "You look tore up and wore out, city boy. Whatchew been up ta?"

I rolled my eyes. "If I answered your dreadfully colloquial inquiry in detail, my dear woman, we would collect several hours of overtime tonight. The short version is Tommy Lee Helton's older brother J.J.—who no one involved in this fiasco ever thought worth mentioning—either killed his brother or has come here from Fort Campbell, Kentucky to act as a vigilante and find out who did."

Bettye blinked her hazel eyes several times. "What?"

"Wait, sweetheart, there's more. I deftly avoided both a physical confrontation and having to shoot that oversized Polish Leviathan, Bill Koronkiewicz, who has occupied a spot on our suspect's list until only minutes ago."

Her shoulders dropped, and she sighed. "Oh, Lord have mercy. Please do not shoot someone while you're workin' for me."

"Pfui. Your cousin said almost the same thing. I'll try not to."

"Speaking of Janetta, how's she doin'?"

"It's only taken her a few days to undo any administrative horror John created and get the office organized. She's an excellent worker. Almost as good as you. *And* she's even got a theory of biblical proportion on who killed Tommy Lee Helton. Five will get you ten she could be right."

"Biblical?"

"She's going with the Cain versus Abel card." Having no better idea, I shrugged. "Could be. Especially since that brutish monster I mentioned seems to have a decent alibi for the times he could have been involved with any of this business. Now we've just got to eliminate his bosses or anyone else over at the paper mill."

"Are those people really viable suspects?"

I shook my head. "Honestly, no. Tommy Lee was no more of a threat to them than any of the other environmentalists. Koronkiewicz popped up only because he and the kid went nose-to-nose one day at the picket line. But, as I said, the Kronkster has two pretty good alibis."

"How much longer do you think this might take? We have to address the Jake Quarles murder."

"Since they're most likely connected, but separated by a long time, in essence, we are. We're beginning to get bogged down and could use some help with what will amount to mostly phone work. Can you break someone loose to handle that for us, if the J.J. Helton angle leads nowhere?"

"I guess so. How much time are you talking about?"

"Not much. We only need a background investigation on the victim's girlfriend and then a location on Jake Quarles' ex-wife and son. Someone good should interview them."

"I suppose you'd like Bo Stallins to handle this for you?"

"Sure. But the first order of business is for a 'wanted for questioning' alarm for James Lee Helton to go out with your signature."

"After that, how soon do you think it will take you to close this out?"

"If the Cain and Abel thing pans out, perhaps very soon. If that fizzles, dig out your Ouija board, baby. I haven't got a clue. How are the searchers making out?"

She let out a long breath. "They're costing me a fortune and finding absolutely nothing."

"Swell. Do you have someone watching the rental cabin, or is Prospect PD handling that?"

"After John worked those two nights," she said, "I didn't want him staying awake overnight and working the case all day. He's not a young man, ya know. Between our cars and the three Prospect sector cars, they all pass by the cabin at least twice a tour. The ladies have 9-1-1 on speed dial. I think they're all right. And they seem content with our protection efforts."

"You're very protective of my Irish partner, but I suppose you're right. People still get assassinated with top-notch security details crawling all over them."

Bettye got up and walked over to a window that overlooked the public parking lot and gave her a view of US-321 heading east toward Townsend. I took a moment to admire her navy blue skirt and silky white blouse that fit her as if it was custom made.

Since I had nothing positive to say about the case, I decided to change the subject. "I see what you're spending your new inflated salary on."

She turned. "What?"

"Silly woman. Your outfits."

She smiled. "You like it?"

"No, I only mention it because you're ugly, and your mother dresses you funny. That's the third new thing I've seen you wear this week. You already know you're beautiful. You don't need me to tell you."

"Well, thank you, Mr. Sam Smarty-Pants Jenkins. And how do you know they're new?"

"I may no longer be a police chief, but I still know everything."

"If that's true, who killed Tommy Lee Helton?"

"I'm getting old. That must have slipped my mind."

———

AFTER LEAVING BETTYE TO THE LAST FEW MINUTES OF HER workday, I made my way downstairs and out the front doors. Just as my foot was about to hit the blacktop, I noticed Titus Haggerty walking toward me out of the door from which they release freed prisoners. He wore a dark blue sweat suit and carried a large brown paper shopping bag. When he saw me, a big smile crossed his face. He was only fifty-seven but looked old enough to have been a foot soldier on the First Crusade. I wanted to avoid him, but that didn't seem to be in the cards.

"Hey, Mr. Jinkins!" He yelled like a little kid meeting Bozo the Clown for the first time. "You doin' aw rot t'day?"

As he approached, I saw that he looked clean and shaven. His hair was combed, and his teeth appeared somewhat whiter. Even though the breeze was at his back, I couldn't smell the old Titus all the cops at Prospect PD knew and loved.

"Hello, Titus. You're looking absolutely...hygienic. I guess the warden gave you some new duds?"

"Yessir, brand new. And a pair o' sneakers, too."

He picked up his left foot to show me his jailhouse boat shoes.

"Even cleaned my old clothes fer me." He held out the paper sack.

"Good for you. How's the chow inside nowadays?"

"Real good." He tilted his head and gave me a conciliatory look. "I mean kindly like better than I've been havin' at home. And I ain't had a drink since Mr. Alcock arrested me. Amazin' what ya feel like when ya wake up and ain't hung over."

"You've got a whole new world ahead of you." I wondered how long it would take before he went on his next three-day bender.

He smiled and clutched the paper sack like a child brown bagging it on their first day of kindergarten.

Since he didn't smell like marinated road kill, I thought I'd do my good deed of the day.

"I'm heading east. Need a ride somewhere?"

"Jest goin' home ta Prospect."

"I forget where you live. You navigate, and I'll drive."

"Thank ya, sir. First trailer park on Doc Beasley off o' Sevierville Road."

"Okay. I'm parked over there." I pointed to my borrowed sheriff's car.

After pulling out onto 321 Titus said, "I heard 'bout ya finally findin' Jake Quarles' body."

"Yeah. You probably heard he'd been murdered."

"Yessir. Seen it on the TV news. Jake the Snake. Now, Jake, he was a good ol' boy. Sorry ta hear 'bout that."

"Friend of yours?"

"Sorta. He's younger 'an me by a year or two, but I used ta drink with him back when I was still workin'."

"And he was alive." I mentioned that only to put his reminiscence into perspective.

Titus shook his head affectionately and with a look of fond memories on his face. "Ol' Jake was always the life o' the party. Yessir, surely was."

"We'll start investigating Jake's death as soon as we finish up with another case. A kid named Tommy Lee Helton was found murdered in the same wooded area where they found Jake. If you knew Quarles, we'd like to talk with you about him."

"Yessir. Be happy ta he'p. Heard 'bout the Helton boy, too. Funny, ain't it? Him bein' Jake's natural borned son."

CHAPTER FIFTEEN

"SAY THAT AGAIN!"

I must have spoken too loud again. Titus jumped.

"Do whot?"

"Tommy Lee Helton was Jake Quarles' son?"

"Uh-huh."

"How do you know this?"

"Jake done told me."

"And you believed him?"

"Sure. Jake was quite the lady's man."

"And he told you about an affair with Jewel Helton?"

A fat man on a vintage Harley-Davidson pulled out of the hospital parking lot across the road and goosed the accelerator as he headed east on 321. He was running cut-out pipes on the Harley that sounded way over the legal noise limit of eighty-eight decibels. Each time he shifted and increased speed, the bike let out a long growl until, in the distance, we heard only a gentle purr. I turned back to look at Titus.

"One night ol' Jake was three sheets ta the wind and lookin' kinda down. So we'uns got talkin', and he tells me what a good-lookin' woman

Jewel is and how much he'd like him and her to tie up proper like, but didn't think that could ever be, them both bein' married ta other people, that is. Then he started explainin' more."

"Were you sober? Are you sure he wasn't just bragging?"

"I mighta had me a couple drinks, but I remember bein' sober as a judge. And you didn't know Jake. He didn't have ta make up no stories. He had him plenny o' women. Plenny o' good lookin' women. Word is Tommy Lee ain't the only kid can call Jake Daddy."

"Jesus H. Christ." I shook my head. "Do you know if Jimmy Helton knew about this?"

"Cain't imagine he didn't. The boy looked jest like Jake."

———

As soon as I dumped off Haggerty at the fleabag trailer park, I called John Gallagher.

"Are you home now?" I asked.

"Yeah. Terri and I finished half an hour ago. What's up?"

I told him about Tommy Lee's parentage.

"Jeez. That's all too close for comfort. Two bodies. Land owned by the same person. Now we hear the victims are father and son. And before I locked up the office, Bill Werner called. The third bullet, the one Dr. Mo took out of Tommy Lee, came from that same gun as the first two. I was gonna call you tonight."

"Perfect. I thought it might."

"I did, too."

"I'm glad Bill didn't put us on the bottom of his to-do pile. We owe him."

"Yeah. Let's take him to lunch and hit up the sheriff to cover the bill."

"We're gonna need a relaxing lunch after this is over. Now, only one more piece of evidence to go. If Mo matches the DNA of Jake the Snake and Tommy Lee, we've got 'em cold. But if we wait much longer, J.J.

may leave the area for who knows where and it might take us forever to catch him."

"How can you be sure he's still around?"

"I can't, but we've got to work on the theory he is and not waste time finding him."

"I'm with ya, Boss."

"I'll call Bettye tonight. Let's meet in her office tomorrow to work out a strategy. We might need a couple more bodies to efficiently pull off something. She'll have to spare a couple men.

"What do you think?" John asked. "Jimmy killed The Snake when he found out he was banging Jewel, and J.J. croaked Tommy Lee?"

"Who the hell knows? These people are too weird to understand. We need that rifle. Could be Jimmy did one and J.J. the other, or...Shit. Mix and match. Your imagination is the limit."

"If we find the gun, maybe BATF can trace it back and see if Jimmy or J.J. bought it."

"If they bought it through a dealer. If one of the Heltons picked it up on a casual sale, we might never know much more than who bought it first. And that could be anybody."

"With luck, one of them will have it in their possession."

"Yeah," I said. "We'd better invite Moira to our meeting with Bettye and talk about search warrants."

"We got enough for probable cause?"

"Not really, but maybe we can get creative. Maybe the alarm Bettye initiated on J.J. and his van will get some action. Can't be too many 1992 vans around the county."

"If he's still around."

"You're doing it again, John. You're raining on my parade."

"Sorry, Boss."

"After tomorrow we should get more information from the parents. Jewel will have to knock off the airhead act, and Jimmy will either play ball or get locked up."

"We gonna hit them separately?"

"Sure. Jewel first. We'll get her at home. Although we might need a

Prospect cop to keep an eye on her if she goes out tomorrow morning. I'll call Harley and square that away."

"Want me to tell Terri?"

"Can't hurt. She might not have any more time off, but if Harley assigns a person to tail Jewel, it makes sense to use Terri."

"I'll call her."

"Good. See you tomorrow."

———

SHERIFF BETTYE LAMBERT REARRANGED HER MORNING SCHEDULE to accommodate our meeting. Her uniform of the day was a fitted, sleeveless white dress decorated with black lace at the top that would have been suitable for an appearance on a late night talk show.

I arrived first and couldn't resist another comment about her new wardrobe.

"Nice dress, Betts. Can I get a job as your janitor or shoeshine boy—anything where I can see what you're wearing each day? I'm fascinated by your wardrobe."

She gave me a million-dollar smile "Aren't you just the sweetest man?" Then she put an edge on it. "But, Sam Jenkins, don't you ever let *anyone* in this building hear you say somethin' like that. Understand?"

"I get your point. These hillbillies are the biggest rumormongers on the planet. But I hate myself for not telling you to wear plainclothes more often when we worked at the PD."

"Will you stop?"

"Your clothes are anything but plain."

Before she could throw something at me, John Gallagher walked in wearing his usual goofy smile. When he opened the door to Bettye's office the smell of fresh coffee drifted in. I wanted to recommend Cynthia for a commendation.

"Hi, Sheriff. Hi, uh, partner. Howz it goin'?"

"Mornin', John." Bettye said and retreated behind her desk.

In addition to the goofy smile, John wore a pastel green sport jacket, pale yellow shirt and salmon-colored slacks.

"John," I said, "you look like a squad dick from Palm Beach PD."

"Nice, huh? I bought these before we left Boca. I figgered I'd dress up for our important meeting."

Moira Menzies, the new interim district attorney, walked in before I could throw out another snide remark about John's outfit. A youngish-looking man wearing a light blue shirt and tie and gray pleated slacks followed her. A gold and silver oval sheriff's department shield hung on his belt along with a holstered Glock automatic.

"It looks like we're all here," Bettye said. "Sam, John, I don't know if you've met D.L. Joiner. He's the new lieutenant in charge of CID."

We all shook hands and took seats in front of Bettye's desk.

"Before we start," Bettye said, "Would anyone like coffee?"

Joiner passed. John and Moira were interested. I knew Bettye would have a cup, so I ordered one, too. Bettye buzzed her efficient secretary.

"I'm goin' to let Sam lead off," Bettye said, "because he's got all the information and some of its new and very important."

"Last night I inadvertently received a bomb dropped on me that we could have used a week ago."

I told them what Titus Haggerty said the evening before.

"Did you confirm this?" Moira asked.

"I've already asked the ME to match the DNA of both the murder victims. That doesn't happen overnight, but he's put a big rush on it. As soon as we leave here, we'll try to find a blood type for Jimmy Helton to see if he could possibly be Tommy Lee's father. John and I doubt he is. If we get a quick eliminator, questioning him will be a lot easier. But suppose we can't get any record of his blood type and we have to rely on DNA? Let me back up a little and tell you why waiting for the DNA results before pushing forward immediately might be a bad idea."

I was interrupted when Cynthia walked in looking perky in a pink blouse and gray skirt, carrying a tray of cups and an insulated beaker of coffee.

John acted as server and after everyone held what they wanted, I explained Janetta's Cain and Abel theory and how J.J. could, at any moment, leave the area and disappear completely.

"All this circumstantial evidence surrounding J.J. is getting very close to that 'reasonable cause to believe' line," I said. "If we could find him, we'd question him. But so far the guy has been able to stay hidden. Our lives would be easier if he doesn't leave the county."

"You believe the story about Jake Quarles being Tommy Lee's father is credible?" Moira asked.

I pulled a current photo of Tommy Lee and an older driver's license photo of Jake from the case folder and handed them to Moira.

"The informant said they looked alike. I think they do. They're not twins, but the kid looks a hell of a lot more like Quarles than Jimmy Helton."

"You're right. Could be." Moira handed the pictures to D.L. Joiner.

"As Terri Donnellson from Prospect PD mentioned, the kid had pale blue eyes, while Jewel and Jimmy Helton both have brown. Supposedly, there's only a twenty-five percent chance of that happening. Jake, on the other hand, has the same eyes as the kid. Same sandy hair and face structure, too."

"We'll know when Doctor Rappaport finishes the DNA tests," Moira said. "I'd be more comfortable if we had that information."

I nodded. "Yes, but that comfort might give J.J. the opportunity to get lost for a long time. There are just too many coincidences here for these things not to be connected. Right now, we need to latch on to J.J. He's got some explaining to do about that phony ploy at the rental cabin. There was no legitimate reason for that."

"No, certainly not," Moira said. "If you can catch him in the van, the rifle or a recognizable gun case might be in plain view. Unless he's built in some sort of storage place. In that case, don't search the van without a warrant. Don't impound it and pull one of those spurious 'inventories to safeguard the defendant's property.' Those aren't flying much anymore."

"I know. That's why I'd like to apply for a warrant before we find him. What's the worst we have to do, ask for extensions every twenty-four hours? I'm willing to do that, because if we toss the van, we'll find the gun. I doubt he'd chance stashing it somewhere not under his control. A guy with a sniper's mentality wouldn't do that. With the gun, we tie him to two murders and the shooting near the gravesite. Finding the Army tent equipment would be a bonus putting him at the scene of two of those events"

"Sam," Moira said, "you know what we need for a warrant as well as me. Properly prepared, and with the right judge, we can get one for the van. But suppose it's empty?"

I shrugged. "Then I hope we can *convince* him to spill his guts. I'd love to search the Helton homestead, too, but I don't want to fill out the warrant application just to get turned down. Even I can't get that *creative* to get in there. We've got nothing but suspicion right now. But that suspicion may turn into probable cause after another conversation with Jewel and Jimmy. They've been telling big fat porkies ever since we've met them. Just for spite, I should charge them with obstructing."

Moira nodded. "With a little more information, we could probably prove that in court."

"One thing to keep in mind though," I said. "Maybe Jimmy killed Jake the Snake and then gave his rifle to J.J. who took it with him on his Army journeys. I know it hasn't been logged into his company's arms room, but he has private quarters in an NCO barracks, which although subject to periodic inspection, is still as close to a private residence as you can get for a single guy in the Army. So for all these years, one way or another, the gun might have traveled far from Prospect, Tennessee."

"Okay, I'll find a sympathetic judge," Moira said, "and we'll get the warrant for the van, but I like the idea of confronting the parents with this new information before you kill yourself looking for J.J."

"Great minds work alike."

"How can I help with this?" Joiner asked

"I'm going to suggest that the sheriff calls off the search along Cricket Branch. If J.J. knows that area and he doesn't want to be found, he won't. According to people at the 327th Infantry, he's pretty good at his field craft. So, you get Sergeant Bledsoe and the deputies back to regular duty. But if we locate J.J. and need assistance to take him off, we'd like a couple of people."

"Look," Joiner said. "I've never been a detective, and I only got command of CID six months ago. I'll have to defer to you here."

"Okay, thanks. It's John and me and maybe one or two people from Prospect PD. How about one detective for general support and at least one crime scene investigator to take custody of the van and anything we find in it? I'm thinking Bo Stallins and Jackie Shuman—David Sparks if you can spare him."

Bettye stepped in. "That sounds reasonable. This is a double homicide and attempted murder of a police officer."

————

JOHN SWITCHED OFF HIS CELL PHONE AFTER TAKING A QUICK CALL from Terri Donnellson. "Was all that too easy?"

It was just after ten o'clock as I turned east on 321 heading toward the Helton residence, outside of which Terri had been sitting all morning.

"Sometimes you get lucky," I said. "Moira is making the applications based on my affidavit. That saves me a trip into a judge's chambers. She'll call as soon as the warrant gets signed. Then all we have to do is find J.J. and the van."

"Might not be that easy."

"With luck we can shock Jewel into telling the truth."

"Terri says she's been outside the house since quarter to eight," John said. "Jimmy's truck was already gone, but she can see Jewel walking around inside."

"Good. Ten bucks says either she or Jimmy knows where J.J. is or has spoken to him recently."

"J.J. is sort of a man without a country," John said. "Every cop and Federal agent is looking for him. He can't go back to Fort Campbell. He's an *unconvicted* fugitive."

That gave me an idea. "John, I could kiss you. Get Bettye on the phone. Have her tell Bo Stallins to call the credit union on post and all the banks around Fort Campbell and freeze any accounts he finds for J.J. Then call the credit bureaus and get numbers for his credit card accounts and call security at those companies and put a stop on any cards he has. Cut off his cash and he can't buy food or gasoline. We'll starve the bastard out."

He laughed. "Boss, you're mean."

"He's a soldier. He'll understand. If I can't capture his heart and mind, I'll squeeze his balls in a vice."

————

JOHN AND I PULLED INTO THE HELTON'S DRIVEWAY IN OUR borrowed black Ford. Terri was sitting in her British Racing Green Mini Cooper across the street. We met her in the middle of the road.

"She's inside," Terri said. "I've seen her walking around occasionally. She looked out at my car once. Doesn't seem concerned."

"Maybe the stupid thing isn't an act," I said. "If I saw someone sitting for hours in a strange car across from my house, I'd call the PD."

John grinned. "But you're suspicious of everybody."

"How do you want to handle her?" Terri asked.

"I've been thinking about that. I've gotten nowhere with her by being nice. How about a good cop—insane, vindictive, hateful, homicidal, lunatic cop act? I volunteer for the latter."

"Maybe Terri should go with you and start off," John suggested. "You know, like woman to woman. Then if that's goes nowhere, you can always go nuts."

"Yeah. All right."

John made that obnoxious grin he uses when he wants to break my chops. "Ya know, Sam, I'm surprised you're so pissed at a good-lookin' woman."

"Good-looking, yes. But she's about as appealing as raw sewage. I *hate* her."

"Sure you want to do this, boss?" Terri asked. "Maybe John and I..."

"Yeah, I want to be there. I can control my emotions. How about you stay outside, John? Make sure if Jimmy or J.J. show up, they don't disturb us. If either one pulls in, call Prospect PD for backup. Then call me. If my cell phone rings, I'll assume it's you, and we'll be ready to take one or both into custody as soon as they walk in the door."

"Sounds good. I'll park down the road a little."

Terri and I approached the house, and she rang the bell. A moment later, Jewel answered the door wearing jeans and a man-tailored, button-down white shirt. She smiled like someone on valium, her eyes having an almost far-away look.

Terri tinned her and smiled. "Hello, Mrs. Helton. I'm Officer Donnellson from Prospect PD. I believe you know Investigator Jenkins."

"Yes. Hello. Can I help you? Have you found something new?"

I wanted to strangle her.

"We'd like to speak with you," Terri said. "May we come in?"

Jewel forced a quasi-smile. "I suppose so. Please excuse the mess. Our cleaning lady hasn't been here in almost a week."

We followed her into the living room. The place looked like something ready to be photographed for Better Homes and Gardens. Nothing was out of place, and I didn't see any dust. To the casual observer, the Helton home looked unlived in. I figured Jewel probably spent her days hanging from a closet pole like a bat.

Jewel planted her shapely backside on the sofa, while Terri and I sat in the oversized upholstered chairs across a four-foot square cocktail table from her.

Terri began with, "We need to talk about your oldest son, J.J."

"As I told Mr. Jenkins, I haven't seen him or heard from him for some time. You'll have to contact him at his army base."

Terri continued, and I felt as useful as a mushroom growing on a log —kept in the dark and fed on horse manure. "His company commander told me J.J. is signed out on extended leave. He gave his destination as your home."

No inflection, no emotion, no truth, just, "Oh?"

I couldn't help myself and certainly couldn't keep my mouth shut.

"Mrs. Helton, at the moment, J.J. is our number one suspect for the murder of Tommy Lee and other crimes. Are you hiding the truth?"

Jewel began blinking a mile a minute. "That's not possible. Tommy Lee was his brother."

Still calm and rational, I said, "Yes, it is possible. And we believe it's true and provable in court. At the moment, J.J.'s whereabouts are unknown. We want him for questioning and have sent out a nationwide alarm for him to be apprehended."

"Why on earth would you do that?"

Terri surprised me with her next comment. "Please stop the act, Mrs. Helton. Your son has been positively identified as being in this area." Her voice elevated a notch. "And I was one of the people someone shot at in the very spot where we found Tommy Lee's body. We think J.J. took that shot. Now, I'm going to let Mr. Jenkins tell you what might happen to J.J. if he doesn't turn himself in."

She had sugarcoated that one and handed it to me on a spoon. I thought Terri was pretty good at this interrogation game.

It was time for the Sam Jenkins 'Scare the living daylights out of a loving mother routine'.

"Listen carefully, Mrs. Helton. I'll reiterate an important point that Officer Donnellson made. We need you to stop the clueless act. You're not a stupid woman. Attempting to make us believe you are only makes you appear guilty of something. So, let's knock it off, and start from scratch."

She dropped her eyes and just as so many embarrassed subjects do, she began checking the condition of her manicure—which looked pretty good to me.

I figured while she was staggering, it was time to hit her with another knockout punch. "We know that Tommy Lee was not your husband's child."

She looked up, first at me and then to her right at Terri. Her mouth opened, but no words came out. Average people aren't difficult to crack.

"Now that we know J.J. exists," I said, "something both you and your husband hid from us, it was easy to learn about him petitioning a court to become an emancipated minor and leave home. Sixteen-year-old boys don't do that every day. Your alienation of affection toward J.J. stemmed from Tommy Lee being the younger son and serious discord between you and your husband over your affair with Jake Quarles. Even your in-laws knew all this. That's why they financed J.J.'s legal expenses. This secret is out. Are you willing to discuss things honestly now?"

Jewel shrugged timidly. "I don't know how much more I can tell you except the affair with Jake didn't last long."

"Long enough to get pregnant and change your life forever," I suggested.

She nodded slowly. "Yes, you're right."

"Mrs. Helton, you would have to have been in isolation for the last week not to know that the first body we found—on land once owned by your husband's family—was Jake Quarles. Who killed him nine years ago? Jimmy, your husband or J.J., your son?"

She began to cry.

"I only slept with Jake because Jimmy had so many affairs with other women. I felt betrayed. Sometimes I felt like the whole county knew about Jimmy's other women. And the boys knew all about them. So did their classmates. You know how school children can be so hateful. They teased both my boys about Jimmy being a cheat. I just wanted to hurt him like he hurt me. I wanted to get even. And Jake was so charming."

Terri spoke in a soothing, almost motherly tone. "Mrs. Helton, we're going to clear those two homicides. There's no doubt about that. We'll either charge your husband or your oldest son, or both. It's inevitable. If you and they cooperate, we can allow the district attorney to offer them a plea bargain to save the state time and money and to save you and your family members grief and time in prison. We're not heartless, but we're not going away either."

Jewel swallowed hard and continued to blink rapidly.

I sat forward and gave her my stern Dutch uncle spiel. "Jewel, you're not out of the woods either. Based on your lack of cooperation and the lies you've told, you may be charged as an accessory. So count yourself in on this and think how you might feel getting sentenced to jail time. If you perpetuate this lie, we'll see no reason to offer you any leniency or do you any favors. Then think about J.J. You two may have had your differences, but I can see that he still means a lot to you. Every cop and Federal agent in the country has your son's picture and the description of his van. This morning the sheriff started having his bank accounts frozen and stops put on his credit cards. He will not be able to buy food or gasoline. If he wants money, he'll have to steal it. You want him shot after he attempts to stick up a liquor store?"

More tears ran down her cheeks. She shook her head. And I needed to keep pummeling her.

"He can't hide forever. We need him and Jimmy to tell us exactly what happened—about now and about nine years ago. Someone *must* answer for those two deaths. J.J.'s best option is to walk into a police facility voluntarily. Your husband will have to do that, too. We plan on finding him after we leave here and get his side of the story."

Jewel placed three fingers and the thumb of her right hand on her forehead, her chin hanging low, almost resting on her chest. She didn't look as if she had much stamina left. I planned on hammering away until she cracked.

"If J.J., who is currently a suspect in two murders and the attempted murder of a police officer, prefers to stay on the run, some zealous cop might think it necessary to use deadly force to apprehend him—and the cop would be covered by law."

It took Jewel a long moment to speak, but she managed to force out, "You'd kill my son? Tommy Lee is dead, and you'd kill J.J.? You'd leave me with no one?"

So much for Jimmy.

Jewel locked her dark eyes on Terri and asked, "Would you do something like that?"

To which Terri replied, "No police officer leaves home for work hoping to kill someone, Mrs. Helton. However, as far as we know, J.J. is armed, and his Army supervisors say he's a well-trained soldier—potentially a dangerous man. I was a soldier, too, Mrs. Helton. I know what

J.J. is capable of. I wouldn't expect *any* officer to risk their life taking your son into custody. We don't know what J.J. might do if he's cornered. Police officers must protect themselves and do what's necessary."

Jewel Helton began to bite the cuticle of her manicured right index finger. "Please don't hurt my son."

"Did he kill someone?" I asked.

She covered her face with her hands. "Yes," came out softly, and she wept.

"Now the worst is over. Tell us where he is," I said. "If you can, tell him to give himself up. Suppose he's not guilty and your husband is? And some cop confronts him, and he resists, or he's frightened and hesitates too long? He'll either die doing so or he becomes a cop killer. Who will give him a break then?"

"Oh, sweet Jesus." Her voice sounded strained and congested. She pulled a tissue from her front pocket and wiped her nose.

"Help us find him, Mrs. Helton," Terri said.

Jewel shook her head. Frustration showed on her face. "I don't know where he is. He doesn't speak to me. He hates me for what I did—for the affair and for Tommy Lee being born. I was young then. I didn't know what I was doing. I don't know how to find J.J."

"Do you have his cell phone number?"

"He won't answer my calls."

"Let us worry about that. Give me his number," I said, rapidly losing patience.

She did, and Terri entered it into her phone.

"Does J.J. contact your husband?" I asked.

"Yes. I don't know when they spoke last, but J.J. will talk with Jimmy."

———

TERRI STAYED WITH JEWEL HELTON TO START OVER AND GET HER version of everything on paper— going back many years. She would also prevent Jewel from calling Jimmy or J.J. and saying something not in our best interest.

John and I headed for a jobsite in Townsend where Jimmy was supervising the construction of a log home half the size of Delaware. We found him sitting in his truck looking over the plans for the house.

"What is it now?" he asked. "There's a contract. I'm on a deadline here. If I can't finish on time, this job will cost me money. As you can guess, these people have enough cash to buy more lawyers than me."

My patience is not infinite, and I let Jimmy know. "First order of business, Mr. Helton, is you lose the attitude, or we'll put you in cuffs. If you want to play the hotshot contractor, too busy to help solve Tommy Lee's murder, we'll just charge *you* with that crime *and* the murder of Jake Quarles, the boy's real father. Does any of that strike a familiar note?"

His face dropped and paled instantly. Ordinarily a handsome man, Jimmy's long and blanched face reminded me of a strip of limp and fatty bacon.

"You think I...?"

"We know you've lied to us, Mr. Helton, and evaded and omitted the truth ever since we've met. We think you're full o' shit. We think you've been in contact with your son—J.J. — recently. We know he's around here."

His eyes became saucers, blinking like the motor drive of an expensive camera.

"Yes, Mr. Helton, we know about J.J., so, don't try any of your impotent bullshit on us. You *will* talk to us, and you *will* help us find J.J. Of course, you have the right to bring in a lawyer. But if you do it that way, we'll play hardball, too."

"What are you talkin' about?"

"You go for at least accessory to a pair of murders—if you don't confess to one or two yourself. While you're up to your ass in a legal quagmire—that means mud, Mr. Helton—J.J. will be pursued as a fugitive and perhaps shot and killed while resisting arrest. Has that all sunk in?"

He nodded but remained mute.

"Let's take a walk over to our car. I don't want one of your workers—who are on this deadline—to disturb us."

He agreed, and soon enough we stood in the shade near the trunk of our Ford. Jimmy looked every inch the gentleman contractor wearing starched khakis, a Brooks Brother's seventy-five dollar, Tattersall shirt and highly shined work boots.

"If you cooperate, Mr. Helton, we'll do what we can to make life easy for you, Jewel and J.J. It's too late to deny *anything* because we just left your wife who confirmed *everything* we know and filled in the blanks where we had questions."

His eyes looked like he was floating on a plain somewhere above the spot where we stood. Calling him confused would have been an understatement.

"What do you mean you'll do what you can?"

"Cooperation always goes a long way with the district attorney. She's always amenable to saving time and money by staying out of court. She'll let your lawyer negotiate a reasonable plea to satisfy the people of the state of Tennessee and give you the best possible deal."

He blinked and shook his head as if he wasn't sure what had just happened.

"And if I just say nothing?"

"Ha. Go ahead. Tennessee has the death penalty. We have a search warrant for J.J.'s van. With what we learned yesterday and today, we can get one for your home and everything you own. We want the gun. We want confessions. One of you pulled the trigger—on Jake Quarles and on Tommy Lee. The shooter—or shooters—is eligible for a lethal injection. The accomplice gets life without parole. Jewel goes away for an undetermined amount of time for perpetuating this fantasy. Everybody goes down the chute, and we get paid every other Thursday."

His eyes couldn't have gotten any wider. "You don't fool around, do you?"

"I like to get my way. If I don't, I will go for your throat. If you make my life simple, I'll stand by my promise and help out you and your family members."

He ran a hand from the top of his head down the back and squeezed his neck. "Sweet Jesus have mercy. What the hell do I do?"

John took a shot answering his question. "Under the circumstances —the Jake the Snake thing, the trouble between your sons, everything— you could easily claim you and J.J. suffered from extreme emotional distress. That limits your liability. I'd go for that. If you don't..." He shrugged. "You're all screwed."

Jimmy stared off into space, possibly seeking some divine intervention. I didn't want him to spend too much time thinking.

"Let's start with an easy question, Jimmy. Did you kill Jake Quarles for stealing your wife? His actions are not something many men would have stood for."

Jimmy shook his head. "No, I didn't shoot Jake."

"Can we assume J.J. did?"

He closed his eyes momentarily, then gave me a hard stare. "Y'all are askin' me ta give up my son?"

"We're suggesting you save his life. You need to stop a charade that hasn't worked and start all over. You all made mistakes. Perpetuating them has to stop—now. You need to tell the truth."

The same hand that rubbed his head and neck went to his chin. "Can I trust you?"

I took a moment to stare into his eyes. "Yeah. You can trust me. Remember what I said about getting paid every other Thursday? It's all the same to me. You and J.J. can die or rot in prison, or you can walk away with a better deal than you're entitled to. I honestly don't care."

His entire face hardened, and his eyes narrowed. "You're one cold son of a bitch."

"I've had lots of practice. Did J.J. shoot Quarles?"

After a very long moment, he responded. "Yes. A long time ago— after he learned what Jake did to Jewel."

It took two to tango, pal. Mommie never mentioned any coercion.

"That's why he seems to hate his mother?"

"Yes. More than once, he heard us fightin' over her affair. He took it hard. None o' this was his fault."

And what did JJ think about all your affairs?

"And he also shot Tommy Lee?"

Jimmy covered his face with his hands and shook his head. "Man, I need a guarantee here."

"You want a guarantee? Buy a toaster oven. I've got your futures in my hand. You cooperate, or I'll flush your lives down the crapper."

Jimmy groaned like a gallows in use. After another protracted moment, he answered. "Yes, J.J. shot Tommy Lee."

"Do you want to elaborate on that or let J.J. explain for himself?"

"That boy hasn't had it easy. Tommy Lee was basically a good boy, but he always dug away at J.J., sayin' how their momma liked him best. And Jewel wasn't much help. She stuck up for Tommy Lee every time J.J. messed with him. Wasn't J.J.'s fault. All the trouble started when they was younger. I need ya ta swear you'll go easy on my boy."

John took a shot at him. "I think I speak for us all when I say we won't oppose any plea bargain the DA offers. We don't have to let you deal, but we will. You've got our word. You all broke the law, and you gotta pay something. But you're a hardworking guy, and J.J. is supposed to be a good soldier. Your wife is just a woman caught up in a family problem. We can give you a break. So will a judge."

A red tail hawk landed on the branch of a maple tree only thirty feet from where we stood. It eyed up a small squirrel slowly hopping across the gravel driveway of the building site. I wanted to throw a rock at the hawk and yell, 'This isn't a salad bar,' but didn't think that was appropriate. We must have worried the hawk, who did nothing. Finally, the squirrel reached the tree line, and the hawk flew to another tree further down the road.

I looked back at Jimmy and watched him nodding again. It looked as if it gave him some form of comfort.

"Whose rifle was it?" I asked.

He took a deep breath. "I bought it for J.J. when he turned eighteen. But it's his."

"Does he keep it in the van?"

"He does. Almost lives in that van—old thing. He takes good care of it."

"Has he been staying with you since he went on leave?" John asked.

"No. He won't stay at the house when Jewel is there."

"Long time to hold a grudge," I said.

Jimmy nodded. "He's that way. Always has been. Don't matter with who. J.J. just trusts himself. He's always been a loner. He'll talk ta me, but he's his own man."

John asked, "Where's he been all this time?"

"Could be in the van. Could be campin' out. J.J. knows those woods better 'en most anyone. Ever since he's little, he walked those woods. Times were I couldn't find him when I wanted to. If he wants to stay hidden out there, you won't find him."

"I can understand that needle in a haystack theory," I said, "but where is he hiding his van?"

"Could be anywhere. I didn't ask, and he wouldn't tell me anyway. Probably say, 'You don't want to know.' Thinks he's an Army spy or somethin'."

"You going to call him and get him to come in voluntarily?"

A spark of defiance passed over Jimmy's face. "You gonna call off this "wanted dead or alive" thing you got on him?"

"Not until he turns himself in."

"Jesus! You don't give an inch, do ya?"

"We will *after* J.J. is in custody."

He closed his eyes again and looked like he was struggling with the toughest thing he had ever encountered. Undoubtedly, he was. He didn't need much of a nudge.

"Tell you what," I said. "I was one of the cops J.J. took a shot at in the woods. I still can't figure out why he did that. Stupid move. But as a gesture of good faith, I promise I'll forget about the attempted murder of a police officer or reckless endangerment charges that could come from that—if he takes responsibility for what he did to Quarles and Tommy Lee."

"Will that make a big difference?" Jimmy asked.

"What do you think?" I said.

"You better believe it," John added. "You don't want to go into court with the attempted murder of a cop hanging over your head."

"I can call him. I can try."

CHAPTER SIXTEEN

WE DROVE JIMMY HELTON TO OUR OFFICE IN A STATE OF CASUAL custody—not yet under arrest, but not allowed free locomotion either. He, John and I sat around Terri's desk while Janetta watched Jimmy call his son. No doubt embarrassed to death, he hadn't acknowledged her presence. It sounded like J.J. picked up on the fifth ring.

"Daddy?"

"Yeah, son."

"What's up?"

"We got us a problem."

Silence for a long moment.

"What kinda problem?"

"I'm arrested, I guess. By two men from the sheriff's office. They know just about everything. You gotta...You gotta come and talk with them."

"Do what?"

"You gotta give yourse'f up, son. Come, and talk with these men. We're at their office in Maryville, not the Justice Center."

"Daddy, that ain't gonna happen."

"J.J...wait a minute. You better talk with this man. Give him a chance. Hear him out."

Jimmy handed me the phone.

"J.J.?" I said. "My name's Sam Jenkins. You need to listen for a couple of minutes."

"You tracin' this call? You are, I'm hangin' up, and I'm outta here."

I couldn't help a quick laugh. "Kid, I'm not a TV cop. It's possible to triangulate your position from cell towers or some shit like that with the right equipment, but we're sitting in my office on your father's phone—there's no trace. I need you to listen to what I've got to say."

"You got one minute."

Wrong answer. "Bullshit, sergeant. You sit your ass down and listen up. When I say you can hang up, you can, but not before. I was the guy you took a shot at. You owe me this much. Got it?"

Another moment of silence.

"I hear ya."

"Okay, you're in a jackpot. The sheriff sent out a nationwide alarm for every cop and Federal agent alive to pick you up. By now your bank accounts and credit cards are frozen. You can't get any more money than what you've already got in your pockets. We've identified your van. Soon enough every TV station and newspaper will have your picture plastered all over Tennessee and every surrounding state. You've got no place to go. I promised your dad and mother that I'd allow the DA to give them a reasonable deal if you turned yourself in. You, too, get that good deal."

"Yeah, right."

"It's the truth. Don't be stupid. Your lawyer will get a guarantee. But if you go on the run, your parents go to jail, and sooner or later you will, too...if you're still alive. And make no mistake, you *will* get arrested, or the cops somewhere will kill you. This one is a no-brainer, sport."

"You ain't found me yet."

"You're not listening. Unless you turn yourself in *your parents go to jail*. No chance of probation or a good deal. They go down the shitter because of you. *This is on you*. We may not have you yet, but there are a lot of cops in the country, and then there's the FBI. When you run, the Army will classify you as AWOL, and you can add every MP and CID agent in the world. That sound like a good life ahead of you?"

"You want me to confess to murder? You crazy?"

"It's what you've done, right? You think you can hide forever?"

"Gimme a minute ta think."

"That's not on your dance card, pal." I let out a long breath. "J.J., you did what you thought you had to do. I understand that. We all do. But you only get one chance to get in front of this. Now's the time to come in and talk. Tell your side of the story. Or you can run and end up dead like Dillinger or Bonnie and Clyde—your choice."

"I need ta talk with my daddy."

I let out another sigh, seeing more evidence that I never should have been a hostage negotiator. "Sure." I handed the phone back to Jimmy.

"Son?"

"Yeah, Daddy. You trust this guy?"

"Yes, I do. But we ain't got much choice."

"Sweet Jesus, Daddy. Man, I gotta think."

"J.J., son, he gave me his word. You come in, you, me and your mamma can get some kinda deal. You don't, and you'll either get shot or arrested, and we go to jail. If they have to bring you in that way, they'll ask for the death penalty. You want that? Believe him, son. He don't care if you or me or your mamma lives or dies. But I believe he's honest. He's not tryin' ta hoo-doo ya. He talked about not chargin' you with tryin' ta kill him if ya give up."

"I wanted ta kill him, he'd be dead."

"Damn it, son, he knows that, but a jury don't."

"So?"

"So give yourse'f a break. Give me and your mamma a break. We can't do no jail time. It's over. We're done. We never thought what ya done was a good idea, but after it was over, we tried ta protect ya. Now we just gotta try for the best we can get. Understand?"

"And you trust this guy?"

"I said I did. I trust 'em both."

"What's his name?"

"Jenkins."

"Lemme talk ta him again. You sure he ain't tryin' ta trace this call?"

"We're just on my phone in his office. No equipment or nothin'. No trace."

"Okay, put him back on."

Jimmy handed me the phone.

"I'm back," I said.

"What's gonna happen ta me?"

"You killed two people. You'll have to do jail time."

"Life? Am I gonna die in jail?"

"Look, your father has plenty of money for a good attorney. The lawyers can get together and work out a deal. When you plead guilty, the DA can agree to give you something good to save time and money on her end. Your lawyer will know all about this. Ask him when the time comes. I can't tell you exactly what the end result will be, but they will probably combine the two crimes and get a favorable sentence. Keep your nose clean in prison, and you get out for good behavior in less than half the sentence time."

I thought I might be making headway, but then he slipped back to square one.

"Why should I trust you? Maybe I should take my chances. Who says you're gonna find me?"

I wanted to shout. "You're starting to piss me off, son. You've spent enough time in a combat zone to know what it's like to be afraid twenty-four hours a day. If I have to come after you, you'll think twelve months in Afghanistan is like a long weekend in the Magic Kingdom. Come in here and let me give you a break."

He began breathing heavily into the phone. "Oh, man." A long moment of silence followed. "Okay, how do we do this?"

"You agree to come in?"

"Maybe."

"Make up your mind!"

"Okay, okay."

"Good. You come in. I arrest you. We talk. You tell your side of the story. That's it."

"I'll do this, but just you and my daddy can be there. Not no bunch o' other cops."

"You're close. We can do this in my office and not the Justice Center, but it's you, me and my partner. I can't allow your father to be with us, but you can see him right after we're finished."

"Goddamnit."

"Listen, Sarge, I'm sure you can understand that any boss of mine would think it's too dangerous to have a civilian present."

The line went dead for a long moment, then, "Yeah, okay."

"This has got to happen, son."

"How soon? I want a little time."

"What are you waiting for? I'm going to send our secretary home now and have your dad taken to the Justice Center to wait for us. You don't need time. Get your ass over here."

"Give me an hour."

I sighed audibly. "Okay, but if you ditch your gear all deals are off. I want you, the van, your rifle and everything you own at my place in one hour. Agreed?"

"Where do I come?"

I gave him the address and directions.

As soon as I hung up, I called Bettye and asked for a backup team and a car to transport Jimmy to the Justice Center. John called Terri and instructed her to hand Jewel over to Prospect PD for her own safety and to eliminate the possibility of J.J. taking his mother and possibly Terri as hostages.

"What are you doin'?" Jimmy asked, after hearing me ask for reinforcements. "You said just you two and J.J."

"Those other people will stay outside. Sorry, but I don't know or trust your son. If he's got some mischief in mind, I want him outnumbered. If he's good to his word, he's got nothing to worry about."

"Jesus have mercy. He's gonna know. He's good like that."

"We'll see. He doesn't really have a choice, and he doesn't call the shots."

Jimmy leaned forward in the armless chair where he sat and covered his face with his hands.

"Look, Jimmy, your kid will get a fair shake. I promised that, and that's the way it'll be. But if he comes in here shooting, I don't plan on coming in second best."

"I never shoulda done this."

"If you mean cover up J.J.'s murders, right. You should not have done that. If you mean cooperate, yes, you should. It was the right decision. Otherwise you'd be spending the rest of your life in jail."

He looked up at me like a man with nothing left to live for. "Please don't kill my boy."

"It's all up to him now."

———

Terri Donnellson had taken a written statement from Jewel Helton, called for a Prospect PD car to transport Jewel to the Justice Center and dump her on a DA's investigator to proofread the statement and consult with an ADA about what to charge her with and what to do with her after arraignment. John and I waited for a pair of deputies to arrive to take Jimmy Helton into custody and do basically the same thing with him.

Then, since we had time to kill, we waited for the reinforcements I requested. After a short time, D.L. Joiner and Bo Stallins pulled in wearing bulletproof vests over their street clothes. Bo carried a shotgun.

"Here we are," Joiner said. "I wanted ta get involved. Two more uniforms are on the way, and Shuman and Sparks, the crime scene investigators ya wanted, are standin' by."

"Good. I'd like you guys to hang out next door in the furniture shop. This guy is really twitchy, and you know he's dangerous. He's got at least one firearm—and he's good with it."

"You don't want more help in your office?" D.L. asked.

"For some reason he grudgingly agreed to meet with only John and me. There's no place for you to hide except in the little restroom that he might check. In his situation, I would. If he found you, he might shut down or go nuts."

"Okay. Where do you want the two uniforms ta be?"

"We've got to get their marked car out of sight. Let's have one man take the unit behind Auto Pro, across the street. They're good guys and won't object to us using their lot as a staging area. The other man can sit in their waiting room and keep an eye on our parking lot. If J.J. smells a rat or just changes his mind, the inside man can call the car up front, and they can do what's appropriate. I'll dial your cell phone and keep the line open so you can hear what's going on with us. If this guy gets hinky, you can communicate with the uniforms by radio and come to the rescue."

"Sounds easy enough," Bo said.

With Lieutenant Joiner lacking experience, John and I were relying on Bo to keep a lid on the backup team.

Answering Bo, I said, "Who knows? So far, not much of this makes any sense. I hope he was just really hateful toward our victims and not a certified psycho."

"I guess we'll find out soon enough," John said, looking at his watch. "I'll take you guys next door and tell Sergeant Chucky what's happening."

———

At the one hour mark, J.J. had yet to make an appearance.

"This son of a bitch is playing games," I said, looking out the window toward the parking lot and the street. An old man on an even older bicycle rolled past on the roadway. A small scruffy-looking dog sat in the basket between the handlebars.

"Maybe he changed his mind," John suggested.

"Maybe he's been lying all along and wanted another hour to get a head start to...who knows where."

I picked up the open cell phone and spoke to D.L. Joiner. "You listening to us?"

"You're comin' in loud and clear. What's next?"

"Next is me getting extremely pissed off. But, I say give him another half hour. Every cop around has the description of his van. Have your dispatcher broadcast an update to be extra alert and not to initiate contact but report any sightings and follow him discreetly."

"I'll have Bo call the duty officer right now."

"Okay. Now we wait—again."

John seemed just as antsy as me. He must have looked out the window into the parking lot every five minutes and checked to see that his Detective Special was loaded a dozen times.

After another thirty minutes, D.L. spoke loudly into his end of the phone link.

"You hear me over there?"

"Yeah," I said. "We're here—alone, as you can guess."

"How much longer?"

"Shit, I don't know. You need the uniform cops elsewhere?"

"We did pull 'em offa patrol. There's only two cars plus the traffic unit and a supervisor watchin' the whole county."

"Okay. Send them back on the road. And I guess there's no sense in you two hanging around either. John and I will hold the fort until closing time."

"Okay. We'll stop in before we leave."

A few moments later, D.L. and Bo entered the office.

"Damn shame this didn't go off as planned," D.L. said. As he spoke, he pulled on the Velcro tabs and removed his protective vest. "Damn thing is always so gat-dag hot." He shook his head. "I'll ask again—what's next?"

"Damned if I know. Other than upgrade the alarm on J.J. from *wanted for questioning* to *wanted for multiple murders*. When you get back to the office, tell Clete Dunn in the DA's office to process Mom and Dad accordingly. Thanks to J.J., their deals just slipped into the toilet. Let them feel what it's like to pay a high bail. Tomorrow I'll get together with Moira and talk about getting an indictment warrant issued for J.J."

"Okay, I'll git 'er done."

"Thanks, guys."

The two county detectives left, and I made a quick call to Bettye.

"Your people are on the way back to the barn. Our guy, that miserable... didn't show up."

"Oh, hell. Have you heard from him?"

"Not since he agreed to surrender. Maybe he saw the uniform cops or the marked car and got nervous. I'll call his cell phone and see if he answers. Then John and I will wait."

"Okay, Sammy. Let me know what happens. Call me at home if it's after five. And please be careful."

"You got it, boss."

I tried J.J.'s cell phone. It rang seven times and went to voice mail. I left a message and snapped my phone shut.

"Bastard won't answer," I said.

John shrugged. "Not much more we can do but wait."

Twenty-five minutes after Joiner and Stallins left, and as John and I were killing time, a car door slammed outside the office. We both snapped up in our seats and looked at the office door. John drew his revolver and held it low beneath the desktop.

A moment later, our door opened. But it looked as if no one was there. I also drew my handgun.

The ten seconds between the time the door swung open and a face peeked in felt like an hour. The face then disappeared to the left of the doorjamb.

I ducked down behind the desk where I'd been sitting. John did the same.

"You Jenkins?" came from outside the building.

"Doctor Livingston, I presume?"

"Do what?"

"Come in, J.J. We've been waiting for you. You're stylishly late."

"Yeah, and you didn't exactly keep your end o' the bargain."

I sighed. "Well, you've got me there. But it's just the three of us now. The other cops went elsewhere. They're gone."

"I know. I seen them leave. I ain't stupid, ya know."

"Neither am I. Unless you call waiting an extra hour for you stupid. Are you coming in, or are we going to talk through the tin building?"

"You got a gun on me?"

"Of course, we've got guns. *We're* not totally stupid. I assume you've got the rifle."

"Holdin' it."

"Then come inside, but don't point that thing at me, or I will shoot."

After a long moment, "All right. Hold your fire. I'm comin' in."

"Do it slowly."

He stepped into the open doorway holding the scoped rifle at port arms. An all black semi-automatic pistol was tucked into the waistband of his jeans. The rifle had an olive green composite stock, heavy barrel and enough knobs on the scope to make me think it was a variable focal length affair with range finder capabilities. A real homemade sniper outfit.

I halfway expected him to show up wearing a wrinkled set of Army camouflage and being unshaven and unwashed. Instead, he wore pressed jeans and a maroon polo shirt and looked like he had just cleaned up and shaved. Like the rest of the Heltons, J.J. was good-looking—recruiting poster quality, with short dark hair. The tattoo of the air assault wings was just where Sue Brown described on his left forearm. A stylized Screaming Eagle, representing the 101st Airborne Division, decorated his upper right arm and peeked out from beneath his short sleeve shirt. His arms were strong-looking with thick veins running up his biceps.

So far, he made no threatening moves.

"Come in, and hand me your weapons," I said, still using the desk for cover.

J.J. entered slowly. John and I stood up. J.J. stepped up to the desk that separated him and me and just stood there, his eyes shifting rapidly between John and me. He had yet to speak.

Then the window to my right shattered. Glass fell to the floor and a long shotgun barrel showed up pointing straight at J.J.

"Freeze!" a voice said.

I wondered if our unknown assistant had just caused J.J.'s apparently peaceful surrender to go south. I had no idea how volatile J.J. might get and anticipated him turning the rifle at the window or toward John or me and trying to go out in a blaze of glory.

J.J. didn't exactly freeze, but his slow movements were the correct ones. He released the wrist of the rifle stock and raised his right hand. With his left still holding the forestock, he extended the rifle away from his body and toward the outside wall of the office. I wanted to look toward the broken window to see who had interrupted our negotiations, but dare not take my eyes off J.J.

"John, what's going on?"

He let out a long breath. "Uh, our landlord just came to the rescue, Boss."

"Chuck?"

"We've only got one," John said. "Scared the shit outta me. I'm gettin' too old for all this drama."

"Ease up, Sarge," I called out so Chuck Cullum could hear me. "I'm going to take the man's rifle."

I holstered my revolver and stepped around the desk. J.J. had a surprised look on his face. His eyebrows were raised as far as they could go, and his eyes were as big as white walnuts.

"I'm just as surprised as you," I said. "Stand easy, and I'll take the pistol first and then the rifle."

He did nothing.

"You got rounds in the chambers?"

"Pistol. Not the rifle. What are you tryin' ta do?"

"Nothing. We didn't know this was going to happen. We'll smooth everything out. Don't worry. We're cool. That guy's a retired soldier, not a cop. He owns this building."

I pulled a Beretta 92 from his pants and then grabbed the Remington rifle just below his grip.

"Any other weapons?"

"Not on me."

"John, check him for me."

John gave J.J. a quick pat down. "He's clean."

"Sit down," I said.

As J.J. took a seat in the chair next to the piece of furniture known as Terri's desk, I addressed my reinforcements. "Stand down, Sergeant Cullum. The situation is under control. Come on in."

Sergeant Chucky withdrew the barrel of his old Winchester shotgun from the broken window and walked into the office.

I handled the introductions. "SFC Charles Cullum, meet Staff Sergeant Jimmy Lee Helton."

Neither man spoke.

"Thanks for looking out for us, Chuck."

"Uh-huh. Saw him with that rifle and thought ya might need a little he'p."

I nodded. "We appreciate it, but J.J. here says he comes in peace. Isn't that right, J.J.?"

"That was the plan."

"But thanks anyway."

"Uh-huh," Cullum said. "No sweat."

John asked, "Uh, Sarge, you know of anybody who can fix us up with a new window before we go home?"

Chuck snapped the safety button of his old .12 gauge to the on position. "I'll take care o' that."

I dropped the magazine from the Beretta and popped a round out of the chamber. "This an Army gun?"

"Negative. Private purchase."

Happy that we didn't have to involve another Federal agency with the case of a purloined Army pistol, I pocketed the loose nine millimeter round and placed the gun on Janetta's desk. I opened the bolt to check the chamber of the rifle and saw three .308 rounds sitting in the magazine. None ejected from the chamber. I handed the rifle to John. He picked up the pistol and walked both weapons back to his office.

"J.J., you ready to talk about everything?" I asked.

"I need ya ta tell me 'bout the deal first."

I smiled. "If you don't like the deal are you going to escape?"

"Am I under arrest?"

"Not yet, but you can't walk out of here."

"If I don't like the deal, I just won't say nothin'."

I nodded. "Okay, that's reasonable. Before we start, my partner—his name is John Gallagher, by the way—is going to call the sheriff and tell her to have her cops relax. No reason for them to keep hunting you like a rabid dog any longer."

"The sheriff is a woman?"

I grinned and confirmed that. "Is she ever."

He nodded. "Okay."

John picked up the phone on Janetta's desk and made the call.

"Here's the deal as I see it," I said. "It's simple, really. You've got two murders to answer for, Jake Quarles and your brother. Correct?"

He nodded.

"Your lawyer will iron everything out with an assistant district attorney, but basically, I believe they'll agree to combine both deaths and allow the negotiated time to be served consecutively—two charges like it was only one. You've got a good military record they'll consider and no other convictions. Your mom and dad will have their lawyers ask for a deal where, for their cooperation, they get charged with minimal crimes, and because they're first offenders, most likely they get away with probation."

"And no death penalty for me?"

"Correct. That was understood."

"And you'll forget about the shot I took at you?"

I nodded. "I can make that go away, but I want to discuss that incident and a couple other things with you."

"I coulda killed ya, I wanted ta."

"I understand that—and I believe you. People say you're a good shot. But we still need to talk about that and other things I don't fully understand."

He nodded.

"You ready to explain everything and when we finish put it all in writing for the DA?"

"I guess."

"We've got a little audio recorder here. Any problem with that?"

He shook his head. "No."

John finished on the phone and pulled a chair up next to Terri's desk to be part of the conversation. When I mentioned the recorder, he went to the appropriate drawer in a file cabinet to get it. He sat down again, got comfortable and turned on the little machine.

After identifying all members of the conversation and allowing J.J. to waive his rights to a lawyer, I began with, "Let's start with Jake Quarles. When did you learn that he was Tommy Lee's father?"

"Don't exactly remember, but I was just a kid. I heard Momma and Daddy fightin' once, and he said it. She didn't deny it. Screamed back at 'im sayin' it was his fault."

"Second question. You were in the Army nine years ago when Jake died. What brought you back here and why did you decide it was time to shoot him?"

"I just got back from six months in Iraq—my first deployment in the Middle East, a short tour. I hated it over there. Too many troops gettin' killed. Support troops—truck drivers, mechanics, clerks, too many non-combat types. They aren't supposed ta get killed. Those people—the terrorists—they didn't care who they killed, long as we's not Muslims. 'Course some of us *was* Muslims and good soldiers, too. Decent people. I figgered next time I went, I might get hit, and I'd leave this earth with unfinished business."

"So you wanted to take care of Jake—this unfinished business—and do it in case you didn't get another opportunity. You had all that resolved in your mind?"

His answer came out as unemotionally as if he was admitting to shoplifting a candy bar. "Yep, that's about it."

"How'd you do it?"

"Easy really. Just followed 'im some. He did a lot o' drinkin'. Every night after work, he was mostly too drunk to notice me. Then right place, right time—wasn't much of a shot."

"Then you took him to the land your father used to own and buried him."

"Cabin wasn't bein' used. It was an easy walk inta the woods."

"Why did you use that land?"

"Wasn't Daddy's no more. I figgered no more buildin' would go on, and no one would mess with the grave."

"Except the wild dogs and coyotes."

"Yeah. Except them. That didn't bother me none."

"That was a long time ago. Now we get to Tommy Lee. Why go after him? Your mother and Jake made the baby. Why did you need to kill your half brother?"

He hesitated, moving his head around a bit, taking deep breaths. I looked over at John who was staring at J.J.

Finally, J.J. sighed. "I guess after Afghanistan that last time—it was an eighteen month commitment for us—three months preparation. Twelve months in country as a unit—three months debriefing and gettin' the battalion back in shape at Campbell. I hated most o' them Afghan people, but the work was good—what we trained for. Then the same feelin' I had back before Jake got to me again. Too many troops killed by those damn IUDs or snipers or ambushes. Too many maimed —losin' arms or legs or eyes—all o' that. Things Tommy Lee would never have ta experience. But he always had somethin' ta say about us killin' innocent civilians. Gat-dag bleedin' heart, he was. Don't know where he got that from. He didn't know nothin' about what it was like over there. And if I explained how things really were, he wouldn't care." He chuckled. "Accordin' ta Daddy, only thing Tommy Lee cared about was that damn river business. More interested in savin' fish and lizards and shit than soldiers dyin'. That and girls. Pretty Boy, that's what I called 'im. He just wanted ta get his ashes hauled as many times as he could, is all." J.J. hung his head as he spoke. The more he explained, the more agitated he seemed—tense, uneasy, fidgety, picking away at some unseen lint on the leg of his jeans. Finally, he sighed, slapped his thigh and looked up at me. "Boy was never a friend. Never acted like my little brother."

J.J. was an angry and disturbed young man. It was easy to see why an Army psychologist didn't want to trust him with the job of sniper.

"Where did you shoot Tommy Lee?"

Proudly, he pointed to his chest. "Dead center."

I shook my head and tried my best to keep my patience in check. "I mean where did you find him? What part of the world did you determine was the right place to shoot him?"

A slight smile and look of embarrassment crossed his face. "Oh, I get ya. He liked ta go trekkin' before or after work—when he wasn't lookin' ta do some girl, that is. I followed him some. That day he picked a good spot. Kinda remote place in Orr's Valley. He never paid attention ta what was around him. Typical civilian. Wouldn'ta been a good soldier. *Never* knew what was goin' on around 'im—didn't even suspect." He paused and looked at me.

"And what happened then?"

"Like I said, I followed 'im inta the woods a pretty long ways away from everything. I called to 'im. He turned around, and I shot 'im. Wasn't a very long shot either, mebbe thirty, forty meters or so. He never even seen me."

"And then?"

"Had ta carry 'im out and get 'im inta the van. He wasn't too heavy, but that was one hell of a load ta walk with in August. It was hot that day."

"Why did you bury him where you did? Why not right where you killed him?"

"Place where I shot 'im was an old farm the family sold to a developer. They'd be buildin' and cuttin' roads and such pretty quick. Daddy's land wasn't gonna be sold anytime soon and wasn't bein' used. It was an easy spot to dump 'im—considerin'."

"Did you bring Tommy Lee's body in on Cricket Branch—by canoe or boat?"

He looked at me as if I began to turn into a frog right in front of him.

"Cricket Branch? Why would I bring 'im in by water? Be kinda hard dealin' with a body in a canoe. No, I just stopped on the road and hauled 'im inta the woods."

"That was pretty close to the rental cabin."

"Nobody there then. And nobody anywheres along Meissners Station Road for a long ways."

"Why did you camp out near the body?"

"I shot Tommy Lee after he had finished with work and dinner. It was late in the day, and I needed ta eat somethin' myse'f. Didn't want ta finish diggin' the grave then. Lotsa roots in the soil in there. Was hard work. Woulda been too dark when I finished. Too many bugs. Only takes a few minutes to erect a two man tent."

"You had food with you?"

"Uh-huh."

"Why didn't you sleep in your van?"

"Had other stuff in the van. Besides, it was a nice night, and I always liked sleepin' outside. And he didn't start ta smell bad yet."

Obviously, the Army had hardened J.J. to a point few civilians would ever understand. Any good prosecutor would have asked the same questions. As a defendant, I wouldn't want to explain it that way to a jury and appear stone cold. I began to hope J.J.'s attorney, whomever he or she might be, didn't jump on a defense of mental defect.

"Where did you hide your van while you were on bivouac and all the while we were looking for you?"

He chuckled, once again looking proud of himself. "Was wonderin' why ya never found it. Ya just didn't look in the right spot. 'Bout a half *klick* down the road from the rental cabin and on the other side, there's a cut driveway with a gate. Daddy sold that land ta some folks from Knoxville some time back. He cleared them a site and cut a seat for the house—dumped a bunch o' gravel, too. Wasn't much brush or weeds. Then somethin' happened. They got divorced or somethin', and they told him not to build. That gate looks like it's locked with the chain, but it ain't. Just gotta unwind the chain and drive in. The lock is there, but I guess Daddy lost the key and just left it closed, but not connected to another link."

"Where did you hide Tommy Lee's car?"

"Not far from where I shot 'im. Just drove it up a dirt track and left it. Figgered if somebody ran across it, it would look like he'd been out hikin' and never came back."

So much for the best intentions of Sergeant Hugh Bledsoe's search team, my army of volunteers and the best laid plans of a modern police organization.

"Silly us," I said. "We should have looked farther afield."

He smiled again and shrugged. "You think I could have a soda or drink o' water?"

I nodded.

"I'll get water from the fridge," John said.

"Thank ya, sir."

"Now, let's talk about you taking the shot at me and the two other cops."

"You, actually."

"Me? Why was I so lucky?"

"I seen ya around when ya found Jake's body. Looked like you's in charge. Other cop in uniform was young. And that girl in the GI cammies, I didn't know what her story was. I figgered you's the one ta get the shot close to."

"To scare me—us—off."

"Yes, sir. I coulda hit ya real easy. None o' y'all knew exactly where the shot came from. Then I was outta there before ya could react. Figgered if ya thought the area wasn't secure and ya might get killed at any time, ya wouldn't do much lookin'—fer a while anyways."

Sounded good in theory but would have played out better in a remote village in Afghanistan. I wanted to say, 'Gee, you should have been a sniper.' But that might have driven him up a wall.

I settled for, "Classic psy-ops."

"Yes, sir. Exactly. See, you know." Once again, the soldier, proud of his skills.

John placed a twelve-ounce plastic bottle of spring water on the desk next to J.J.

"Thanks." He twisted off the screw cap and took a long drink.

I shifted in my seat, felt a dull pain in my lower back and crossed my left leg over the right.

"Why did you pull that electric company scam on the ladies at the rental cabin?"

"Oh, that." He grinned. "Not sure. I guess I wanted ta see if anybody recognized me."

"And if someone did?"

He shrugged and took another pull on his water bottle.

"What does that mean?"

"I just needed ta see, is all."

Sure it was.

"Would you have killed them if someone had recognized you?"

"Didn't have to."

I nodded, finding it more and more difficult to imagine how the man's brain functioned.

"Now, J.J., we're down to the last question. It's something that's been confusing me all along. Why did you hang round after you shot Tommy Lee? Why not just bug out and get away from all the people looking for you? Get back to the safety of Fort Campbell?"

"Why?"

"That's what I said."

"Huh? I wanted to see my mother."

"You haven't spoken to her in years. Why now?"

"Just wanted to."

That bit of laundry didn't wash.

"To tell her you shot Tommy Lee?"

He looked at me with those dark, almost black eyes. Not Jimmy's eyes that were as shiny and hard as winter rain on new blacktop, but rather, lifeless eyes with a classic thousand yard stare, something you only get from seeing and doing too much in ways the average Joe never knows.

"No. I wouldn'ta told her that."

"Then talk about what?"

He looked down and searched for more nonexistent lint on his pants leg. "Just talk."

"Did you tell your father you wanted to see her? He would have arranged for you two to meet."

"I didn't."

I tried a different tactic. "I knew your first sergeant's father when I was in the 82nd. We had a few things to talk about."

He perked up and smiled. "Well, I'll be. You was with the 82nd Airborne?"

I nodded. "For a short time. Your first sergeant says you're a good soldier."

He nodded. "Good to hear. I like the first sergeant. Some in the company don't. I do."

"Your CO thinks you're a good man as well."

"Captain Roselli said that?"

"He did."

"Well, I like him, I guess. He's a good officer—for an I-talian."

"Uh, yeah. Of course. Look, J.J., if you're such a sharp trooper, why would you jeopardize getting captured when you could have called your mother and asked her to meet you somewhere out of the county?"

"Meet me?"

"Yeah, somewhere the cops weren't looking for you so diligently."

He shrugged. "I'm not sure."

"Come on, Sarge, we're just talking here. These two shootings are past history. The worst is over now. You know what's going to happen. Why try and bullshit me? You won't be charged with thinking of doing something illegal. Getting an idea isn't a conspiracy. Did you want to kill your mother to close this circle? It only makes sense."

A small grin crossed his face. "I never said I wanted that."

CHAPTER SEVENTEEN

We packaged up J.J. Helton with a pair of Peerless, nickel-plated bracelets and sent him off to the Justice Center with two deputies who were told to deliver him and the audio recording of his confession to DA's investigator Cletus Dunn and his sharpest stenographer.

I called Bettye to make sure she could clear her calendar and stick around for me and my final explanation of the Quarles-Helton murders.

John and I locked up the office, leaving the broken window for whomever our landlord assigned to repair his building. Outside we looked over J.J.'s Ford van. The body had been painted as close to Army olive drab as he could get, with the bumpers and other usual bright work colored flat black. He had it converted to four-wheel drive and lifted up the suspension to provide extra ground clearance. A ladder attached to the rear gave him easy access to the oversized roof rack. There were four jerry cans of gasoline lashed down in custom-made brackets attached to the rear doors. A homemade tactical vehicle. A team of crime scene investigators were on the way to impound the van and begin processing it.

We walked into the furniture repair shop to again thank Chuck Cullum for his assistance (which almost blew our entire investigation—

but it was the thought that counted) and then headed for home. On the way, I'd stop at the sheriff's property bureau to voucher J.J.'s Beretta automatic and Remington 700 murder weapon with instructions to have them sent to the TBI firearms ID section for comparison testing. Finally, I'd end my day by having an audience with the sheriff herself.

Thirty-five minutes after I walked into the Justice Center, I found myself slumped in a guest chair facing Bettye Lambert who sat in the matching seat, both of us a couple feet in front of her desk. Only a few other workers were in that part of the building that held mostly administrative offices.

"Do you have a bottle in one of those drawers?" I asked.

She gave me a motherly smile. "I have a bottle of perfume."

Disappointment caused my shoulders to involuntarily drop several inches. "I can't *drink* that."

"I know, darlin'. Should I get you a cup of coffee?"

I tossed my head back and sighed deeply, attempting to convey a theatrically delivered message. "Caffeine is the last thing I need now. I may appear dreadfully calm and heroically cool, but, my *dahling*, I have a terminal case of after-action fidgets that the entire staff of the Mayo Clinic couldn't understand. I-Need-A-Drink."

"I know, Sammy, but I'm sorry, you're gonna have to wait."

"Pfui. I'd even settle for two bottles of beer."

"Still can't help you."

"The next time I come, I'll bring my own scotch. Save it for me. For emergencies like this."

Bettye tilted her head and looked perfectly understanding. "Are you finished?"

I raised my eyes to see her with my head still hanging like a condemned man. "Hardly. Would you like a synopsis of what happened and what we learned?"

Another conciliatory smile. "Of course I do."

I only put up with her patronization because I love it.

"Okay, lady, here's the poop from group..."

My story of J.J.'s involvement was easy to explain and took me less than fifteen minutes.

"He wanted to kill his mother? And probably the women in the rental cabin?" Bettye sounded as if she couldn't grasp the possibility.

"He wouldn't admit that, but I think so. He's one troubled dude. Killing doesn't mean any more to him than chopping down a tree."

"Troubled? He's psychotic."

"Well, yeah, but don't say that too loud, or his lawyer may hear you and jump on that as a defense."

"Who's his lawyer?"

"Yet to be named. But since his old man isn't short of disposable cash, I'd guess the best money can buy."

Her eyes popped open. "Joe Costello?"

"That's who I'd pick."

Her eyes narrowed accusingly. "You didn't suggest him, did you?"

I shook my head. "No, not this time. And don't look at me like that. I'm not going to assist the defense team. I don't want to interfere with fate."

"Thank goodness."

I shrugged. "But maybe he deserves to get 'candled' by a good shrink. Maybe he should be hospitalized rather than introduced into the general population of one of our fine penal institutions."

She scowled at me. "You can think so, Sam Jenkins, but don't you ever suggest that."

I opened my mouth, but she didn't allow me time to speak.

"And don't tell me you didn't want to. For God's sake, he shot at you, and you entertain the idea of him getting some kind of good deal?"

"But he didn't hit me—on purpose. Look, Betts, this poor schlep had his head constantly scrambled as a kid. His parents' fault all the way. Okay, so did I and hundreds of other children who didn't live with Donna Reed and Carl Betz, but it seems to have hit him harder than usual. Then at age eighteen—and his timing was really lousy here—he joined the Army. And lucky him, does eight years of hard tours, going places where religious fanatics were shooting at him, where he had to shoot people—maybe belligerents who just happened to be women and children. And he watched while oodles of his comrades got blown up or maimed and sent back to the US in a body bag or lacking some or all of the extremities with which they left home. These are things no young person should be subjected to, but historically many are. It's not easy to live with these memories when you've got a healthy, robust mind. This guy began his military career as a closet nudnik, and fate never allowed him an easy time of it."

She nodded slowly. "So what do you suggest?"

"I suggest nothing. I told you what I think. Now, let the kid's mouthpiece and Moira Menzies duke it out and decide his fate. But I'll tell you one thing, boss-lady, if they come to reasonable terms that include a long stint in some secure funny farm, I won't oppose it."

"You've always had a soft spot for a soldier, no matter what they do."

"That's oversimplified and not exactly true. But I was a soldier once when I was young. Gee, that sounds like a book or movie title." I flipped my hands up in mock surrender. "You get my point. Perhaps through no fault of his own, Jimmy Lee Helton became something of a victim himself. I think we should let those head-shrinkers the county pays look at him and decide. I just hope they're not crazier than he is."

Bettye gave me one of those smiles that turn me into a-hundred-and-eighty-pounds of Silly Putty. "As usually, Sammy, you're right. Let's let the chips fall where they may."

———

ANOTHER DAY, AND AS PHILIP MARLOWE MIGHT SAY, ANOTHER twenty-five smackers. Why is it that every time I sit down with Moira Menzies to do business I feel like I really earn my money—or do I end up in the hole?

"I read the transcribed statement you took from Helton," she said. "I've got to hand it to you, Sam, the questions you ask usually nail these people cold. There's no doubt what was in his mind. Makes proving culpability easy."

That certainly sounded positive.

"Aw shucks, ma'am. You're making me blush."

But life is not all positive.

"I just wish you would have gotten him to waive his right to an attorney in writing."

"He did so on the audio tape. Okay, maybe I didn't read him the card verbatim, but I'm sure Clete got a signed waiver before J.J. scribbled his name on the written statement."

"Oh, he did. I just wish you were better acquainted with Ernesto Miranda."

I really didn't need Moira's version of in-service training. "Hey, I'm only a lowly PI who refuses to watch TV cop shows and learn what to do in the real world. What do I know of Miranda versus Arizona, that landmark Supreme Court case of 1966 and Ernesto's claim of having his 6th Amendment rights violated? What I do remember was *Ern-nes-to's* second trial where he got re-convicted—inevitable discovery or some minor point like the cops had a damn good case without the lousy confession."

"You're showing off."

"When Jimmy Lee Helton walked into my office—which is not a police facility—he was brandishing two firearms and behaving like a paranoid Looney Tunes character. When he settled down and started talking, I didn't want to interrupt his free flow of information. I saw that as spontaneous admissions on his part. It's all on the tape."

"Spontaneous because he knew you'd crucify his parents if he didn't confess."

I shrugged and didn't even try to hide my smile. "And your point is?"

"My point is, hotshot, that I hope your bosom buddy Joe Costello doesn't file a motion to suppress the statement. By the way, did you recommend him to the Heltons?"

"No, Ms. Interim DA, I didn't. I assume Jimmy Helton asked his business attorney who the best criminal defender was. So what? With the parent's statements implicating Jimmy in both deaths and all the physical evidence, you can't lose. Joe isn't stupid. His best strategy would be the defense of not guilty by reason of mental disease or defect. And maybe that's the best result for everyone concerned. J.J. is a walking time bomb. Talk to him for a few minutes. He explains his abhorrent conduct as reasonable and inevitable under his circumstances. He's functional, but from another planet. Costello will hire the best liberal shrink around and introduce testimony that J.J. isn't capable of distinguishing right from wrong. But that will only be one doctor's opinion. Maybe yours will say the opposite."

"Do you think he can't distinguish right from wrong?"

"Of course not. He's totally lucid, just monumentally twisted. He's not a sociopath. My best clinical description would be he's freakin' nuts. His head must feel like a tornado inside when he's not engrossed with being an infantryman. For fifteen years, he's trained to kill people efficiently. He spent eight of those years actively practicing his craft in real time with the blessings of Uncle Sam and all his generals.

"If we wanted to give justice a chance, maybe we should get him examined by someone highly skilled at spotting abnormal psychological problems and let them voice an opinion.

"Maybe the kid should spend the rest of his life in a rubber room and not pumping iron and gobbling up steroids in a prison gym."

Moira closed her eyes and shook her head. "Why do I think you've got someone in mind?"

"I do. Sharon Rubenstein. She's in Maryville and a better choice than those second string head doctors the county has on retainer. Mo Rappaport recommended her, and I asked for help with that Leary-Pitts horror show. She's good at her job—better than any FBI profiler I ever met. From what I see, she plays it straight down the middle—not a bleeding heart lefty nor a right-winger who says, "Kill 'em all and let God sort 'em out."

"I don't want this guy to walk."

"Neither do I. But maybe the slammer isn't the place for a guy who's risked his life so often for his country. Would you have a problem with seeing him locked away in a mental hospital?"

"He might get out."

"Of course he might. And in a run-of-the-mill state slammer he might get out early for good behavior with little or no serious shrink time."

She took a long moment to think before responding. "All right, I won't argue with that. The correctional system isn't famous for providing the best care for the cons who need it most."

"See if Joe brings up the mental defense. If he doesn't and wants to suppress the confession, offer it as an alternative to trial—contingent on *your* psychologist's recommendation."

"My psychologist?"

"Our psychologist."

————

I finished with Moira at quarter after eleven and called Bernadette Gavin.

"Have you been listening to the local news?" I asked.

"Yes. You arrested Tommy's brother. My God, how could he?"

"It's a lot more complicated, but the quick answer is, he's nutty as a fruitcake."

She sighed. "You're about a subtle as a calving glacier."

I laughed. "That sounds like something I might say. Sorry, I'm not a social worker or known for my political correctness."

I heard a soft chuckle. "Really?" But she continued with a serious question. "What were his reasons?"

It took me a moment to formulate a correct answer. "J.J. is a troubled soul and probably has been for many years. I'm not making excuses for what he did, but I'm not surprised. If you knew the hidden family history, you'd understand."

"I'm not sure I want to."

"I understand. Professionally, it would be fascinating, but personally, you'll have to decide if that serves a purpose. It certainly won't bring Tommy back."

She took a long moment to comment. "Do you think I should know everything?"

"I'm only a sidewalk psychologist...but basically nosy, and I would want to know. I'd say hearing the entire story might allow you to move on more easily. You might even spread the blame around more evenly and not focus your anger on one person. The parents are passively responsible for their sons' lives and mentality. I won't say Tommy Lee was doomed from the start, but neither one of the Helton boys were dealt a winning hand. It's your choice."

Another pause.

"I'd like to know. I think. Will you tell me? I'd rather not learn by sitting through a trial."

"Of course."

"And can I thank you and your partner for what you've done?"

"He'd like that. But there was a third and fourth member of the team who had important parts in finding Tommy's killer. A kind word to them would be nice, too."

"I guess I should take you all to lunch, shouldn't I?"

"We can discuss this over lunch, but I won't let you pick up the tab for the four of us. It's on me. Or maybe I can get the sheriff to pay the bill—I'm no hero."

She laughed. "Okay. But someday you must let me pay for a lunch. It's only right."

I let that one slide. "For this next time, we all should go somewhere more private than the Shrimp Dock," I said. "You like Italian food?"

"Of course."

"Good. I know the owner of the Villa Napoli in Maryville. He'll give us a quiet corner. Today good for you?"

"I guess so."

"Can you take a late lunch, 1:30 or so?"

"I'll take a half day off."

"You're sure?"

"Yes."

"Then let's make it 1:30. If you get there first, tell Rosie, the hostess, you're meeting me. She'll take you to table 35."

"You have your own table?"

"It's Nick's table—the owner's. He lets me use it."

"Wow, I know a guy who gets his own permanently reserved table in a classy restaurant. Too bad you're a cop."

"Hey, go easy on me. I stick up for all you tree huggers."

"Fair enough. 1:30 it is."

"Okay. See you later."

———

BERNIE GOT ALONG FAMOUSLY WITH TERRI AND JANETTA AND listened patiently for John and me to explain J.J.'s involvement and motivation behind killing Jake Quarles and Tommy Lee. I left out my conjecture that he waited around looking for an opportunity to kill his mother and came close to eliminating four of New Milford's finest ladies. No doubt, Bernie would have enjoyed a Movie of the Week more, but she accepted the Helton family tragedy like a real trooper.

Nick Cutrone put out a top-notch spread, and we killed two bottles of wine during the two and a half hours we spent at table 35.

After lunch, John and I drove back to Meissners Station Road to tell the ladies of the 'Guild' roughly the same things we had gone over with Bernie Gavin.

We learned that Chamois was healing nicely and had a final check up with the vet the next day. They had all intentions of packing up and driving back to Connecticut the day after but claimed that they would return for another holiday on the peaceful side of the Smokies.

Where else can you book a vacation that includes major roles in a murder mystery?

———

DOCTOR SHARON RUBENSTEIN SPENT THREE HOURS WITH J.J.

Helton, attempting to determine his suitability to stand trial. She characterized him as only semi-cooperative. After the interview, she would neither state definitively that he was as crazy as an outhouse rat nor was he living totally in a real world. Her official diagnosis went into much more detail.

In the end, her findings became irrelevant because J.J. refused to allow Joe Costello to accept a deal for a plea of not guilty by reason of mental disease or defect. He wanted to stand trial, perhaps thinking the average Blount County juror would see his actions as reasonable and justified or just inevitable and forgivable.

The proceedings lasted only four days. Most of the witnesses were called by the prosecutor, the newly appointed chief assistant district attorney, my old friend, Shelby Johnson. Joe Costello cross-examined Sharon Rubenstein and called a psychiatrist from Knoxville to comment on J.J.'s mental state. His parents were called to testify to the long-term events that contributed to J.J.'s decision to kill two people. It was the first time I saw Joe floundering for a purpose.

My testimony lasted longest and, in my opinion, ranged from helpful to the prosecution to not so bad for the defense. I played it straight down the middle and let the chips fall where they may. I doubted any juror thought J.J.'s actions came from a sound mind, but a verdict of not guilty based on his instability was not an option.

After only four hours of deliberation, the jury foreman delivered a verdict of guilty. Two days later, the judge sentenced J.J. to twenty-five years to life. But because of extenuating circumstances, he did so with an unusual recommendation to the Department of Corrections for placement into a facility with the best psychological rehabilitation program in the state. J.J.'s opportunity for parole would be determined only after several qualified doctors concurred that he might be fit for integration back into polite society—if ever. I didn't see that as a probability.

Jewel and Jimmy Helton pled guilty to several reduced charges, and each received sentences of five years supervised probation.

————

THREE DAYS AFTER THE CONCLUSION OF THE TRIAL, RALPH Oliveri called with news from our friend with the FBI in Asheville.

After a weeklong nighttime surveillance, agents dressed in haz-mat suits were present when an employee and his supervisor at the Cataloochee Paper Mill discharged more gallons of toxic waste into the Pigeon River than anyone cared to estimate. A quick analysis of the polluted water directly below the mill allowed the Feds and their warrants into the building the next day to arrest the owner and CEO. He promptly gave up the two employees who did the actual release and spilled the beans about his collusion with the county's chief deputy sheriff and a lieutenant from the patrol division. He also implicated two senior officials from the county's Health Department.

Neither Donal Curry nor Bill Koronkiewicz were implicated in the ongoing wholesale pollution of the waterways of North Carolina and Tennessee. The two former marines were, however, out of a job when the Feds closed down the paper mill.

Bernadette Gavin was ecstatic when I told her the news about the mill before it became common knowledge. She promised to inform all her cronies at the Smoky Mountain Ecologists group.

————

THE ONLY ITEM REMAINING FROM THAT MISSING person/multiple murder case was to pick up our final paychecks. Bettye Lambert asked me to see her personally rather than wait for the finance section to mail out the individual checks.

"I knew you'd solve this one, Sammy. And look what happened. You not only cleared the Tommy Lee Helton case, but a nine-year-old unreported homicide to boot."

"Am I good or what?"

"You keep askin' me that, and I agree. You're the best, darlin'."

"Great. Can I have our money? I hate to sound mercenary, but I don't do this stuff for the people of Blount County out of the goodness of my heart."

"That's what I wanted to talk to you about. Joe Henshall in finance questioned one of your expenses."

"Oh? What's his beef?"

"He kinda wondered why you needed to spend $167.81 for lunch at the Villa Napoli."

I shook my head, half expecting someone to balk at that one. "Bureaucratic nincompoop. That was for me, John, Terri, *your cousin* Janetta and Bernadette Gavin. Bernadette provided us with invaluable information on not only Tommy Lee, but the people at the paper mill who initially were our prime suspects. But you know about them. Tell Henshall to go back to counting paperclips and not to second guess your *special investigator*."

"I guess the bill that accompanied your voucher didn't explain everythin'. Just so I can tell him somethin', why was the check so high?"

"High? That was downright reasonable for five people. The lunch specials were only $16.95 each—dirt cheap for what you get. You know, I've taken you there."

Bettye nodded and waited for me to finish my explanation.

"You get five choices, for godssakes. And Nicky even threw in salads for free because he likes me. It's not like I took these people to the Hilton or some *really* high-priced joint. And there were only two bottles of wine at thirty bucks each, that ridiculous 9.25% sales tax we have to pay and a twenty percent tip. $167.81 was a bargain."

She frowned. "Did you really need two bottles of wine?"

"For five people? I think so. You and I can polish off a bottle between just the two of us. That's only a couple glasses each. Is the man a cretin? How about the times John and I ate junk food and never charged you because we were pressed for time? Or when we ate that toxic waste from your jail's kitchen? I don't pad my expenses. Tell him to bug off."

"Okay, okay. I've got a check for you, and I'll explain things to Joe. But next time maybe could you order iced tea or something a little less expensive?"

"Iced tea and good Italian food? Just shoot me. I don't think I want to work for you anymore." I figured sulking might be the best tactic.

Bettye walked around from behind her desk, bent over and kissed me on the forehead. "Yes, ya do, darlin'. If you didn't help me solve these big cases, who would?"

THE END

If you enjoyed *Sins of Eden* and would like a free copy of the award winning *A New Prospect*, simply go to
www.waynezurlbooks.net

Don't miss out on your next favorite book!

Join the Melange Books mailing list at
www.melange-books.com/mail.html

Perks include:

- First peeks at upcoming releases.
- Exclusive giveaways.
- News of book sales and freebies right in your inbox.
- And more!

ABOUT THE AUTHOR

Wayne Zurl grew up on Long Island and retired after twenty years with the Suffolk County Police Department, one of the largest municipal law enforcement agencies in New York and the nation. For thirteen of those years he served as a section commander, supervising investigators. He is a  graduate of SUNY, Empire State College and served on active duty in the US Army during the Vietnam War and later in the reserves. Zurl left New York to live in the foothills of the Great Smoky Mountains of Tennessee with his wife, Barbara.

Zurl has won Eric Hoffer and Indie Book Awards, and was named a finalist for a Montaigne Medal and First Horizon Book Award. He has written seven novels and more than twenty novelettes in the Sam Jenkins mystery series.

www.waynezurlbooks.net
www.facebook.com/waynezurl
www.twitter.com/waynezurl

ALSO BY WAYNE ZURL

A New Prospect

A Leprechaun's Lament

Heroes and Lovers

Pigeon River Blues

A Touch of Morning Calm

A Can of Worms

Honor Among Thieves

A Bleak Prospect

Sins of Eden

From New York to the Smokies: A Collection of Sam Jenkins Mysteries

Murder in Knoxville and Other Sam Jenkins Mysteries

The Great Smoky Mountain Bank Job and Other Sam Jenkins Mysteries

Graceland on Wheels and More Sam Jenkins Mysteries

www.ingramcontent.com/pod-product-compliance
Lightning Source LLC
Chambersburg PA
CBHW050510260626
47157CB00004B/1262